Southpaw

by USA TODAY bestselling author
GINGER SCOTT

Southpaw

AN ENEMIES-TO-LOVERS SPORTS ROMANCE

GINGER SCOTT

Thank you.

I usually save this for the acknowledgements but what can I say, there is something about baseball that gets me all sentimental. So dear reader, thank you for spending your time on my words and this little story of my heart. I hope you enjoy it as much as I did.

XO
Ginger

This one . . . I wrote this baby for me. ♡

"Love is the most important thing in the world,
   but baseball is pretty good, too."
      ~ Yogi Berra

CHAPTER 1

I should say no to the shot of tequila Kiki is swaying in front of me in her open palm. Is she swaying it? Or do I *think* it's swaying?

See. I should say no.

"I'm beyond buzzed, Keeks. I should go home and sleep off this entire asshole of a day." I take the shot from her hand as I say these words; the liquid already down my throat. I've blown past buzzed. Hello, bathroom floor when I get home.

"When men we waste our time on propose to other women with the same damn ring they gave us, we're allowed to get shitfaced." She's right. I've earned a night out. And I earned that drink. And the four that came before it.

Before I have a chance to slip back into my self-pity party, I plop the shot glass on the tabletop and take my best friend's hand, leading her out to the dance floor that has distracted me quite nicely for most of the night. McGill's is a college pub with everything. Dance music, check. Frat

1

boys who like to dance, check. Big screens on every wall with various games on constant stream, triple check. It's where I took my first legal drink, and it's where my friends and I solve all our problems. Unfortunately, it's also the official bar for the Arizona Monsoon triple-A baseball team. And that fucker my friend mentioned before—the one who wasted my time and proposed to another girl with the ring he gave to me less than a year ago—yeah, his shit is all over this bar. Corbin Forsythe is a goddamned Monsoon legend. And he'll be pro-ball royalty one day. Only, someone else will be his queen.

I know my best friend is trying to push me to the other side of *moved on* by dragging me out tonight, and the last few times we've been here, I haven't felt the pangs of heartbreak from seeing his signed jersey and the wall dedicated to his various newspaper and magazine clippings. I ripped the photo of him and me celebrating the day he got called up from the wall two months ago, so I don't have to stare at that anymore. But those TVs on the wall are incessant tonight, and apparently Corbin Forsythe proposing to Meghan-nobody after his start for Texas last night is still big news. Probably because he did it seconds after the Gatorade was dumped on his head. While he was still on the field and talking to the post-game reporter about throwing a complete game shutout. On national TV.

"I hope that ring turns her finger green," Kiki shouts in my ear. The music is thumping in here, yet somehow I can still hear the proposal news blaring from the TV across the bar.

I twist my lips into a soured pucker.

"It's a really nice ring. Remember? I've seen it," I say, squeezing my left hand into a ball at my hip, still feeling the burn of where it wrapped around my finger for an entire month.

"What an asshole. Who asks for their proposal ring back?" my friend says, waving away the story showing on repeat on the TV before blowing at the loose hairs sticking to her glistening forehead.

A few people dancing near us glance my way, and whether it's real or imagined, the sense that they're staring at me with pity for being the jilted ex instantly chips away at the thin emotional armor I've worked really hard to construct.

"Hey, you know what? I should go. That last shot is hitting me hard." That's not a lie. My feet feel like bricks and my arms are tingling. I begin shuffling my way backward to the bar when Kiki reaches forward and grabs the strap of my small crossbody purse.

"Keeks, I'm tired. I really want to go home."

"Liar," she says through pursed lips. Her hands have moved to my small bag and she's unzipping it as she stares me down. I drop my gaze to her grip and force a yawn.

"Seriously, I am truly tired." I'm also a lot of other things—emotional, embarrassed, angry, jealous—but tired definitely factors in. My spine straightens when Kiki tugs on my bag again, and my eyes snap to hers.

"Sutter, I know you. You aren't going home from here. Admit it." Kiki's hard, knowing glare breaks through even the foggiest of drunk goggles. My attempt to dispute her claim lasts an entire two seconds before I exhale and let my shoulders slump.

"That's not fair. Billy's place is closer by like, uh, several miles. He's my brother, and he doesn't care when I crash there."

"One, he does care," my best friend says as she reaches into my purse and pulls out my phone.

"*Pffft*, he cares when I come over to talk about *him*. But he doesn't care when I come over to sleep." Drunk as I am, even I don't believe the bullshit coming out of my mouth. Since I moved out six months ago, my brother has relished the idea of owning a bachelor pad. I've barged in on a few of his dates with my own late-night breakdowns, and while he tolerates me in the moment, his cold shoulder for the following week gets the point across.

"Sutter, you haven't given in to the urge to wallow in your old bed in a month. Don't let today set you back."

My old bed. *Our* old bed. I lived in that room with Corbin. I made plans in that room, with Corbin. I believed in him—in that room. I know it's self-inflicted emotional torture every time I step foot in there, but there's a tiny element that still feels good too. *That's something a heroin addict would say.*

Kiki palms my phone and lifts a single brow before looking down and tapping on the screen. She slips it back inside my purse seconds later, zipping my bag closed. Placing her palms on my bare shoulders, she squares me with her and forces me to look her in the eyes. "Your ride will be here in six minutes. And it will take you to *your* apartment. The one you were so excited to live in by yourself. The one that is super inconvenient for me, but away from everything you found triggering. And you'll tuck yourself in and wake up with a nasty headache in the morning. But . . . you won't have broken your streak."

"What streak?" I question, gravity pulling my body down a little more than it did a minute ago. I'm not sure if that's the tequila or the lecture.

"The streak of not giving Corbin space in your heart and head that he doesn't deserve." She holds me steady and doesn't let go until I nod. I sell it with a salute just to make her happy, then I let her march me out the door to the curb. After a few minutes, the black Camry driven by a woman named Natalie pulls up to take me away, just like the ride share app said she would.

"You can do this," Kiki says to me as I fall into the back seat and swivel my legs into the car.

"I can do this," I echo.

I'm a liar. I'm totally not doing this. But I can pretend for Kiki. I don't need to drag her down with me. She should enjoy her Friday night, and dance with the cute guy who kept trying to get her attention away from me. She's put her own good times aside for me too many times lately.

I wait until Natalie takes me a full block away from McGill's when I clutch my bag against my chest and utter, "Shit!" It's a lame plan but it's the best I can do with little notice.

"Everything all right?" Natalie glances over her right shoulder.

"Yeah, I just realized my friend has my credit card. You know what? I'll get out here. I'm sure I can catch her," I say, my hand already on the door handle.

"Do you want me to wait?"

"Nah, it's okay. It might take me a little while, and I can request another ride for later. You know how it is when you start talking to your friends."

Before she has a chance to counter me and offer to wait as long as it takes, I pull a twenty from my purse and toss it into the front seat. "For your trouble," I say before exiting the car and walking back toward the bar.

I spend the next several seconds in paranoid freak mode, glancing over my shoulder until rideshare Natalie pulls away and finally turns a corner. The second she does, I do a one-eighty and slog my way to my brother's apartment five blocks away.

The scent of freshly watered grass cuts through the desert air, the breeze cooling it and letting me know I'm almost to the building's entrance. I don't have to check the time to know it's eleven thirty, when the outfield sprinklers cycle through. The smell is enough of a reminder.

I don't give in and look across the street to the gates of the Monsoon Ballpark. I don't need to. I have that view memorized. After all, it was my view for five years of college and grad school. Tucson was my home well before college, too. We moved here from Oregon when I was five and Billy was eight. Back then, being the kid of the Monsoon head coach was epically cool. Billy and I have coveted this apartment building since we were in grade school, and when Billy got the chance to rent a unit here as a college student, I begged him to let me stay during the weekends while I was in high school. He merely tolerated me for a few weekends, but the older we got, the closer we grew. He was between roommates when it came time for me to start at the university, so I moved in.

Corbin was only supposed to do a stint on our couch while he waited for a host family to come through. But after a few weeks, the only move he made was from the couch to my bed. He stayed there for two years—*two seasons*. Then he got the call. The one every ball player waits for. He said he'd come back during his breaks, and I could come stay with him on mine until I finished my masters. Then we'd set a date. He came back only once, and it was to take back his ring. I always thought it was *my* ring.

Since that day, this building and its stupid, amazing view has lost its appeal. I still have a key, though. My brother knows better than to ask for it back. As much as I hate this place for all of its reminders, I'm not ready to quit on it. Sometimes, I need to get my fix. To slip under the comforter that my brother has yet to throw away, to smell the sheets and pillows that still make up my old bed. *I'm a pathetic junkie.*

I punch the code for the building's side door and teeter my way down the hallway past the laundry room and maintenance office to the charming Art Deco style elevator. My thumb presses the green button and I hold it there for a few extra seconds to make sure it reads my request. As much as I love the quirks of this building, I don't miss the way shit's always breaking. If the ground weren't wobbling so much, I'd take the stairs to the third floor. But risking getting stuck in the elevator for the night is a better option than potentially rolling down concrete steps end over end.

When the door dings and slides open, my mouth stretches into a sloppy smile. I'm almost home. Well, not *home* home, but in a place where I can drown in my feelings until I pass out. I'll set my alarm and trot my way out of here before Billy wakes up. It will be as if I were never here. No witnesses.

The elevator door begins to close when a hand grabs one side and shoves it back open.

"You're gonna break it," I mumble, laughing at the sound of my voice. I sound like my mom. Layers of blonde hair zigzag across my face, and the bangs I've been growing out have slipped free of the pin I secured them under earlier this evening. I spit out the strands sticking to my lips and rub my hand over my face with the vigor one uses to clean a window. That's when I see the body attached to the arm that cut my elevator ride short.

Standing at least six inches taller than me with dark hair tucked under a State ballcap and blue eyes that somehow make this seventy-year-old elevator feel fancy, my interloper stares down at me with an annoyed expression. Plump, kissable lips in a straight line. Why isn't he smiling? *Am I smiling?*

Uh, you interrupted my elevator ride, dude.

"What floor?" His mouth pulls in on one side as he blinks at me.

My God, does he smell delicious. Too bad every other clue points to ballplayer.

"Three," I respond.

He taps the button with his knuckle then backs toward the opposite side of the elevator, leaning against the wall before pulling his phone from the pocket of his gray joggers. His white T-shirt is damp from sweat, and the ends of his hair curl around the back of his hat. He's been at the gym—probably the Monsoon gym. Typical. This building is full of guys trying to prove they're special by working out late at night.

My gaze drops to his shoes, and I chuckle lightly when I see they're New Balance turfs. Of course they are. I bet he's a pitcher.

When the elevator dings, I run my hands through my hair to clear my face and exit to the right. It takes me a few seconds to realize that Mr. New Balance has gotten off behind me. He never pushed another button. My eyes dart from my right periphery to my left, and my bat-like hearing tunes in to his gait. He's keeping up with me step for step, and the farther down the hallway I go, the more my chest tightens against the firing beats of my heart. I don't have a lot at my disposal—tank top, jeans, and a cotton shirt tied around my waist. My purse isn't very heavy, so I'm not sure swinging it at him would do any good in fending him off.

As my brother's apartment door comes into view, though, I remember the small bottle of dry shampoo spray I wedged into my bag at the last minute. I unzip my purse and plunge my hand in with a few steps to go, and before I reach the apartment door, I spin on my heels, pop the cap from the spray, and blast my follower's eyes.

"What the fu—!" He takes a few strides back and bends forward, quickly bringing the bottom of his shirt up to his face and holding the cotton against his eyes.

I pound on the door and fumble for my phone, dropping it in my manic state.

"Shit!" I scoop it up and shove it in my pocket then turn to the door and beat it with both fists. "Billy! Let me in! Help! Billy!"

Within seconds, my brother flings the door open and I fall forward into his chest.

"Sutter, what are you doing here?" My brother's large palm covers my shoulder, and he steadies me as he bends down to look me in my crazed, drunken, panicked eyes. His gaze flits up a second later, just as I hear my attacker groan his way into the doorway.

"Oh, shit," Billy says, moving his hand from my shoulder to the bridge of his nose.

"Oh, shit? I think you mean, quick Sutter, get inside and call the police," I say, moving myself so I'm now standing behind my brother's large frame. He seems completely fine with the fact Mr. New Balance is hobbling into the apartment and closing the door behind him.

"Sutter, I was going to tell you . . ." Billy begins.

"This is Sutter?" the man says, gesturing toward me with one hand while still holding his shirt up to his face with his other. He puffs out a short laugh that I'm pretty sure wasn't meant to be nice, then meanders into the kitchen where he bends over the sink to splash water in his eyes.

"Billy? How does he know my name?" I round on my brother again, tugging at his T-shirt so he turns to face me.

His palm runs over his scruffy chin, then he glances over his shoulder to the sink and back to me, his hand still covering his mouth as he speaks.

"I had to take on a roommate to afford the rent. And I didn't think you were going to break your lease and move back anytime soon, so I—"

"Billy?" I swallow down the tequila-tinged bile threatening the back of my throat.

"Don't say my name like that," he says.

"Like what?"

"Like . . . like Mom does."

"Billy, Mom says your name like that when she's disappointed in you. And I maybe have a good reason to be disappointed." I step to the side to fully take in the new roommate. He's finished washing out his eyes, and taken his shirt off completely to use as a towel. He's practically carved from marble, and before I made his eyes bloodshot orbs of misery, they were pretty phenomenal too.

"Before you say it, yes," my brother says. I snap my gaze back to him, ignoring the one locked on me from the other side of the kitchen counter.

"He's a ballplayer. You took in one of his boys?" That's how we always referred to my dad's players. Even Corbin was one of Dad's boys. I bet despite what happened between us, my dad still considers him as such. My dad doesn't have to like you personally to make you one of his.

My brother's head cocks to one side and his shoulders shrug. His mouth draws in tight. I hold his stare for a few solid, awkward seconds, mostly because the adrenaline is wearing off and the tequila is really working against me. Finally, the rest of if clicks.

"A pitcher? He's a fucking pitcher?" I point toward the guy, my hand still clutching the now empty bottle of dry shampoo.

"Hey, I'm in the room, by the way. Yeah, me . . . the fucking pitcher. And I'm not entirely against filing assault charges," he says as he tosses his shirt on the counter and marches over to my brother and me. His hands on his hips, right where his waistband sits along a ridge of muscle on his super-toned stomach. Corbin was taller, but he was never built like this. He had a softness to his middle. Nothing soft going on here.

"Eyes up here," he snaps, jolting me out of my ill-timed drool fest.

"I know where your eyes are!" I fire back, as if that's any kind of defense.

He shifts his weight and chews at the inside of his mouth for a beat before smirking.

"Whatever. It's late, and I've got a bullpen in the morning. I'm going to bed." With a wave of his hand, he strides across the living room and into the bedroom that I considered my spare for as long as I needed it.

When the door slams shut behind him, I spin to face

my brother again and push hard against his chest. Billy's twice my size and doesn't move an inch.

"Look, Sutter. I didn't go out and find some replacement for Corbin to move in here and shove in your face. I've been struggling to make the rent on my own for a few months, and Dad said Jensen was stuck because his host family bailed. I was going to tell you in the morning, I swear."

I nod as I process the facts as he says them, but buzzed as I am, I'm not too drunk to realize Jensen has been living here for more than a day or two.

"So, is that a week after he moved in? Two?" I squint up at him and drop my fist to the center of his chest with a thud.

Billy sighs.

"He's been here eight days. But I swear, I really was going to tell you tomorrow. I was working out how. I knew you'd get like this."

"Like what?" I hold my palms out, a small part of me realizing how ridiculous and unfair I'm being but not loud enough to cut through my rock-solid self-righteous exterior.

"Upset, Sutter. I didn't want you to be upset. More upset than you've been lately." Billy's shoulders tick up briefly with earnest defeat. His eyes round with that pleading look he always gets when he's in trouble. He's been making that face since we were kids, when I would tattle on him for not sharing or for skipping his homework. I was a brat sometimes.

Unable to maintain eye contact because of, well, guilt, I shake my head and move toward the couch. I'm still sleeping here.

"What about my stuff?" I've purposely dragged my feet clearing my things out completely because it makes for a good excuse to stop by. It's a thinly veiled excuse that both Billy and Kiki have called me out on. But like the rest of my pathetic behavior, it endured their criticism.

"I boxed it up. It's in my closet," he says. "You wanna get it now?"

I huff out a short laugh.

"No. But I'll take a blanket. It's been a long day and I might be a little drunk." I turn back to the couch and Billy helps pull the cushions away.

"A little drunk?" He scrunches his face, mocking me.

I shake my head and shrug.

"You see the news today?" I know he has. My brother wakes up to *Sports Center* and he manages a golf resort, the kind of place that breeds locker room gossip. And the guy on track to be the youngest Cy Young award winner ever dropping to a knee post-game is definitely good gossip.

"I saw," Billy croaks. He doesn't meet my gaze, instead pulling the remaining cushions away from the sofa and stretching out the pull-out bed on his own. I flop down face first the moment it's level with the ground.

"So . . . the spare blankets are in, uh . . ." he chokes out.

I roll to my side and crack an eyelid open to see him point toward what used to be my room. Now Jensen's room. I roll my eye and close the lid again.

"It's fine," I say, flailing my arm at him to leave.

"You can have mine—"

"I'm fine," I cut him off. My brother still wears the same cologne he did in high school, and I can't stand the smell. It stinks of teenager and gas stations.

"Alright, well . . ." He's hovering because my brother is

13

a fixer. It's why he didn't want to tell me he let another baseball player move in before he had a full story worked out to ease my mind. And he wants to fix me now, patch up my feelings and hurt. It's sweet, and it's why he's my favorite human. But he can't fix the shit I've got going on inside. He can't make me believe in people who aren't him or my best friend.

"Good night, Billy. I'm sorry I'm a mess." My words are muffled by the mattress my mouth is mashed up against.

"It's okay," he says, nudging my right foot that's dangling from the end of the bed. I laugh into the mattress, loving his honesty. No *"You aren't a mess, Sutter."* Simply an *"It's okay."*

The sound of the light clicking off is followed by the creak and click of Billy's bedroom door. I roll my face against the abrasive sheets that never get changed on this thing and push my hair from my face. It takes me longer than it should to toe my ankle boots from my feet, and even longer to unwrap the overshirt from my waist. I fashion it into a blanket to cover my shoulders, and shift in the bed so I can stare at the door that used to be mine.

I'm not sure how long I've been staring at it when it opens. I shut my eyes in a panic, not wanting to get caught —not wanting to face him again after the way I acted. I suppose I've found a way to keep me away from this place for good.

With my eyes closed, my other senses take over. Jensen is trying to be quiet, but the wood floors in this building make sneaking around impossible. The floorboards creak under his weight but stop maybe a few steps from the side of the couch. He must have showered, because the dulled mix of cologne and sweat he emanated in the elevator has been replaced by a clean cucumber scent. The floor creaks again, his footsteps getting fainter as he heads back to his room. I crack my eyes open for a quick glance, but his room is dark. When his form fills the frame again, I snap my eyes closed and hold my breath. He's not wearing a shirt, and I didn't get to stare long enough to know whether those were boxers or sweatpants. More creaking floors prelude a whoosh of air over my body as a blanket unfurls, covering me from shoulders to toes. The weight is nice, like a hug, and the fabric is warm, as if it's already soaked in someone's body heat. *Jensen's body heat.*

He treads back to his room and closes the door, and I keep my eyes closed for nearly a minute, grasping the edge of the blanket and bringing it to my cheek. It's soft, and small threads tickle my face. It smells like he did in the elevator. When I feel safe enough to look, I open my eyes and wait for them to adjust to the dark, taking in the hundreds of tiny fabric squares stitched together and tied with threads every few inches. Someone made this blanket, and I wonder if it's the kind of treasure that stumbled into his possession or one that was made with love and affection, the kind my mom put into the things she made for Billy and me before her mind wouldn't let her anymore.

Whoever it was made for, it was stitched with care. And it's not the comforter I came here looking for tonight.

CHAPTER 2

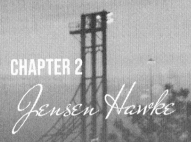

Jensen Hawke

I haven't woken to a smell like this in ·ages. I'm not completely sure whether I've already eaten the bacon or if I simply dreamt it, my mind under the control of the smell wafting under my door.

Rolling slowly to my side, I wait to stretch my arm and test its mobility. It's been more than a year, but I still hold my breath every morning anticipating the pain to be there again. It hasn't come back yet, and if I do things right—*and if I'm lucky*—it won't. That's what the doc says.

My intuition, however? That's another story. It's tainted by years of disappointment. Those people who preach that hard work is the key to success have never touched a baseball. I know what I'm capable of. My numbers before surgery were as good as—nah, they were better than—half the guys who went ahead of me in the draft. But baseball is the same at every level. Talent can get you a tryout, but money and who you know? That gets you on the roster. And my parents? They're nothing but a pair of hypocrites. I doubt they even know I'm in Arizona. I'm not a headline-

17

making player, and since we don't really talk anymore, as far as they know I'm still in the farm system in Alabama. Of course, they probably forgot I was ever there, too.

I was the last kid placed on a team in Little League. Always the alternate for All Stars because my family didn't feel like fundraising for uniforms. I got cut my freshman and sophomore years, and when I made the team my junior and senior years, my role was the bullpen pitcher used against the shit squads because my coach had two sons on the team he started for the games that mattered. Both of his boys skipped college and work security at a storage facility now. The only reason I made the college roster was because I persisted as a walk-on for State and grinded my way into the starting rotation after proving myself as a reliever.

Work ethic. That's all that matters. At least, it's all that *should* matter. My sister says it's exactly that attitude that holds me back. Amber has always been the ray of sunshine. She makes time for everyone and anything. She's never been burned the way I have, though. I don't waste time on things that aren't going to move me forward. My relationships with people are strictly business. The last time she and I talked, she said it's why everyone thinks I'm a difficult asshole and won't give me a shot. I don't know; maybe she's right. It sure as shit ain't my arm. Of course, that was before my UCL tore in Alabama. I'm determined to be one of those guys who comes out of Tommy John surgery with an ax to grind and a superpower to back it up. It's half the reason I was all right with the trade that sent me to the southern Arizona desert. The staff down here is renowned for turning stitched-up arms into cannons. And as long as I don't disintegrate under this damn unforgiving sun, maybe I'll be this year's Cinderella story.

Dishes clank against the table outside my door, and I inhale the scent again. It's enough to motivate me to move my arm and test how it feels. Relief floods my chest as I stretch my arm over my head then across my body, flexing my muscles, and bending and straightening my elbow without a single nagging, painful reminder that it exists.

Rolling out of bed, my feet hit the floor just as my phone buzzes with a message. It's my sister, but I'm not in the mood to read her multi-paragraph fairytale text. You'd think she'd stop trying so hard with me. I never respond to her little stories of positivity. They're annoying. And I'm pretty sure they're made up. But that's the difference between us—she's all sunshine and happiness while I'm stone-cold reality.

I toss my phone on the bed and slip my hoodie over my head before wading out into hostile territory. Billy's sister was not what I expected based on the limited info he gave me when I moved in. He made her sound quiet and a little reclusive. But half a can of some baby-powder-smelling stuff in my eyes paints a totally different picture.

Billy's back is to me in the kitchen, so I'm quiet as I sneak into the living room where my quilt is folded neatly on the arm of the couch. Unless his sister is in the bathroom or hiding somewhere, it seems she's cleared out. As much as I didn't want to face her, I did want to take credit for the blanket I gave her. I don't need her bad-mouthing me to her dad, and I'd rather be the guy who gave her a blanket when she was cold than the "fucking pitcher" she referred to me as last night.

I clear my throat to get Billy's attention and he glances over his shoulder, a pan in his hand over the stove.

"Hey, man. I hope you're hungry." He nods toward a pile of pancakes and a plate filled with bacon. "Eggs ready in a second."

I hope he doesn't expect to make this a regular thing. If I weren't starving, I'd refuse to join him because I don't want this setting some precedent. We're roommates. We split bills. That's what this arrangement is. I didn't realize Coach was setting me up with living arrangements with his son until my shit was in the room and it was too late to find an alternative.

"I, uh, usually grab a protein something," I say, stopping myself short of blurting out something rude. My mouth is watering, so I give in and pick up a piece of bacon. It's thick cut. God, how I have missed thick-cut bacon.

"Right, well, eat if you want. Honestly, I was going to make this meal no matter what. It's my flaw," he says, turning toward me and dividing the eggs between two plates. He sets the pan in the sink then pushes one of the plates toward me and offers a quick shrug.

"Your flaw is bacon?" I say, my tongue practically pulsing with ecstasy from the piece I just devoured.

"Ha, no. That's a perk of my flaw."

I lift a brow and give in, taking the plate he pushed toward me and tossing a few more pieces of bacon on top of the eggs, then adding two pancakes with a fork. I move to the table where Billy set out a bottle of syrup and some butter.

"I'm what you might call a *pleaser*. My dad will tell you it drives him nuts. I'm the one always running around during holidays making sure everyone is happy and nobody feels left out. And I do things like, oh . . . I don't know . . . make huge breakfasts for people the morning after a huge misunderstanding that was probably my fault."

I laugh out once because I appreciate his candor.

"So that was Sutter, huh?" I acknowledge, popping another bite of bacon in my mouth.

"Yeah, that was her." He sighs, adding pancakes to his plate then taking the seat across from me at the table. "And if I told her you were here, she probably never would have shown up. At least not until her nosiness got the best of her. My bad on that."

I nod, not totally understanding but also not really wanting to know more than I need to.

"She didn't want to stay for pancakes?" I ask as I drench the pancakes in syrup. There is more sugar on this plate than I've had in weeks.

"Oh, no. She told me my stupid pancakes weren't going to fix things and then left the minute I pulled out the pan." He halts his loaded fork a few inches from his mouth then looks up at me. "My sister had a thing with our last roommate, and—"

"None of my business," I cut in. Truly. I want to know as little as possible. "And her loss. These pancakes are great."

I grin through another bite.

"Good. Glad you like it. Anyhow, I'm sorry about all of that," he says, gesturing toward the living room. His brow knits and his head tilts when he spots my blanket. Before he has a chance to make it something more than it is, I confess motivations.

"Yeah, that was a peace offering. I don't need your sister telling your dad what an asshole I am."

He nods with instant understanding as I shovel more food into my mouth.

"Smart. Won't matter, though," he says. I cough and drop my fork on my plate.

"What does that mean?"

Billy looks up from his plate again and laughs when he takes in what I'm guessing is my ghost-white face.

"No, I don't mean that she'll torpedo your rep with my dad. I mean, she doesn't *talk* to my dad. Sutter holds grudges, and she's never wrong. Even when she's wrong." Billy grimaces. I nod.

"Well, no beef between us. And no need to overcompensate again with breakfast. This was great, though. If you leave the dishes, I'll take care of them," I say as I stand and deliver my plate to the sink.

"I got 'em," he says with a wave of his hand. "All part of my penance."

"All right," I say, wiping my hands clean with a towel.

Billy gets up and moves toward me, but I exit the kitchen galley and give him a nod and utter *thanks* before we exchange a truly awkward bro hug.

By the time I shower and get ready to head to the field, Billy's gone. He manages some hoity-toity golf course up in the hills. He's offered to give me a free pass at least six times, which I now realize is probably part of that flaw of his. I wonder if he'll stop offering if I take one. Probably not until he actually sees me out there on the links. And then I bet he'd try to join me for the round and comp me a drink or two. As desperate as this guy is to be liked, I'm as eager to be left alone.

I snag my quilt from the couch and toss it on my bed before grabbing my gear bag. When I get back into the main room, the door to our apartment is wide open. I peer into the kitchen and lean forward to look down the hall, where Billy's room is still dark.

"Hey, man. You forget something?" I say, dropping my bag at my feet before taking a few measured steps toward his room. When he doesn't answer, I slam the apartment door shut and hold my breath to see if I hear anyone.

"Hey, it's me!" Sutter says, rounding the corner while hugging an oversized box. She freezes when our eyes meet, and her mouth forms an O.

"For someone who doesn't live here, you seem pretty comfortable coming and going as you please," I say, relaxing the fists I had formed at my sides. I'm not sure which I prefer—a real intruder, or Billy's sister.

She juts her hip and adjusts her grip on the box, and maybe if she weren't sneering at me, I'd offer to take it.

"For your information, I was getting my stuff. And I have my own key, which my brother likes me having for emergencies. So, there." She shuffles the box in her arms again and marches toward me.

So there? "Did you seriously just try to make your point with a *so there?*" My pulse races with irritation. "I thought you were a burglar. What if I attacked you?"

She stops near the door and presses the box between her chest and the wall in order to free her hand and reach the knob. She tosses her hair over her shoulder with her glance and smirks.

"And how well did you do when you attacked me last night?" she says.

My jaw drops and for the few seconds it takes her to

maneuver the door open, I'm stunned speechless. I snap out of it as she steps out into the hallway.

"Uh, excuse me—who attacked whom? And you're missing the point." I pull the door closed behind me and sling my bag over my shoulder before locking it, not that locking it does much to keep some people out. She's halfway to the elevator by the time I turn around.

"Hey, Sutter. Let me get that for you," some old guy with a cane and black-rimmed glasses says as she fumbles around in an attempt to press the elevator button.

As I step up beside her, he looks me up and down and spits out a short laugh. It takes me a beat to realize he's making commentary on me not helping her.

"She sprayed me in the face with powder," I blurt out, holding his eye contact for a full breath then turning my attention to Sutter, expecting her face to be full of shame. It's not. Instead, that irritating smirk has crept up a little higher. *Shit.*

"You probably deserved it," the old man grunts, sticking his cane into the doorway and pushing the doors wider as Sutter steps in. He glares at me. I don't dare let him hold that thing open for me.

"You first. I insist." I motion with one hand, holding the door with my other arm.

"Damn right," he mumbles as he steps in next to Sutter. The two of them share a look and the old man's shoulders shake with silent laughter. *Awesome.* I'm sure somehow this guy is the team owner, and with my luck he'll follow me to the stadium and cut me loose right there.

The doors creak shut, and the small space feels instantly tighter.

"Let me carry that to your car for you," I say with a sigh.

"I'm fine," Sutter insists, shifting the box that is clearly too big for her arms to wrap up completely.

"Come on. You're making me look bad."

"Hmm," she grumps. She and the old man share another glance.

I shake my head as the back of my neck warms.

"Just to the car," I plead.

She turns to me, box and all, as the elevator doors open, then takes one step backward into the hallway. I step forward to block the door from shutting between us.

"To my car," she reiterates. I can see her friend staring at me in my periphery. He's invested in this more than any normal person should be.

"Yes." I glance at him. He doesn't even flinch.

I turn my attention back to Sutter and our eyes lock. It feels as though I'm in a negotiation with a mob boss, one where the heat lamp is turned on my face and a guy holding a pair of pliers is anxiously gripping them off to the side. There's something working behind her eyes—a distrust hidden in her slight squint. Her eyelids seem desperate for sleep. They're heavy but fighting to remain alive and alert, which I guess after rolling in drunk at about midnight totally checks. But it's more than that. If disappointment had a human form, I think it would look like Sutter. Same clothes as last night, same white button-down tied around her waist, hair twisted into a messy pile on top of her head, but not the kind that looks neat and intentional. And she's irritable.

"Here." She finally gives in, pushing the box into my

arms with a bit of a thrust. I think she simply got tired of me looking at her. Judging her.

The box is lighter than I expect, and a quick peek into the poorly folded top reveals what looks like photo albums and maybe a few documents.

"You take care, Sutter. And don't be a stranger," the man says as he heads in the opposite direction from us —*thank God*. I follow Sutter's lead toward the main road.

"He seems nice," I joke.

She tosses a laugh over her shoulder, and as pissed off as I want to remain, the sound pushes a short-lived smile into my cheeks.

"You're lousy at making first impressions, you know," she says, stopping at the crosswalk that leads to the stadium. She presses the side of her fist into the walk button then drops her hands into her pockets, squinting against the bright sun.

"I'm sorry. I'll learn to greet new people with a hefty dose of mace instead." I add a little bite to my tone.

A hint of a smile touches her lips, and she glances at me for a second.

"It was dry shampoo," she says with a slight tilt of her head.

"The fuck is dry shampoo?"

My response is genuine, and it makes her laugh hard—a real, full laugh this time. One that lasts long enough to not evaporate in the breeze. And the smile that goes with it touches her eyes.

I follow her across the street when the walk sign blinks, and she makes a hard left toward the ticketing offices. There must be another lot over there, one where her dad parks.

She probably left her car there last night. Unless . . . unless it's at some bar. The bars are a few blocks from here. And I've got a throwing session to get to. We're still walking.

"Where are you parked?" I have a bad feeling about this.

"At home. Come on, we better catch this bus," she answers, pointing to the city transit pulling into the bus lane a full block ahead. She begins to jog, and my legs automatically follow for a few steps before my suspicion kicks in.

"You're messing with me, aren't you?" I say.

She jogs a few more steps away before stopping and falling forward with both hands on her knees. And here I thought I made her laugh for real. This display right now? At my expense? That's a real laugh. That other one was merely a warm-up.

"I really thought you'd get on the bus," she cackles.

"Aw, man. Not cool!" I straighten one finger that's wrapped around the box to point at her and dip my chin. "Not. Cool."

She stands up straight and holds a fist to her mouth.

"Sorry, yes. You are right. That wasn't nice," she says, barely containing the gurgles begging to break free behind her words.

"Where's your car?" My voice is stern. Now, I'm actually pissed.

"It's seriously at my house. But my friend is driving around the block. She'll be here in a few seconds," she says, coming toward me with her arms out. A gentleman would insist on holding this box until her friend shows up, but screw that. I hand it back to her without an ounce of guilt, literally washing my hands in the air for show after I do.

"Your dad doesn't like us to be late for things. I suppose you know that, though." I pull my phone from my pocket to check the time. I'm still early, but that's not the point.

"Not if you're his favorite," she says with a roll of her eyes.

I'm not sure what that comment is supposed to mean, but based on the little Billy told me, I'm guessing it has something to do with her beef with her dad.

"Okay, well, whatever. Not helpful. And quit breaking in. I live there now, not you." I'm walking backward as I lecture her, but I'm still close enough to catch every detail of her unimpressed expression.

A silver sedan pulls up to the curb, slowing as the driver rolls down the passenger window. I'm guessing it's her friend. The woman has short black hair and she's wearing oversized sunglasses that she pushes on top of her head as she leans against the steering wheel to stare at me.

"Girl, who's this?" Her mouth is hanging open with a mix of surprise and some sort of predatory fascination that makes my neck turtle.

"He's Billy's new roommate. One more of my dad's boys." Sutter jerks open the back door and shoves her box inside, crimping the side with the door as she slams it shut.

"Better get to it. Wouldn't want to be late," she says without giving me another glance as she slings open the passenger door and climbs inside.

The car thumps with music as it pulls away, kicking up some letter-sized envelope in its wake. I stare at it for a few seconds, debating whether I should pick it up or ignore it—

ignore the last thirty minutes of my life. My conscience wins out, though, and I step into the roadway and snag it before the next rush of traffic comes through.

It's addressed to Sutter, which means it probably slipped out of that ratty box. It's from some law firm, and it's sealed, so it's probably something new her brother was holding for her. I tuck it in my gym bag and vow to forget about it the moment I hand it back to her brother. And I sure as hell better not be there when she swings by to get it. Something about that girl feels risky, like she's a temptation that could bury me in problems I have zero business—or interest—stepping into. The kinds of things that would quickly rule me out of becoming her dad's favorite.

CHAPTER 3
Sutter

If Kiki hadn't gone home with Shawn, the guy she met at McGill's last night, I probably would be taking the bus home right now. She left her car at the bar and walked back to Shawn's place after closing McGill's down. When she woke up in his bed this morning, she found herself on the second floor of a frat house. It's not that twenty-five is that much older than twenty-one, but clerking in the county judicial system *is* a long way from keg stands and frat parties.

Kiki crept out when the sun was barely up and called me on the sneaking suspicion that I disobeyed her orders to go directly home. She was able to bail me out of Billy's place before I had to eat one of his apology pancakes. Instead, we met up for all-you-can-drink strong coffee at the diner by the bar.

Rehashing the whole night with Kiki fired me up enough to obsess about getting my box of crap out of there as soon as possible. If only I'd waited one more hour.

"So, are we going to talk about him? Or are we going to

pretend that boy back there is not fine as hell?" Kiki teases. We haven't even made it a full block away. I can still see him in the passenger mirror.

"What's to talk about? My brother got a new roommate without telling me. That was him." I shrug, prop my elbow by the window and chew on my thumbnail.

Kiki coughs out a laugh, but I hold my ground and keep my focus on the storefronts and patio diners to my right.

"When you told me about your night, you did not once mention that new guy Jensen looked like that," she says.

I check my mirror to see if he's still in view, but he's nothing but a speck near the stadium.

"They all look like that."

"Uh, no. They do not," my friend retorts.

I roll my head against the headrest and meet her gaze long enough to roll my eyes at her.

"You're just jaded because of that asshat you almost married," she shouts in anticipation of the argument she knows she'll get from me.

"Wow! That's harsh," I roar.

Kiki laughs me off. Kiki never liked Corbin, not genuinely. She tolerated him for me, but when she and I went out alone, she wasn't shy about ripping him apart one annoying flaw at a time.

"Girl, Corbin looks like an accountant compared to that fine specimen back there. That's all I'm saying." She holds out an open palm as if presented an indisputable closing argument. I pop my mouth open to disagree, but then bite the tip of my tongue and laugh.

"Okay, you might be right," I decide. I've got to stop defending Corbin, even in dumb debates about guys who may or may not be better looking than him. He doesn't deserve to win.

"Thank you. And no *might* about it. I *am* right."

I shake my head and relax into my seat.

My friend manages to remain silent for almost an entire minute, and I foolishly assume she's moved on.

"You know . . ." The way her voice dips at the end triggers a deep inhale as I brace myself for whatever she's about to suggest. "You could maybe leverage this newfound friendship. As a way to finally finish that thesis you started two years ago."

"Kiki, there is no friendship to leverage. And I've moved on to a totally different thesis topic anyhow," I sigh out.

"Yeah? Is that why you're almost done with your master's degree and ready to turn that huge-ass chunk of research in for peer review?" She purses her lips and levels me with her *I-told-you-so* glare, which has only gotten sharper with her law degree.

This time, her look might be justified.

"That's fair," I say.

I'm down to seven weeks and a few days until my deadline with little to show but a pile of research papers and case studies that have zero correlation to one another. The most I've done with any of the materials in the last few months is shuffle the boxes from my living room to my bedroom and back again. My specialization is motivational therapy and personal growth coaching, which my dad always says sounds like a nice way to say self-help grifter. He doesn't believe in the psychology, but I know it works. I've *seen* it work in his world. With Corbin. My coaching sessions with my ex started naturally at first—just a girlfriend trying to help her boyfriend be his best. But when he started racking up strikeouts, I decided to start documenting things and correlating my work with his numbers. The metrics were proof. And Corbin fully bought into my research.

Until he no longer needed it. Or me.

Now I can't seem to settle on a new topic. And I've already pitched my professor seven of them. At this point, I'm tempted to write my thesis in a memoir style about the slow descent into madness of a twenty-five-year-old woman who let a man derail her dreams. I'm not sure I ever really had dreams, though, so not sure what my hypothesis would be.

Kiki stops in front of my building and shifts into park. I roll my neck and groan, almost wishing at this point I'd taken the damn bus.

"Okay, okay. I hear you. My lips are zipped on the topic. It's just that I think you could use a distraction. Call it a rebound! Besides, it would be pretty sweet if you motivated that adorable boy back there to become even greater than the so-called *Rocket* Corbin Forsythe. Am I right?" She hits me with a crooked smile that I can't help but mimic.

"Roger Clemens was The Rocket. They call Corbin *Sweet Heat,* which I always thought sounded lame, but—" I stop when I meet her blank stare, washed with that sleepiness she gets when I nerd out about baseball. *Back to the things Kiki's interested in.* "But yes, you are right. Jensen is adorable," I relent. We laugh in unison as I get out of her car and grab my box from the back seat.

"Think about it," she says through the open window.

"I'll think about it," I concede.

My friend holds up a pinky for me to mimic in a swear but I merely lift the box in my arms a hair higher.

"That counts as a pinky swear," she shouts as she pulls away.

I don't think it does.

I dump the box in the hall closet and nudge it to the back with my foot. I'll deal with it later. I spend the next thirty minutes laying in my bathtub with the shower water beating against my head, face, and chest. I feel downright rough after last night, as if I spent the night riding out in the desert in an open-top Jeep. I decide to pamper myself on my day off with a pajama day and the comfort of old episodes of *The Office*. I nuzzle into my oversized blanket and pull it up to my chin, clutching it with my fists as my head sinks into my pillow. The way my laptop taunts me from the end of my bed, though, is making pajama day hard to enjoy. Relaxing on the weekends has gotten harder as my thesis deadline—the generous, two-month *extended* deadline—approaches. Since my head is already filled with emotional racquetballs, maybe I should at least *try* to get rid of a few of them.

Reluctantly, I sit upright and pull the computer to my lap. I flip it open and immediately laugh at my last attempt at a presentation that's still open on the screen. I've been working part time in human resources for the local school district as a way to pay the bills, and actually tried to convince myself that using my degree to create truly motivational yet mandatory HR training modules would be the awe-inspiring breakthrough I needed for my thesis. The bee clipart followed by a record amount of bee puns says otherwise. I must have been drunker than I was last night when I came up with this.

Bee yourself and bee amazing. I chortle as I tap the delete key over and over until the evidence is erased. The starkness of the blank page hits me hard. Without the stupid bee puns, I'm literally back to square one.

Tongue firmly pushing against the inside of my cheek, I draw in a deep breath and click on the folder in the upper lefthand corner of my screen. The one titled ASSHOLE. There are dozens of video clips in there, and I hover over the most recent one for several seconds before giving in and clicking it.

"I should get a cut of your first big contract." My voice is an echo from the past. I catch myself smiling at it, mostly because I sound so damn happy. I laughed at my own joke then, and I'm laughing now hearing it on the video. Corbin is overexaggerating his motion, and I vividly remember this moment in time. I could close my eyes and my mind would mirror the visual on my computer screen to perfection.

"I can hear the documentary narration now. 'He was just a boy from Arkansas with nothing but raw talent, and then he met the brilliant Dr. Sutter Mason and she unlocked his untapped potential.'" I snap the computer shut at his words before I hear the sound of his pitch smacking into the catcher's mitt.

I really should get a cut of his next contract extension.

Of course, back when we filmed this for my thesis, we were partners for life . . . or so I thought.

So much work wasted. So much of my heart wasted. I flip the screen back open and immediately X out of the video clip before it can continue. I count the number of files and reach sixty with several left to count so I decide to stop. All I need to do is edit these together and narrate them, cutting in with my own videos where I explain my methods and the mental coaching that clearly correlates to Corbin's success on the mound. It's all right there—a final interview and the last test for metrics for my hypothesis. I'm sure if I swallow every ounce of my pride and ask, Corbin would let me run the tests and sit him down for one last interview. But it's more than the fact sitting across from him might turn me into a murderer. I simply don't want to give him the attention. I don't want him to be the star of my thesis. To be published in the university psychology library. To evermore be linked to me and my profession.

I click open a browser and type Jensen's name into the search bar. His name doesn't get the kind of hits Corbin's does, but the first video to come up has nearly a million views. Curious, I click to see what seems to be the last inning of a no-hitter for Clarence College on the Texas-Oklahoma border.

"Jay Hawk! Jay Hawk!" the crowd shouts in unison. I smirk at the clever nickname. It's also pretty sexy. Certainly, more alluring than Sweet Heat.

I flip to my stomach and prop my chin on my stacked fists so I can watch things unfold on the video. This doesn't seem like a big game for any reason other than Jensen possibly finishing a complete game no-hitter.

The video is shaky, clearly someone's cell phone from the third baseline, but it's steady enough to get a clear picture of every tick in Jensen's routine and windup. He's a lefty, which automatically gives him a mental edge over the right-handed hitter in the box. Lefties are . . . weird. I don't know why, but ever since I was a little girl, I knew they were somehow more special than the rest of the bullpen on my dad's teams.

Jensen's first two pitches are straight fastballs—strikes that the batter lets go right by. Nothing special about them, and probably totally hittable. But they came out of a lefty's hand, which makes them automatically . . . *weird*. He ends up getting the guy out on a slider that skips in the dirt, and the catcher tags the batter before he leaves the box.

Two batters to go. I'm sure I could scan down the comments to spoil the ending, but I'm invested. I want to see this play out. Even the video's title is vague—A COLLEGE NO-NO? The question beckons—did he do it?

I'm holding my breath as Jensen walks to the back of the mound and presses the ball between his hands, working the leather and threads in his palms, likely hoping they leave just enough moisture behind to give him that extra edge. He wears his hat low, and I'm fairly certain he's smeared eye black down his cheeks. My brother used to do that when he played Little League. Of course, he was never any good at the game, much to our father's disappointment. But he had the intimidation appearance down pat.

Jensen stares down the next hitter as he makes his way into the batter's box, and doesn't give him time to get comfortable, firing in a fast ball that baits him to swing. It's a blooper pop out to the third baseman, and the chants of *Jay Hawk* grow louder. Whoever is filming is jumping up and down, and the motion nauseates me, so I tuck my forehead into my palms for a few seconds. I continue to listen, my pulse mimicking the rhythm of the background noise—the stomping feet and chanting crowd. I pop my head up in time to witness the lengthy stare-down between Jensen and a hitter I recognize as last year's major league Rookie of the Year.

"Oh, shit!" I pop up into a sit and pull the laptop on my knees so I can get extra close. I'm more tempted to cheat now, to fast forward or read the comments. Kendall

Simpson hit a record-breaking number of home runs last year for Pittsburg. And staring at this college version of him shows that he has always been bigger than the average player. His legs are the size of regular people—whole people. And his arms nearly bust out of his sleeves.

This video either has a million views because Jensen did the unthinkable, or because Kendall Simpson spoiled a potential no-hitter. My palms are sweating and I'm watching this showdown four years after it actually happened. I cover my mouth and study every frame that passes as Jensen sets up just as he did with the two batters before. I tap mute on my computer. The crowd noise is distracting, and I'm not sure I want to hear them if this goes wrong. The person filming is wound up enough, and if this pitch lasts much longer I'm going to throw up from motion sickness caused by the recorder's jittery hands.

Jensen's knee comes up, his pause sitting at about the same length as every other pitch. His head forward, shoulders in a perfect line, glove out then tucked. His leg kick lands straight and he's ready the second the fastball leaves his hand.

And then suddenly the ball is gone—jetting four-hundred feet over the right field wall as Kendall Simpson drops his bat and makes a slow jog around the bases.

I hit pause and stare at the frozen image for a few seconds, my mouth agape under my palm. I don't think I've blinked once since this at-bat started.

The field is marked by a line of players, starting with Jensen, and stretching all the way out to the visiting bullpen filled with pitchers, each with their gloves and throwing hands on top of their heads as they stare off into the black night where the ball left the light. I tap play and let the victory lap play out, but my eyes remain on Jensen. As everyone turns back to the field and gets ready for the next hitter, he stays put, staring at the outcome of the last one. I bet he thinks about this moment every time he's on the mound, subconsciously if not directly. It has to be lodged in there. *How could it not?*

Jensen's hands haven't left the top of his head. His back is still to the plate. Even as his coach comes out to pull him from his almost epic game that will now go down as a one-hitter he couldn't finish, or worse, if his reliever lets him down, he remains fixated on that terrible, awful result.

I run the video again, this time full sound, and I focus on the crowd—the way it turns against him with the swing of a bat. Then I dive into the rabbit hole of other links that came up with my search, reading about his injury, about his up and down outings, about his frustrated coaches and the inevitable criticism from the baseball pundits who haven't thrown a ball in years.

Jensen Hawke is going to fail with my father if he is anything like these blog posts say he is. And it won't have a damn thing to do with mechanics. His problem is in his head. Just like Corbin's was.

I flop back on my bed and pinch the bridge of my nose, knowing my solution is right there on that computer screen. I also know I could do Jensen some good. We could help each other. I've had those thoughts before, though, and it got me nothing but a hurt, angry, jaded heart. But maybe that's the armor I need to be absolutely clinical with Jensen. Maybe he's actually the perfect test subject come along at the right time. And maybe, like Kiki said, I can help turn Jensen into a better pitcher than Corbin ever will be.

My lip ticks up at that thought. I'm not proud of the jolt of serotonin this revenge fantasy gives me, but I like it. I like it a lot. Enough that I grab my phone from my side table and fire off a text to my dad, asking if I can watch practice tomorrow. It's the first thing I've written to him since I texted the word ASSHOLE in all caps. I'm not big on the idea, but for the sake of finally finishing this damn thesis, I'll go ahead and swallow my pride.

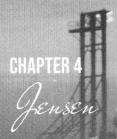

CHAPTER 4

Jensen

For a girl who is apparently holding a grudge against her father, Sutter seems awfully comfortable talking to him right now. She's been here all morning. First in his office, then tailing him around like she's his intern or some shit. If she's holding a grudge, it must be invisible. I sure as shit don't see evidence of it.

"Hey, earth to Jensen." A glove smacks the side of my calf, reminding me that I have important things to do out here. I look down at Dalton—the catcher who got traded with me—as he squats, ready to catch my slider and work out some things. He's a decent guy. Older, married with a baby on the way. It means he's not hip on hitting the bars after practices and games. All business. And he has a good track record of working with lefties like me.

"Sorry, yeah. I was wondering if Coach was going to come by," I ramble, my eyes scanning back to the batting cages, where he's now nodding as Sutter flips through pages of some packet in her hands.

"Sure you were." Dalton snickers.

I grimace down at him before heading toward the bullpen mound.

"What's that supposed to mean?"

Dalton hits his glove with his fist a few times before stretching it out toward me and calling for the ball. I rotate my arm slowly and toss the ball his way for a few warm-up throws. He holds the ball in his hand and rotates it a few times before throwing it back.

"You know that's Coach Mason's daughter over there, right?" He pushes his mask up on his head and meets my eyes.

"Yeah, so what? I live with his son. I met her, sort of. She's . . . a lot," I say.

I throw the ball back and it snaps in Dalton's glove. He pushes his mask back down then fires the ball back.

"Okay, good. I just wanted to make sure you weren't getting stupid ideas or some shit. I've seen this story before, and the player always loses. Always."

"Yeah, I hear ya," I respond. I want to add that I don't have time for drama or high maintenance princesses with daddy issues, but I hold my tongue if only to prove that I'm focused and not some young punk who listens to his penis first. I also don't want to give the topic more discussion than we already have, and I definitely don't need to start talking about how tempting Sutter is. Because while I have zero interest in hooking up with anyone, Sutter Mason is definitely the apple in my Garden of Eden.

She's built like an athlete, her arms toned and her legs muscular. Her hair is a dusty sort of blonde, and the way it's tucked underneath the Monsoon hat she's wearing is sexy as hell. The tight jeans, bright white shoes and T-shirt make her stand out among a field full of gritty-ass ballplayers. I'd like to say that's the only reason I was staring in her direction a few minutes ago, but it's not. She's hard *not* to look at when she's nearby. She's been eye-fucked at least a dozen times this morning by some of the other guys.

"Okay, let's see what you've got," Dalton says, setting up for my slider.

I shake off all thoughts of Sutter and focus on nothing but the visual in my head—the perfect pitch. I bend down and let my arm hang as I breathe out before standing tall and coming set with a deep inhale. I let the ball fly and it skips the dirt right at Dalton's knee as it dives.

"Not bad. You're still giving it away too much, though. I think you're falling to your right too much," Dalton says, tossing the ball back.

I nod, but I don't think he's right. My line was fine. It's something with my grip or my release. I just can't seem to find the feel lately.

I go through the motion again, coming set the same as before, breathing in then out. This time I remind myself fractions of a second before my pitch to watch my release. The ball never dives, clipping the outside of the strike zone. This time, Dalton doesn't offer any feedback.

"Shit," I mutter under my breath the second I catch his throwback.

"He's right; you're falling off to the right. And that time you tried to overcorrect with a different release point." Coach Mason's voice startles me, but I keep my cool, shaking out my arms as I turn to my right where he's standing next to the pitching coach and his daughter. *Great. An audience. With her.*

"Okay, I'll watch that," I say, pulling my lips in tight to keep my mouth shut. He's wrong; I'm not falling off. I am overcorrecting, though, and if I try not to fall off with this pitch, I'm going to be adding another layer on top of whatever my real problem is.

I can see the three of them hovering in my periphery, fingers linked into the fence, Sutter clutching that stack of papers to her chest, Coach crossing his ankles as he gets comfortable. That means he's going to watch every pitch. This isn't the product I want him to see.

I breathe in deeply through my nose and calm my pulse, rolling my shoulder and letting my arm hang until I feel a sense of calm. This used to be my money pitch. It's the reason I'm here. It's the paycheck pitch, the one that will take down giants if I can just remember how to fucking throw it.

Standing tall, I inhale and hold my breath an extra beat before beginning my motion. The result is better this time, but that had zero to do with my mechanics. I willed that ball to behave correctly. I know. Coach knows it. Assistant Coach Benson knows it. Sutter probably knows it too with my luck. It's why nobody talks.

Dalton throws the ball back and our eyes meet for a quick glance. He's not saying it, but I swear I read his glance to mean he agrees with Coach. Fine. I'll try watching my line.

I dig into the bullpen rubber with my left foot and shake my arm out at my hip as I clear my mind. It doesn't help that I'm looking right into Sutter's eyes like this. She's facing the sun, so her hat is pulled low to shade her face, but I can see her lashes and the creases from her squint, and it's enough to let me know she's staring back at me. I stare at her as I kick at the dirt and work my foot in, looking away briefly only to lean forward and lock my aim onto Dalton's glove. Deep breath, long hold, then exhale. This time, I skip the second inhale, instead fueling myself with some good ol' fashioned irrational hostility as I turn back to look Sutter in the eyes one last time. She's lifted her chin, which lets the sunlight under the brim of her hat, glinting off her blue eyes. Her expression matches her father's—blank, emotionless, and hard. My head swivels back toward my target and I unleash another pitch. It's the same as the last, only a little more heat and maybe a little closer to the ground. Nothing about it was easy, and nobody says a word. Again.

This routine goes on for my entire session, and after the last pitch, both coaches wander off without giving me feedback. The pit in my stomach widens and my mouth waters like I'm going to vomit.

"Not bad. You're getting there," Dalton says as he slips his mask off and stands next to me.

"*Pfft*," I huff.

"Yeah, I know. I was trying to make you feel better," he admits before grabbing his water bottle and squirting it into his mouth, then spraying down his face and neck.

I stare at him until he shrugs, then I laugh.

"That's fair. I'd rather have your honesty, for what it's worth," I say.

We both walk to the bench to gather our gear bags and I take out a towel to run over my face. This Arizona sun is brutal, and the humidity off the field has me sweating bullets. It's only spring.

"So, you really want honesty?" Dalton says as we exit the bullpen and head toward the training room. I nod.

"You were falling to your right." He shrugs.

"Hmm," I respond. I look straight ahead and let the

tightness that forms in my chest work itself out without getting defensive. Maybe he's right. Perhaps they all are. My gut still says no, though.

I get a short glimpse of Sutter and her dad speaking down the hall as we enter the facility, and I pause in an attempt to eavesdrop on their conversation.

"Good luck with that. Even if he does sign, I don't think you're going to get the results you think you are," Coach says.

"We'll see," Sutter responds, her head tilted defiantly to the side.

She juts out her palm and her dad chuckles before shaking it once. Maybe Billy wasn't totally wrong about the cold shoulder thing. Nothing about this scene feels warm or fuzzy or like daddy's little girl at all.

I dip inside the training room before Sutter catches me watching. I toss my bag in my cubby and head toward the trainer's table so she can wrap my shoulder with ice. The routine is relentless, but it has to be. If I want to make the comeback I imagine, I have to follow their rules. This arm is what keeps me in my job.

"You know the drill, Jensen," Shannon, the trainer, says. In the two weeks I've been here, Shannon has wrapped my arm and put me through various strength drills more hours than I've actually been on the field with a ball in my hand. She's the perfect fit for me—a former military medic who threw discus in college about thirty years ago. She's tough and no-nonsense, which I probably need if I'm going to stick to all the things I need to do to stay healthy.

I hold my arm out in her preferred position and she preps it before packing on the ice. My attention is on the sting of the cold against my skin, but somehow I still sense Sutter enter the room behind me.

"What, did you leave some of your things in the locker room too and come to get them? Or are you stalking me," I gripe. Shannon lifts her focus to my eyes for a beat, and smirks.

"They're wrong, you know," Sutter says.

I chew at my tongue, sorting out what she means without actually asking. I can't.

"Who's wrong?" I keep my eyes on the work Shannon is doing, but I hear Sutter's steps as she moves closer.

"Your problem isn't that you're falling off too much to the right," she says.

My mouth ticks up on one side instinctively, because I like being told I'm right.

"I know," I say.

Shannon stretches out the wrap so she can contour it around my shoulder, and she chuckles at my clipped response.

"Don't get me wrong, you may be falling off to the right. Right, left . . . I don't really know about that stuff. I just know that's not your problem." Sutter moves around the table and takes a seat on the one behind Shannon. My trainer isn't fazed, but I am.

"Pardon me if I don't take your feedback seriously since you *don't really know about that stuff*," I chime back. I'm looking her in the eyes now, and the slight squint that crinkles the corners and the small lift in her cheeks tells me she's not backing down.

"I'd like to help you," she says.

"Pass," I respond.

Leaning forward, Sutter folds her hands over the stack

of papers resting on her thighs. She crosses her ankles as they dangle from the table and tilts her head slightly, looking in Shannon's direction.

"Why are they always so stubborn," she asks my trainer.

"Because they're men," Shannon says.

Fuck. Shannon is not really my ally.

My mouth opens slightly and when Shannon looks up and catches my surprised expression she shrugs and coughs out a short laugh.

"Girl knows her shit, Sparky. I've seen it work. Up to you if you want to take advantage of every tool in the kit. I can only help you with this part." Shannon pats the now fully wrapped ice pack against my arm. I thought her calling me Sparky was a term of endearment, but now that I hear it in this context, I think maybe she was mocking me.

Shannon collects the remaining wrap and heads toward the table in the back of the room where one of the outfielders is stretched out on his back and working through some knee strengthening exercises. I wonder what nickname he gets. I wonder if we're all Sparky.

"I have a proposal," Sutter says, bringing my attention back to her.

"Don't you have a job?" It's a Monday yet she's spending her time here, chasing her dad around and now pestering me.

"I do. I flexed my time because I felt this was important." She hands me the stack of papers she's been carrying around the ballpark this morning. I glance at the top page and read a few key parts:

UNIVERSITY THESIS SUBJECT STUDY CONTRACT

"Ohhh, no, thank you," I say, thrusting the contract at her. She pushes it back toward me as she stands.

"You didn't even read it. Hear my pitch first."

I hold her gaze, mulling over the idea of tossing the pages on the floor and walking out, but there's something to her hard glare. It's as though she's challenging me, and whether she suspects it or not, that's one of my weaknesses. I can't walk away when people test me.

"What's the pitch?" I'm not interested, but listening, or at least pretending to listen, should be enough to make her go away, and I'll look like I heard her out.

"Are you familiar with mental coaching?" She clasps her hands in front of her as she talks, and I note how short her fingernails are, devoid of color and torn almost to the fingertips. She balls her hands together quickly and I glance up to see she caught me staring.

"You bite those things when you're nervous?" I gesture to her hands.

"No. I bite my nails when I'm pissed, and I've been pissed a lot lately. Now answer my question."

Pissed. She's been pissed. I'm the one who threw like shit and got stuck in an apartment with a guy whose sister is, well, her.

"Yes, I've heard of mental coaching. But given your pissed-off nail-biting habits, I'm not sure you'd make the best mental coach." Again, I try to shove the papers back into her hands. She steps to her right and begins to pace. I sigh.

Why am I still here, listening? Why was Shannon on her side? What makes this conversation worthwhile?

"What would you say if I told you that you threw the ball exactly the way you thought you would today?"

I laugh lightly but go silent when she turns and meets my gaze. She leans back against one of the cabinets, folding her arms across her chest. There's a tan line on her wrist where it looks as though a smart watch belongs. She must be outside a lot.

"I'd tell you that I threw the ball the exact *opposite* of the way I thought I would today." I roll up her contract and squeeze it tightly while I hold her stare.

Sutter doesn't flinch, and a confident grin tugs up one side of her mouth. She pushes away from the counter and walks back toward me, stopping when she's about a foot away.

"Liar."

I blink a few times at her bold remark, eventually spitting out a laugh and shaking my head.

"I'm sorry, but we're done." I drop the contract on the training table and push past her.

"In one week, I will have you consistently hitting your spot with the slider. And all we have to do is talk," she says to my back.

I hold up my right palm. "Thanks, I throw my slider just fine," I lie.

"Maybe. But not when people are looking."

Fuck.

I stop about a dozen feet shy of leaving the room and chew on her observation. She's not wrong. And it's *her* father who watched me fail today over and over again. I don't for one minute believe her voodoo psychology will make a difference in the way I throw, but I also don't think having Coach's daughter invested in my success is a totally bad idea. Billy said his dad and sister don't talk much, but they seemed chummy enough today. At least until he wished her good luck with getting something signed. I turn around and my eyes dart to the contract on the table, then shift my attention to Sutter's face.

"Your dad doesn't believe in this shit, does he?" I'm assuming from the bit of the conversation I overheard, but I am pretty certain I have it nailed down.

"He doesn't like to think he does, but he's seen it work. He's just too arrogant to give credit where it's due. Coach Kevin Mason has a reputation to uphold, after all. And if he's not the reason stellar pitching comes out of this farm system then why have him around at all?" She reaches forward and picks up the curled pages, pushing them together as she strolls toward me and hands them to me again.

"Do me a favor. Look at the small case study I've noted on the last page, and if, after seeing those numbers, you aren't a little interested in my experiment, I'll drop it. But" —she slaps the packet against my chest and I reluctantly take it—"If you think those numbers on that last page are doable—that they're in you, in that arm covered in ice— well, you know where to sign. And we start immediately."

She reaches in her back pocket and pulls out a pen, which she also flattens against my chest with her palm. I cover her hand with mine, swallowing it underneath the span of my fingers, and the coolness of her skin tempts me to close my hand around her to warm her up. Thankfully, she pulls her hand away, leaving me only with the pen. I don't need thoughts like that running through my head. If anything, I'm going to throw even *more* like shit if she gets me focused on stuff like warming her hand with mine, holding her hand, touching her.

"I'll let you know," I say, holding the pen up before

tucking it behind my ear. I snag my bag from my cubby and leave her behind, not as much as glancing at the stack of papers in my hand during my walk back to my apartment.

Billy usually doesn't get home until late on his work-days, which is a perfect situation for me. I like having this place to myself in the afternoons. I've been doing a lot of yoga and I don't need an audience for that. Plus, the TV in the main room is huge, and if I'm going to watch my competition and study the guys I want to be like, I want to see them on a sixty-inch screen.

I drop my bag by the door when I come in and carry the contract into the kitchen, leaving it on the counter while I pull out my supplements and the blender, along with the last of my orange juice. Once my smoothie is mixed and the blender rinsed, I give in and pull up a chair to give this case study a proper look. It's a chart for some mysterious SUBJECT A, and she's charted everything from spin rates to true strike versus forced strike counts. The pitcher is a lefty, and this guy's curve differential tracks from a ten mile-per-hour drop to seventeen over what looks like an entire minor season. My gut says bullshit, that this myste-rious person is made up, or that she followed some guy fresh from the surgeon's table to the peak of his recovery. It's not realistic.

I toss the pages back on the counter and head into my bathroom to remove the ice wrap and shower. When I come out, the first thing I notice is the morning news team banter echoing from the living room. Maybe Billy took a sick day or something. Wrapped in a towel, I step into the living room to see if he's camped out on the couch.

"Hey, you out here, man?"

It's as if Sutter was sitting on the edge of the couch

waiting for me to appear. The second I round the corner she jets to her feet and walks toward me, hands shoved in her pockets, her body literally brewing with the energy of a thousand grams of caffeine.

"So, what do you think?" she asks.

My mouth hangs open for a second as I take a quick scan of the room, partly expecting more people to pop out and surprise me.

"Did you break in here? What the—"

"I have a key, remember?" she says, pulling it from her pocket and flashing it to me as evidence before tucking it back in her possession.

"Remind me, why the fuck do you have a key? You don't live here!" I run my palm over my face and through my hair, gripping the wet strands in frustrated shock.

"Well, I *did* live here, and I like having a key. And my brother needs me to check on the place sometimes when he works late, and—"

"Your nearly thirty-year-old brother needs someone to check on him?" *How is this happening to me? How am I living in this situation? This nightmare? I need to move. I—* "Can you get out, please? I'm sort of in the middle of showering."

I grip the towel at my waist and turn toward my room, but damn if she doesn't follow right behind.

"Looks like you already showered, and I've seen men in towels before." She's literally in my room now, the door I tried to sling shut meaningless to her.

I spin around and glare at her.

"How do I get you to leave?" I gesture toward the doorway, partly wishing I had magical powers that would banish her with the motion. News flash: I don't.

"Sign the contract. Let me help you." She crosses her

arms over her chest and juts a hip. Her gaze dips to my waist for a second before coming back up to my eyes.

"I don't need your help," I reiterate, but my defiance only seems to embolden her and she steps closer. My bed between us, we remain in this weird-ass standoff for more seconds than we should. She's stubborn and relentless, but so am I.

"I can make you better." Her tone is devoid of doubt, and the arrogance trips a wire in my chest. I know how this game works, and I don't care who her dad is. I don't give a shit what my trainer's opinion is of this smug daddy's girl standing in my bedroom. And I know damn well the only person who can really make a difference in my pitching is me.

Drawing in a slow breath to calm my brewing temper, I look to my right where the envelope addressed to Sutter still sits on my dresser top. I walk over and snag it then move to her side of the bed, stopping a foot away and tapping the edge of the mail against her forearm.

"Take your mail and go home."

Her tongue pushes in her cheek as her eyes haze a hint. Her gaze remains glued to mine, but her tough-girl exterior seems a little weakened. She reluctantly takes the letter from my hand and glances at it, her eyes dimming more when she reads who it's from. Probably because it's some lawyer. Probably someone suing her ass for breaking into people's apartments while they shower.

"You'll change your mind," she says, stepping back and shoving the envelope in her back pocket. She turns around when she exits my room and I step into the hall to make sure she's truly leaving.

"You can leave the key by the door," I throw out before

she opens it. Her only response is a quick middle finger tossed over her shoulder before she exits. She punctuates it by locking the door with her key from the other side.

Instead of getting dressed and moving on with my day, I head right back into the shower and turn the water as hot as it will go. I'm riled, and I'm not going to be able to focus on anything but her frustrating insistence for the rest of the day. And thanks to a key and some real crap luck in terms of roommates and teams and daddy-daughter relationships, I may end up repeating this entire nightmare again tomorrow. And the next day. And the next. Until I sign some stupid paper that gives her permission to show up and talk to me even more.

CHAPTER 5
Sutter

I was wearing my confident jeans two days ago. Those jeans are the ones that get me to the front of the line at clubs, that flex enough to let me run in cute shoes and tops when I need to get the hell out of someplace, and the ones that make my legs look both sexy and like I might also kick someone's teeth in if I need to. If I could go back in time, I would buy six more pairs. But I can't. And now I'm in my linen shorts and sandals, and feel more like a girl out for tea with Grams than a woman on her path to being a licensed psychologist.

In the confidant jeans, I was bold enough to call my professor and declare I was finishing my original project and it would be done and turned in on time. Well, the *new* on time. I knew in my gut I would wear Jensen Hawke down and get my way, and he would thank me for the life-altering therapy down the road.

In my linen shorts, however? Yeah, this version of me is taking hard stock of the fact it's been two days and Jensen hasn't emailed or called. And I'm feeling less assertive and willing to simply show up at the clubhouse. Both because I don't want to give him a chance to verbally say no again before I come up with a new plan of attack and because I don't want my dad to have the satisfaction of being right.

This is when I miss Mom the most. And maybe it's why I'm here, because even on her difficult days, Kate Mason is often able to give me clarity just by being close to her.

I pull into the parking spot closest to the main office at Lilac Gardens Memory Care. Mom picked this place herself, before things got bad. Most days, she doesn't seem to hate being here. There are others, though, when it's hard to visit.

"Your mom's in her room, Sutter. Good to see you," says the nurse named Jamie who has been here since my mom toured the place with me and Billy a few years ago.

I sign the visitor form and take the badge from Jamie, clipping it on the sleeve of my striped T-shirt. Jamie's warm smile tells me my mom is doing well today. She's good about letting me and Billy know what to expect. She's also good at hearing my frustrations when Dad refuses to come along.

Once I'm through the double security doors, I stroll down the long hallway, past a few open doors where residents are visiting with family members or each other. I refer to this section as the *in-between*. There is a lot of supervision available, and medical care is in the same wing. But it's not quite the clinical setting that's in the next building over. When mom moves there, odds are she won't remember me. I brace myself for it every time I visit because I'm the one who will have to make the call. Billy sees the bright side of everything, and my dad refuses to believe life has changed. In his head, he thinks they're still married and he's an attentive spouse. Both of them know better deep down, of course. What they really want to avoid are hard decisions—*painful* decisions. And I enable them by taking the reins.

I probably should have done my thesis on my own family. But I'm not healthy enough to face that head on.

I get to my mom's door and knock softly since it's partly opened. She's sitting in the winged-back leather chair with the ottoman she insisted we move into this place with her. She lifts up and cranes her neck, looking over the rims of her glasses. I don't breathe until she smiles.

"Sutter! What a surprise." Her voice instantly fills all the holes inside my chest, places I don't realize are void of warmth until I'm in her presence. She gets up from her chair and sets the book she was reading down, along with her glasses. Her arms engulf me in seconds, and I breathe her in. She did her hair today, and she's dressed almost as if she were ready for work. Routine, she always told me, will be what keeps her present. Now nearing my masters in psychology, I can attest that her hypothesis carries some weight.

"*Tom Sawyer*, huh?" I say as we break apart. She follows my gaze to the book, and smiles.

"There's comfort in knowing how a story ends," she says before pushing the ottoman back a few feet to give me a place to sit.

My mom taught the classics in the literature department at the university before she was diagnosed with young-onset dementia and forced into early retirement. It's a rare occurrence, but more likely when a family member has had the disease, and both of my grandparents did. Billy and I have tested for the genes, and though our results came back negative, that worry lingers in my mind every time I forget something.

Dementia is a cruel curse, and it hammers away at a family from every angle. I wanted Mom to live with me in our own place, but she refused. She's the most unselfish person I know, and my brother definitely takes after her. Me, not so much.

"So, what's new in the world today? How is school? And that friend of yours?" She means Kiki. My mom has trouble lately remembering her name. I've learned her tells, though. She says things to get around the words when she needs to.

"Kiki is doing great. And I'm still trying to finish that final research paper. I'll get there," I say, biting my tongue until I get a read on her expression. Sometimes I can talk to my mom about my breakup with Corbin and the unfinished research I have, but other days . . .

"You will. Just keep plugging along," she says, her lips forming her signature *you-can-do-it* smile.

"I saw there's a concert in the garden next week. Maybe we can go together?" I know that will depend on how she is doing that day, and since she moved from her independent apartment to this space six months ago, we haven't been able to make a single social event together. Mostly when I visit, we sit together and read.

"Won't you be busy?" Mom's brow furrows and her head tilts. My stomach tightens because I have no idea *why* I would be busy. And neither does she.

"My weekend is wide open," I say with a smile.

Her mouth bunches and brow lowers even more. I redirect our conversation to her book by reaching over and picking it up, but she's already begun down this new conversational path, one without rules.

"Are things not going well with Corbin?" My mom started asking about him a month ago, maybe two. She brings him up periodically, and I think maybe because he was present when we first helped her move into the apartment.

"Mom, Corbin and I—"

"Oh, that's right," she cuts in with a wave of her hand.

I sit back and exhale, relieved that she remembered. But she hasn't.

"I forgot he's been traveling with the team. You must be so excited to have him home this week, though, for the series. Do tell him I miss his charming smile." The easy curve that touches my mom's lips makes it impossible for me to correct her despite the fire-hot hole burning in my chest.

I stand up and hand her the book.

"I will. I should actually be on my way," I say, leaning down and kissing her cheek as she pecks mine. She squeezes my hand before I back away, and I scoot her ottoman back under her feet before I leave the room. I suck back the tears and emotion that desperately want to ruin my eyeliner and mascara, and count my blessings that Jamie is busy when I check out and leave. I manage to hold it together until I get to my car. Under the cover of my tinted windows and behind the safety of my steering wheel, though, I cry. I let it out hard—the ugly kind that requires Kleenex and blowing. But after a minute, I force it all back down and pull out my phone to see if my hunch is right.

I open the baseball app to check the schedule, and there it is—Texas is in town for a three-game series starting tomorrow. There is zero chance Corbin is passing up an opportunity to be loved and adored by his Monsoon family of fans.

It's not exactly confidence that suddenly fuels me, but the effects are similar. I know full well that I'm buckling up and peeling out of the senior living center on the fumes of rage and a dash of jealousy. There's a pressure at the top of my stomach, right where my ribs part and my insides get soft. It's as if a silver bullet is slowly melting its way inside of me. All of my training tells me now is the time to step back and evaluate my feelings before behaving irrationally, but I've never been good at listening to myself, or good advice at all for that matter. I'm in the Monsoon parking lot right at one. Months of habits formed by visiting Corbin at practice have etched this schedule into my brain, and if my memory is correct, there should be a scrimmage happening on the field.

I dig through my center console for my sunglasses and push them on my face before knotting my hair up in a band on top of my head. My leather bag is still in my trunk from work yesterday, so I take it out and riffle through it as I walk toward the main gates. When I find the notepad and pen, I pull them out then gather myself and put on an air of professionalism. Since the office doors are locked, I check in with the security staff at the gate. It's new people every year so they don't recognize me, and proceed to radio the operations manager—my dad's boss—to check my credentials. It's embarrassing when this happens because for those few minutes it takes them to get the confirmation, the guards always look at me as if I'm here to catch myself a ballplayer-slash-baby daddy. One time, I went ahead and pretended I was because screw them for judging me if that's what I were up to.

"Go on," the guy finally says, handing back my credential along with my leather bag that he has completely left disheveled inside. I do my best to push things back into the right spots as I head down the concourse and through the tunnel to the field.

The sharp snap of ball hitting glove greets me as I step out from the shadows and into the bright sun, and I can't help but smile. There are some things about this game that even a lying ex-fiancé won't ruin for me, and that sound is near the top of the list.

There are few people spread around the stands today, mostly family and friends who are in town. I head down to the third row behind the home dugout. I like the view from here, but more than that, I like the way sound travels from the concrete walls in front of me. I can overhear a lot of secrets from this seat—the kinds of commentary and offhanded remarks that can help Jensen. Plus, when the same critique comes from my mouth that he'll get from my father, I might earn some credibility with him. And since I'm not leaving here without him agreeing to try my methods for at least a week, I'm going to need every edge I can get.

"Well, you're here, so that must mean you duped that poor sucker into your head doctoring." My dad's voice growls behind me, nodules from years of tobacco texturing the deep voice I grew up hearing. I don't bother looking up.

65

"He's almost on board," I answer, purposely exuding an obnoxious amount of confidence.

My dad spits out a laugh and mutters *shit* under his breath as he passes, clearly not buying a drop of it.

"Saw Mom today," I throw at his back. He pauses at the last step before entering the field. That was low to say right now, even for me. But I've got the same messy passive-aggressive tendencies that he does, so he shouldn't be surprised.

He doesn't turn to face me completely, but he does look to his left enough to give me a clear view of the twitch in his jaw before he speaks.

"She having a good day?" He squints from the sun. Years of staring at the sky just like this has etched permanent lines at the corners of his eyes.

I bite the tip of my tongue and will my better self to respond.

"She was reading *Tom Sawyer*, so yeah."

His mouth ticks up a hint and he nods before heading down the steps into the dugout. Some other day I might have told him the truth, that she was confused, and then I'd admonish him for never bothering to visit her himself. But I have more important battles to pick, and my sparring partner just took the mound to pitch to a live batter.

Jensen circles the mound while he works the ball in his hand, letting the batter step up to the plate and wait for him. The pitching coach is sitting a dozen feet behind the mound, guarded by a screen, and I can tell by the way Jensen carries his shoulders that it's getting in his head. The relaxed man I've argued with every time we've met seems instantly uncertain from chest up, yet his legs continue to walk the same circular path as his hands feel every nuance of the ball.

"Alright, Hawke. There's a time limit, you know," the pitching coach says, twirling his finger in the air to urge him to hurry it along.

Jensen nods and digs his foot into the ground against the rubber.

His chest inflates with a deep breath as he settles in and stares at the batter for a beat before leaning forward to get his sign. He nods and stands tall, his shoulders finally relaxing a little before he begins his wind up and chucks a fastball down the center of the plate. The hitter sends it into the opposing bullpen about three hundred fifty feet away.

I push my sunglasses to the top of my head and make a note of everything that stood out. I sit forward after, my hands on my notepad and gaze fixed on how Jensen reacts after failure. He's facing my direction, but his eyes aren't focused on anything in particular. It's probably why he feels he can get away with mouthing *fuck*. My dad is in the dugout at the same sightline I am, and I know he'll remember him doing it. Not that my father is a saint in terms of swearing. I'm pretty sure he was the reason I dropped an F-bomb in first grade. What he *won't* like is any showing of emotion during battle. My dad has always considered this part of the game to be a duel, like an old western shootout with a ball instead of a bullet. And F-bombs? They reek of weakness.

Jensen shortens his pre-pitch routine and comes back with what looks like a slider that fools the hitter for a strike. Like last time, his body and mouth react, this time with more fire. Fire is good. I think it's useful. My dad won't, however.

It's clear Jensen has some magic in his arm. He ends up striking out three hitters in a row with a good mix of pitches before the same hitter who hit one out of the park steps back up and manages to drive a hard ground ball right back at Jensen's feet. He jumps out of the way as the guys waiting in the opposite dugout clap and holler for the batter. Jensen's gaze locks on them, and the scowl on his face creases so deeply I can make out the harsh lines from dozens of feet away.

"Alright, that's good for today," my dad says as he steps up from the dugout and walks toward the mound, meeting Jensen halfway. He slaps Jensen's ass in a show of *good job* as he continues his stroll over to his colleague, where I'm sure they'll share half-critiques before they put the next guy to the test. Just before Jensen steps down into the dugout, he glances up, and our eyes meet. I smile with tight lips. He merely blinks slowly before disappearing from my view.

I jot a few more thoughts on my notepad then tuck it away in my bag before propping my feet on the seat in front of me. My dad walks back toward the dugout as the next pitcher steps up. He doesn't mouth anything to me, but he snickers for sure.

"You'll see," I say, loud enough for him to hear. He shakes his head before disappearing into the dugout again.

I pick at the sides of my fingernails as the next guy gets to work. I'm only half paying attention to him, but his outcome doesn't seem any better or worse than what Jensen had. It's going to be hard to convince him he's on track. I get the sense that Jensen Hawke is the kind of athlete who thinks he should be at his very best without having to make the climb.

Two more pitchers throw before Jensen finally appears again. He steps out of the dugout, his arm wrapped in ice, and pauses as he stares at the opposite end of the stadium. His jaw flexes as he chews at something, eventually spitting what looks like sunflower seed shells into an empty water bottle in his hand. He reaches into his back pocket, pulls out a bag of seeds, and pours more into his mouth before turning my direction and holding the bag up slightly.

"No, thanks. I'm not really into food you have to work for only to spit ninety percent of it out," I say.

He shrugs, and a brief smile plays at his lips. He hides it by mashing them together as he rolls the bag up and shoves it back into the pocket of his baseball pants. He looks at the ground for a few seconds, gently kicking around the dirt before his shoulders finally drop and he walks around the gate to join me in the seats. He plops down with three seats between us, his manspread eating up half the distance. I squint against the sun as I look at him, one of my eyes open more than the other.

"You want my thoughts?" I quirk a brow.

"Nope." He spits a few more shells into his bottle and remains focused on the field.

I nod, wishing I had the confident jeans on. Regardless, I believe I'll eventually get him on my side.

Since he's not ready to hear my commentary about him, I decide to take a different approach, and as a short, stocky pitcher takes the mound to throw, I give my best assessment of what I think might be going on in his head.

"You see how he's smiling?" I note, glancing Jensen's way.

"*Mmm*," he grumbles, clearly not a smiler himself.

"Oh, I'm not saying that's a good thing. It's not, actually. I mean, it can be a tool, sure, but this kid is so desperate for my dad's approval, he's grinning every chance he gets to show how grateful he is for this chance. Watch. After every throw, he looks this way for affirmation. He wants praise. This sport will eat him up."

I don't watch Jensen directly for his reaction, but I keep an eye on him from my periphery and note how his posture shifts and he settles in more to one side as if he's really studying the guy. When the pitcher does exactly what I predict—turning and smiling toward my father and us by default, he chuckles.

"Shit, am I that bad?" he says through light laughter.

"You? No. You don't have his issues." I glance back in his direction and take in his body as he rests in the chair. I'm about to point out how relaxed he seems now when we're interrupted by several voices shouting one name on the concourse behind us.

"Corbin!"

We both look over our shoulders, and my heart squeezes so hard I think it might shrivel up and drop to the depths of my chest within one breath. Every person who works in this building knows who he is, and that charm has not waned one bit. He showers every single person who comes to kiss his ring with ample affection—hugs, pats on the back, handshakes. I'm far enough away to not be easily noticed, which is good. My legs feel completely numb, which puts a damper on any escape plans running through my mind.

"They really love him here, huh?" Jensen says.

"Yep." I turn in my seat to face the field, not bothering to look in Jensen's direction as I drop my sunglasses over my eyes. I can see enough of Jensen to know he's still staring at Corbin's every move, probably hanging on to every word he says. And he should. He could be that good one day—better, based on the little I saw. He'll need to know how to deal with adoring fans and people who consider themselves family since they were with him at the beginning.

"I thought I recognized that voice," my dad says, stepping up from the dugout and climbing a few steps into the stands to meet Corbin. I sink down in my seat and will myself not to be sick as they both come closer.

"Hey, Coach," Corbin says, closing the distance and embracing my dad, giving him a few pats on the back before they both descend into their own little baseball world.

Neither of them bothers to take their sunglasses off, which amuses me a little because I have a suspicion they're hiding their eyes for a reason. While Corbin is my father's so-called prodigy, I know for a fact my dad thinks the guy is an arrogant prick. He told me so when I told him we were engaged. I doubt that opinion has changed, especially since my father had zero ounces of empathy when we broke up.

On the flip side, Corbin thinks my dad is a dinosaur, too old to be relevant in a changing game. I agreed with him when we were together because I resent my dad for a whole host of other things, and it felt nice to team up against him. Now that I'm not marrying Corbin, I can admit to myself that he's off base. My dad doesn't know many things about life—love and relationships right at the top of that list—but the man sure as hell knows baseball. In this one vein, my dad is timeless. Yet despite all that, Corbin still has privilege with my dad—he's one of *his boys*. I've never been able to fully understand how that works, how two people can harbor such dislike yet always make space for each other.

"He sure likes to talk about himself," Jensen mutters at my side.

My shoulders lift with a silent laugh.

"Which one of them?" I pile on, causing Jensen to breathe out a laugh of his own.

"Sutter Mason, how are ya?" And with one small sentence, any glint of laughter escaping my lips is gone.

"Hi, Corbin." Looking up at him from my seat is hard enough. I wonder if he expected a warmer greeting from me. A hug? He was pretty clear about how he wanted to treat our relationship—professional. As if the other stuff was all accidental and meaningless.

"You look good," he says with a slight swallow. His compliment sends a rush of adrenaline to my nerve endings, and I hate that I like it. I'm also glad I bothered with hair and makeup and all of the extras this morning. And I hope me looking good hurts him a little. I hope that swallow tasted of regret.

"Thanks," I say, not bothering to return his favor. "Nice of you to stop by during the series. You know these guys all like seeing you."

I swallow down the bile burning its way up my esophagus. I'm disgusted with myself, the fake words coming out of my mouth in that forced tone, as if I think anything about him being here is nice. When he leaves, I'm going to be stuck with those looks of pity from anyone who knows our story, and there are plenty of those folks still around. This small distance between us is weird, too, and I can feel my hands and feet wanting to move toward him, as if being pulled by a magnet. Habit is a nasty son of a bitch.

"Yeah, well, I figured it's an off day for me, so if I'm late to the ballpark they'll understand. The ownership is good like that. You know, when players are in their home-towns and stuff." Corbin pulls his glasses off to clean the lenses on his crisp white T-shirt. Maybe he wanted a better look at me, or perhaps he simply wanted an excuse to move his wrist and flash his hundred-thousand-dollar watch. I kind of think he was hoping I'd take my glasses off too so he could really dive in and fuck with my head. Fat chance. These lenses are like a shield, protecting me and the year's worth of work I did to get over this asshole.

"You're from Arkansas. So isn't *that* really your home-town?" I snark.

Corbin freezes, his sunglasses pinched between fingers under the fabric of his shirt. His eyes flit up to meet my gaze and he smirks.

"This is home too," he admonishes. He blinks at me slowly before curving his smile into place as his eyes glance over my shoulder. He doesn't want me to make a scene, especially in front of some new pitcher who might idolize him.

"Hey, Corbin Forsythe," he says, stepping into my row and leaning over me with his hand out for Jensen.

"Uh, yeah." Jensen chuckles. "I'm Jensen Hawke."

There's a pause between the two of them and it's long enough to draw my attention to Corbin's face. He drops Jensen's hand and stands tall again, his head tilting an inch to the side as his mouth pulls up in a crooked smile. He points toward Jensen with his sunglasses and laughs.

"Yeah, I recognize you. You've got some stuff in that arm. Man, I wish I had your slider," Corbin says.

"Yeah, well I wish I had . . . your contract, I guess," Jensen responds.

"That'll come. Put in the work, and you'll get yours," Corbin says, sliding his glasses back in place before dropping his hands in his Bermuda shorts and offering a smug grin. He's wearing leather shoes without socks, and his legs look like they've been waxed.

"Hey, good luck," he adds, filling the silent void from Jensen's lack of a response.

"Yeah, you, too," Jensen replies. I catch him nodding, and I'm not sure whether he's starstruck or put off by Corbin. Maybe it's both.

"Sut," Corbin says, turning his attention to me. Sut. I hate the way he shortens my name. *I used to love it.*

I look up as he stares down through his shades and find his hand waiting for mine. My eyes wince a little, and I come close to busting out a laugh. But I don't want to explain things to Jensen. And I already feel eyes on me from everyone else. I power through and shake hands, the entire action lasting only seconds but feeling like forever in my head as every place where our hands meet sparks some old memory of his touch—the first times, the best times, and the last. It's weird how I don't miss it, yet it still burns.

"Take care," he says.

I'm not sure whether his sendoff is for Jensen or me, but neither of us responds as he turns and leaves. In fact, we don't say a word until he's on the other side of the stadium signing balls for rookies fresh out of college.

"He's a real dick," Jensen finally lets out as he gets up from his seat and walks back into the dugout. I smirk in his wake and stare at the empty seat he left behind, a pool of water from where his ice melted quickly drying on the concrete.

The last time I saw Corbin, he was at our apartment door, holding a letter and asking for his ring back. I always thought the next time I saw him in person would hurt like hell. Strangely, though, it doesn't. I've hurt far worse over other things. And maybe I'm relieved I didn't marry a real dick.

CHAPTER 6

Jensen

I've left my sister's text unanswered for twenty-four hours, which is why she's switched to calling me instead. I don't want to have this conversation in a grocery store, but if I don't answer now, she'll just keep calling. And then there's the risk I'll have to talk to her a lot longer because I won't have the excuse of being in a grocery store to keep things short.

I look at her name on the screen and suck in a deep breath in preparation before pressing answer.

"Hi, Amber. Yes, I got your invitation. No, I'm not planning to come all the way to Washington for a party. Anything else?" I rattle through the questions I know are coming, and I know I sound rude, but I don't have time to make a trip to Seattle in the middle of a season start. She knows this because she's marrying a guy who just retired from living the same exact schedule as me.

"And hi to you too, brother. Good thing that party isn't in Washington. I assume a quick jaunt to LA won't be a problem at all," she tosses back, her spitfire sarcasm on point this evening.

I stop right in front of the produce section, basket dangling from my arm, phone pressed to my ear.

"Come on, Amber." I leave it simple this time. She knows I'll show up for her actual wedding. An engagement party is like extra fluff that nobody wants to go to, at least not normal people like me who aren't trying to show off and impress everyone. And the fact my parents actually want to host this—that they are spending money they don't have on it—makes me sick.

My sister sighs into the phone. I pick up an apple and inspect it, as though I know how to evaluate fruit. The longer both of us go without talking, the more her guilt powers squeeze at my stomach. I don't know how she's able to do this through the phone. It's the devil's magic.

"I'll think about it," I say.

"Yay! I mean"—she clears her throat and tamps down her enthusiasm, barely—"That's great. I appreciate it. And if you can make it—which you totally can—I promise to sit you far away from everyone."

I smirk and breathe out a laugh while dropping the apple into my basket.

"You know you are the only person I would do this for, right?" I shake my head and meander around the various stands of pears, melons, and bright red and orange peppers.

"It's not a special day for me without my brother," she says. My heart drops a beat and my eyes flutter closed. My sister is my weakness, even with her relentless sunshine. When nobody, meaning our parents, was interested in seeing my baseball games in high school, she showed up.

Amber is eight years older than me, and she works for a big marketing firm. When I was grinding it out to get a college scholarship, she took time off from her job to play the part of parent. She's the one who filmed my games and sent out emails to coaches, pretending to be me. She's the reason I made the roster at Clarence College. And despite my injury setback and the third year of minor-league wages, she still seems genuinely proud of me, unlike my parents who are waiting for me to get a *real* job.

"I will seriously think about it," I reiterate. I can't promise her my final answer, and deep down, she probably knows I'll end up bailing. But if there's a sliver of a chance I can convince myself to go to what I know will be a third circle of hell for me, I will. I'll do it for her.

"That's good enough. Now, how's the arm?"

I rotate my shoulder on her prompt, testing like I always do. No pain.

"It's good. I've been throwing a lot. I'm a little off, though," I say, my mind instantly replaying those words from Sutter this morning—*you don't have his issues. What issues do I have, then? Wait, no! I don't have any issues.*

"I'm sure you'll figure it out. I believe in you, J. Always have."

I smile at her positive words, though I will never give her the satisfaction of knowing I secretly appreciate them.

"Hope so. Hey, I'm at the grocery store. I gotta run," I say. We exchange quick love yous and end the call.

I make it no more than two steps away from the celery when another incessant female breaks into my day.

"And why do you think you're a little off?" Sutter's ability to pop up out of nowhere is legitimately starting to freak me out.

"Come on!" I grumble as I turn around to face her.

She lifts up her basket, which is full of various spices and some sauce cans and pasta.

"I swear I'm not following you. I was shopping and happened to see you. But since you're here . . ."

I rumble out a frustrated laugh and attempt to walk away. Naturally, Sutter steps right up next to me. I stop at the butcher area, and everything I put down she proceeds to pick up and examine as if she's considering buying it.

"You didn't answer me earlier, you know," she says.

I flash her a quirked brow.

"Why do you think you're a little off?"

My eyes flutter shut with my deep inhale. "You literally are never going to stop, are you?" I throw a pound of ground beef into my basket and glare at her. She simply smiles with tight lips and shakes her head, uttering *uh uh*.

Sutter tosses a pack of meat in her basket and follows me down the supplement aisle. I laugh when she begins pulling bottles down and holding them out to read ingredients, clearly not knowing what she's looking at since the first two things she inspects are for hair growth and sperm count.

"Okay, I will give you one week," I relent. What's the harm in indulging her for seven days? Maybe she'll realize how little she can help, or my obvious unpleasant demeanor will chase her away. Not that it's worked thus far.

"Awesome. One week that I know will turn into your season. I guarantee it," she says, reaching out an open palm for me to shake.

"Hmm, one week. Not an entire season," I assert before

taking her hand. Her grip is firm despite how my hand swallows hers.

"We can start tonight," she says as our hands part. She marches down the aisle with an actual sway to her hips, the kind my sister puts on when she's gotten her way. I might be tempted to stare at the dangerous spot where Sutter's shorts quit covering the back of her legs and flirt with her ass if it weren't for the sudden addition she just slapped on my calendar.

"Wait. Tonight?" I catch up to her in the bread aisle, and she promptly tosses a loaf of Italian bread in my basket.

"I'm not big on bread," I say, pulling it out. She puts it right back in.

"One, of course you don't eat a lot of bread. *Pfft*, annoying. And two, it's not for you. Well, I mean, it *could* be if you ate bread. But since you don't—"

Mouth hung open, I'm left with nothing but this blank stare. I can't even muster a blink. I head to the checkout line with my apple, two pears, a pound of beef, and bread I won't eat, and Sutter hops into the line one cashier over. It isn't a race, yet somehow I find myself constantly comparing the progress my line is making compared to hers, and when I get stuck behind a lady with a stack of coupons, I audibly groan.

"I have a knack for picking right," Sutter says with a wink as she stands on her toes and eyes me over the partition.

"Of course you do," I huff.

By the time I pay for my tiny load of groceries, Sutter is holding four bags and waiting for me outside the door.

"I'm parked to the right. Come on; I'll drive us to your

place," she says. She makes it several steps before turning and acknowledging that I haven't moved.

My scowl must be pretty damn obvious because she drops her head and shuffles back toward me. I'm already carrying bread I won't eat. Now I'm riding home with her. Because we're starting tonight. This is why I didn't want to entertain this.

"Look," she says, popping her head up when she's only a few feet away. Her smile is arresting; I won't deny that. It's the thing that's kept me off-guard since the first time we met, not that she did a lot of smiling while spraying my face with hair chemicals. But there's a real earnestness about her that pokes at my insides. It's irritating, but it's also familiar. I think a part of her reminds me of my sister, and Amber has always been the best person I know.

"I was already planning to make dinner for Billy, and since I've got all this food, and I'm going there anyway . . ." She nods over her shoulder toward her car.

"You just happened to be coming to my apartment anyhow." It's not completely far-fetched, and I do get the feeling she and Billy have a pretty solid relationship. But the timing is still suspect.

"Yeah, I bailed on his make-up pancakes, and while he has this thing about making everyone like him, I sort of have this thing about making people not hate me. Anyhow, I make a mean meat sauce. And if you don't eat pasta, I'll grill chicken."

I glance through the plastic bags to confirm she has chicken in one of them. I don't see it, but the bags are pretty full. The idea of eating homemade sauce is awfully appealing.

"Okay, but then today counts as day one. You get six more after that," I explain.

"Yes, I get how six plus one is seven," she jokes.

I can't help my laugh, and she shows off her smile in return. My eyes settle on her lips, pink and glossed but not in an overly made-up way. They look sun kissed.

We stop at a small white two-door sedan, and she pushes a button on her key fob to pop the trunk. She drops her bags in and I step up to add mine in, pausing when I see three pairs of hiking boots and a mountain bike tire.

"You ride?" I say, nodding toward the treads. I put my bag inside and she shuts the trunk.

"I try." She laughs as she moves to the driver's side. We both get in, and the second she turns the car on the speakers blast out some barely coherent AM station. She reaches forward and quickly twists the volume.

"Sorry, I was trying to catch the Suns game last night and I don't have cable, so I bought some donut holes and camped out in here for the fourth quarter," she explains.

I nod and smile, then study her for a few extra seconds as she adjusts her mirror and backs out of the parking spot. This girl literally sat in her car for a playoff basketball game.

"You a big fan?" I figure being a local and from a baseball family, sports are probably part of her genetics, but then she flashes me the inside of her wrist and I note the seventies-style tattoo with the retro Suns logo.

"Okay, so that's a yes," I respond.

She kisses the inside of her wrist, then rests her hand on the wheel.

"Is that some good luck thing?" I ask.

"Damn right. When I kiss this tat, they do good

things." She pulls her hand back to her mouth and kisses her wrist again. "For good measure."

She winks and smiles again—*that* smile. When I catch myself staring for a little too long, I shift in my seat and rest my arm on the window ledge, the space in this two-door car suddenly feeling about the size of the bobsled ride at Disneyland.

Sutter pulls into a spot that I don't think is really a spot, but she swears she's parked here a million times so that's where we end up. She walks ahead of me into the building and already has her key out by the time the elevator doors open. Billy's already home, though, so we walk right in, the apartment saturated with the aroma of chili, garlic, and cumin. Billy is standing above a pot stirring, and Sutter laughs as she turns to face me.

"Silly brother. You forgot about our dinner plans," she says through a toothy smile.

Goddammit. She made this whole thing up.

I cock my head to the side and purse my lips, leveling her with a look that says this is not a great start to day one of Sutter Mason mental coaching. I'm pretty sure lies aren't a good basis for anything.

"Did I miss a message?" Billy looks genuinely confused as his sister plops down bags of groceries on the counter next to him.

"Remember? We talked?" Sutter's eyes flutter in this awkward pattern that looks like she's gotten her lashes caught in a spiderweb.

"What's wrong with your eyes?" Billy asks.

"Your sister is trying to send you top-secret spy signals because she needs you to play along with her massive fib. Oh, and she tricked me into buying her a loaf of bread," I say, plopping the Italian loaf on the counter. I lean forward and rest my elbows on the counter then gawk at Sutter, a little in awe of her massive boldness.

"Oh, I could have sworn—"

"Ehhhh!" I blurt out like a buzzer.

She scowls at me, and like a child, I lean into her brother to get closer to her with my evil-eyed return.

"Okay, here's the deal," Billy finally says, clanking his spoon against his pot of what is by far the best smelling chili I've ever breathed in. Neither Sutter nor I flinch, but we both turn our attention to him. Or maybe we're looking at the chili. It's hard to say.

"Sutter brought food to apparently *cook* for the three of us," Billy says, making the air quotes with his free hand and shooting a hard glare at Sutter. "However, since Sutter burns water and can't even make pancakes with premade mix, my instincts tell me this chili I was making for the chili contest at work is now going to be three bowls lighter. Sutter, would you like to stay for dinner? And Jensen, I hope you like chili."

"Thanks, bro," Sutter says, slapping Billy on the back as he nods in that way that indicates she has worked him before.

"You don't even cook," I say flatly.

"Define *cook*," Sutter says, moving to the fridge and shoving her bags of groceries inside.

"Unbelievable." My blank stare has nowhere to go. I find myself aghast, yet again, with this woman.

"I'll set the table," Sutter says, pulling out bowls and utensils while I lean into the counter and cross my arms over my chest to study her brother's expression for some damn insight as to what is going on. He meets my glare after a few seconds and laughs.

"Man, if you are looking for some clue into why my sister is the way she is, I got nothing. All I can tell you is there is a reason she's studying psychology, and I think it's got something to do with manipulation."

"I heard that!" Sutter says in a raised voice.

"Good," her brother deadpans.

He gives me a sideways glance and another shrug. I'm left with nothing to do but carry my loaf of bread—which I won't eat—into the dining room, where Sutter has a plate and some butter and is already waiting to break it into pieces.

I duck into my room to change into a clean pair of sweats and my dark gray long-sleeved college baseball tee. By the time I come back out, Billy has filled the bowls with chili and he and his sister sit on opposite ends of the table laughing hysterically.

"Nothing makes a guy more uneasy than stepping up to a bowl full of food while everyone else in the room is in on a secret." I take the seat closest to the kitchen, push my sleeves up my forearms, and pick up my spoon to dig in.

The chili is nearly to my lips when Sutter says, "You think we're laughing now, wait until you see us cackle over your massive diarrhea."

I drop my spoon and sit back to give her a sideways look. Her brother does the same.

"Don't joke about my cooking, Sut. Not cool. Not fucking cool." Billy points his spoon at her then gives me a sharp look before scooping up a bite and swallowing it. He lets out an *ahh* in proof that it's down his throat and he's still alive.

I shake my head and follow his suit, taking my first bite and quickly following it up with two more spoonfuls. It's hot as hell, but I don't even care if my tongue blisters.

"This is incredible," I say in the middle of my third bite.

"Thank you," Billy replies, shooting another glare at his sister.

"Oh, come on. I was joking," she defends, folding her legs up in her chair and scooting in close to hold her spoon over the bowl and blow it cool. Something about the way she looks, the innocence of it, is sweet. She's also adorable with her hair pulled up in this ponytail on top of her head, her face makeup-free, cheeks pink from the sun from today. I smile but quickly look down at my own bowl so nobody sees it.

"Sut, huh? So, since we're going to be working together, can I call you that?" I ask between bites.

"No." Her response is clipped and instantaneous. I look up to check her expression and see if she's teasing, but her face is blank, and she merely digs in for another bite.

I swallow and glance to her brother. He winces a little with a slight shrug.

"Got it. Brother-sister thing."

It's quiet for a few minutes as we all eat, but eventually Sutter reaches toward the bread, taking a hunk and holding it out in offering to me. I purse my lips and utter, "Ha ha."

She winks and butters the bread generously before dipping the corner of it into her chili and taking a huge bite.

"You got any siblings, Hawke?" she asks with a full mouth.

I chuckle at her bluntness, and her lack of manners. It's . . . refreshing.

"I do. I have a sister," I answer. "Actually, you two are a lot alike."

"Oh, I doubt that," she says.

I pause my eating and sit back in my seat with a hard laugh.

"Wow, so sure of that. You're downright punchy," I say.

"Remember when I told you Sutter is never wrong?" Billy pipes in. His eyes shift from me to his sister, who instantly tilts her head and levels her brother with a hard stare upon his criticism. "What? You're never wrong."

They stare at each other for a few seconds but eventually Sutter breaks into a laugh and reaches across the table in his direction, patting the air as if patting his head from a distance. "I've trained you well, my brother," she says.

"And I'm older, by three years," he says, returning to his dinner, shoveling a spoonful into his mouth.

"My sister's older than me, by eight years," I say, stopping short of sharing much more than that.

"So, she's thirty-three," Sutter fills in.

I pinch my brow.

"Uh, yeah," I affirm with hesitation.

"Relax, Jensen. I have your profile memorized. You're twenty-five, which you add eight to and voilà. You don't think I would go into a coaching agreement without knowing the details of my subject, do you?"

Her brother coughs, half choking on a bite.

"You're going to do mental coaching with him?" Billy says. His eyebrows are close to his hairline, which is receding.

"Yes, Billy. It's what I plan to do with my degree, so—"

"I know, but . . . with him," her brother repeats.

There's a momentary wordless standoff between them,

and it's maybe the first time I've seen Sutter pinch her face into a warning look. Billy's the first to break, a short laugh popping from his mouth as he smiles with teeth clamped together. He shakes his head.

"Okay," he gives in, returning to his dinner, his pace picking up with each bite.

There's an obvious chill in the air, and I'm a little offended by the way he said *with him,* but I don't want to delve into whatever family bullshit might be going on. Also, I'm giving this a week. *One* week.

"Truth is, Billy, you could have laced this with arsenic, and I'd still be tempted to walk into that kitchen and help myself to a second bowl." I scrape the last of my helping and practically French kiss the spoon. Billy chuckles, his coldness warming again.

"I'd say dig in, but I really want to win this contest. It's a bragging rights thing," he says.

"Oh, that's not all it is," Sutter teases. She pushes her empty bowl away and sits back, cradling her bread and breaking off a bite at a time as she looks at her brother with puckered lips and a knowing glare.

I chuckle, unable to avoid slipping into the comfortable mood coming back to the table.

"Let me guess," I say, pulling the napkin to my mouth and running it across my lips. "There's a girl."

I glance to Sutter, and she flickers her eyes as a hint, which pulls stronger laughter from my chest. Napkin balled in my fist, I hold it to my mouth to hide my reaction.

"Goddammit, Sutter." Billy gets up from the table and proceeds to take all of our bowls with jerking motions and stomping feet.

"Her name is Kendra, and she's from Hawaii," she says, waggling her brows at me.

"Oh, the islands," I add in.

Sutter shifts in her seat, mostly to lean to the opposite side so she can keep her eyes on her brother, who is now throwing a small fit while rinsing the bowls and dropping them into the dishwasher with extra force.

"She ran the sister property in Maui and was transferred to Billy's resort a few months ago. She's in marketing, isn't she Billy," Sutter says. She might disagree without the facts, but she really is a lot like Amber. This is exactly how my sister would have this conversation with me. If I had an inkling of interest in relationships, that is.

"Well, this has been a fun night for me. Thank you, Sut, for surprising me and coming over to 'cook,'" Billy says, air quoting that word again. He ducks down to look me in the eyes under the row of cabinets above the island. "Jensen, I won't hold this against you after tonight, but right now, man? Right now, you're an asshole too. You guys have a good night, and may she do far less psychological damage to you than she's done to me over the years." Billy tosses the dishtowel onto the counter after drying his hands, and flips the lights off for that half of the apartment before heading into his room.

Sutter and I swivel our heads to look at each other with wide eyes, and after a second or two she spits out another laugh at her brother's expense. She stands eventually, pushing in her chair and holding the back while she pulls one of her legs up behind her to grab hold of her toes and stretch her leg. Sometime during dinner, she must have kicked her shoes off, making herself completely at home, because *of course she did*. Her stretch lasts several seconds, and her balance is impressive, but not as interesting as the cut of muscle on her thigh and the flex of her calf.

"I love him, that's why I tease. He's a great guy, and he deserves a girl to worship him," she finally says, drawing me out of my gawking inappropriateness. Thankfully, I don't think she noticed.

"It's nice that you two get along so well," I say, standing and pushing my own chair in.

Our eyes meet for a few beats, neither of us looking away despite how uncomfortable it feels to stand this close while staring. At least, it's uncomfortable to me. Sutter doesn't seem to *get* uncomfortable. I envy that.

"Fucker left that thing on simmer so we'd have to smell it," she says.

I chuckle.

"I'd swipe seconds except I know how important showing off tomorrow is to him, and I don't want to ruin his plan," she says with a soft click of the mouth.

Clearly not as equipped with interpersonal skills as she is, I grip the corners of the chair back and wiggle the chair to rid my nervous energy. I don't like not having a plan, and this conversation is on an uncharted path. She said she wanted to start her coaching or whatever tonight, but if it's going to involve me talking about personal stuff, I'm not sure I'm in the mood. But then again, *am I ever in the mood?*

"Join me on the couch," she says, probably sensing my unease.

"Oh-kayyyy," I answer, leaving the safety of the table to sit on the sofa on the opposite end as Sutter.

She turns to her side, pulling one leg up and tucking it close to her body. I lean forward and rest my forearms on my knees, clasping my hands. Sutter's gaze seems glued to my threaded fingers, and eventually I break them apart and flash open palms.

"What?"

Her lips twist.

"You always sit like that?" she questions.

My shoulders lift as I shake my head slowly.

"I don't fucking know. Yeah, I guess." I can actually feel the pinch in my brow, so deep the skin folds and is touching.

Her head falls to the side, resting on the back cushion as she blinks slowly.

"Fine," I huff, leaning back and slouching, one arm on the rest, the other limp at my side. The coffee table is too far to kick a foot up, so I just manspread. "Better?"

She grimaces.

"You're faking it," she chastises.

I *tsk*.

"It's fine," she responds. She leans forward and pushes her hand between the cushions, then pulls out the remote and presses power.

"Have you ever watched *Sing for Your Supper?*" she asks. My mouth hangs open for a breath, then snaps shut.

"Can't say I have."

"Oh, good. You're going to love it." She flips through the channels then stops on some obscure cable show where people are pulled from the street and brought into some dinner theater where they are forced to sing whatever song the band plays in front of a full audience.

"This is terrifying," I say after we watch two people go through the torture.

"Yeah, but it's also great, right? I mean, all they know is some dude is offering them a grand to sing a song, and then *boom!*" She gestures to the screen as a backstory plays. I get caught up in the wonder in her face over a stupid show rather than looking at the television. She's mesmerized by these utterly predictable stories, yet it's so heartwarming to watch her watch something absolutely asinine.

"I mean, like, you totally know this girl is going to come out there and really sing, right? That's why they're doing the whole backstory thing about how she used to sing in high school and wanted to go into theater but couldn't afford college or training. She's my age."

Sutter glances my way as she speaks, and I clear my throat and look to the screen.

"It's a pretty predictable formula," I say.

"But is it?" she questions quickly.

I bite my lip and lower my brow, glancing back to her, not understanding. She meets my gaze—the smile. She leans her head toward the TV.

"Watch," she commands.

I stare at her for a few extra seconds before doing what I'm told.

As I figured, the girl is brought into the dinner theater and the band begins playing a song. It's some famous Broadway tune that I vaguely recognize. The girl's cheeks are fire engine red, the house lights not bright enough to hide her audience, and as the band plays, she misses her queue to begin.

"Oh, this one's going to be so good," Sutter hums. She shifts to face the screen, folding her legs up and leaning forward, her chin balanced on her hands, elbows balanced on her legs. Like a pretzel. Her smile is so big I can see an entire half on the side of her face closest to me.

I swallow and look back to the TV.

The camera is tight on the girl's face. She closes her eyes as her lips move with the band's intro, almost like her own version of a dry run-through only she can hear. This time, she hits her mark, and her voice doesn't come out timid or riddled with quivering nerves. She belts, her power so big her hand automatically covers her diaphragm as the audience roars at the pleasant surprise. By the time she's done, people are on their feet and the girl is in tears. So is Sutter.

"Sorry, that kind of stuff always gets me," she says, running her palms under her eyes.

"What about it?" I ask, my own chest fluttering a little from someone else's rush.

Sutter shakes her head and glances up at the ceiling for a breath before dropping her gaze back on me.

"People actually doing it—their thing. No, not just doing it. *Slaying it,*" she says, her cheeks round with this unbridled glee. I give in to my own urge with a half-smile.

"Yeah, I guess that is pretty cool."

"Hawke, that's not just pretty cool. It's fucking amazing," she says.

A joyful giggle actually leaves her mouth as she brings her hands to her face and cups her mouth, her eyes bright and wide enough to reflect the light from the television. Like disco balls at a roller rink. The singer on the TV is being surprised by a talent agent in the audience. It turns out, the audience is filled with them. And within minutes, she has a dozen of them praising her and vying to manage her future—her vibrant, possible, fucking amazing future.

I don't know what any of this has to do with me being able to throw a slider tomorrow. And I'm not sure we're going to talk about me and my issues. But I like this show, and I like how I feel right now. And I like looking at Sutter light up. I like her smile. And the way she can balance on one foot and flex like a champ. I should not have agreed to a day of this, let alone a week. Yet I'm not moving from this couch. I'm glued to it, and I'm ready to watch Sutter celebrate another unsuspecting dinner singer. I'm ready to watch her smile. And nothing about right now is why I'm here in Arizona. Nothing about it at all.

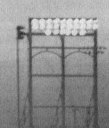

CHAPTER 7
Sutter

Sometime in the middle of the third episode, Jensen fell asleep. I took the opportunity to study him while he rested. Yeah, a part of me wanted to scope out his chiseled chin and late-night stubble along with his incredible body—the tight fit of his shirt across his broad chest and the way his sweats hug his massive thighs. It's been awhile since I let myself indulge in man candy, and wrong as it might be, I indulged. I stopped myself before snapping a quick pic to send to Kiki, but I thought about it a good long while.

Beyond his hotness, I focused on the way he breathes, so much easier than when he's awake. The constant guard he seems to wear like a mask, the one that holds his mouth in a perfect line devoid of emotion, was gone. He's beautiful that way, and if I can get him to bring that same sense of peace—which I know will translate into confidence—to his pitching, he will become his hype.

I woke up before anyone this morning and slipped into the shower. One of the things I miss most about this apartment is how it never seems to run out of hot water, which is good because I've been in here for nearly thirty minutes. I'm hiding. As early as I woke up, my brother will soon be awake too. We're early risers. Always have been. But if it's only Billy and me stirring in the apartment, I won't be able to ignore his criticism.

I could easily distract myself with Jensen last night. I focused on my scheme to force that tense man to relax, to be free for just thirty freaking minutes.

Without the distraction of my goals, though, Billy's warning glance and passive aggressive tone echoes in my head. I understand his caution. His sister is walking down a path similar to the trip she took a few years ago, the one that left her in pieces and made her sour to the idea of opening her heart ever again. But this is different than it was before.

With Corbin, I went into things already in love. I was blinded by it, and maybe I failed at my job because of it. Not that I don't think our sessions worked, but maybe they could have been more productive without the sex getting in the way.

But now . . . with Jensen? There isn't a relationship other than the one we formed and put on paper last night. He signed my contract, the one I created after learning my lesson with Corbin. The data I can mine from him will kick off my career. I know it in my gut.

Of course, I did go and watch him sleep. That's my kryptonite—watching people sleep. Probably because I've always had trouble sleeping myself and I've gotten used to witnessing everyone else in my life drift into slumber. I've grown accustomed to feeding off of their bliss, and like Corbin, Jensen is a beautiful man. But he has habits that Corbin doesn't. He sleeps peacefully, barely moving at all, even to breathe. A question always seemed to linger on Corbin's face. Even when he slept, that man was plagued by uncertainty. When we removed that hesitation from his talent, he was able to dominate on the mound. Shame on me for not realizing that same uncertainty lived inside his heart too.

There's nothing uncertain on Jensen's face when he sleeps; he looks like an actual angel. If only I could read his thoughts and live inside his mind. He seems to be two completely different people asleep and awake. One is wound so tightly he can barely completely fill his lungs, while the other looks so content and at ease. Both of those people might be the most handsome creatures I've ever seen, which brings me back to Billy's warning. Maybe it's good that Jensen suggested a week-long test. As much as it's a test for him, it's also one for me, and if I feel myself getting lost in the potential for fantasy, I have to pull back. I need to focus on the work. My professional future literally depends on this panning out.

With my chest a bright pink from the pounding hot water and my fingertips wrinkled from the long soak, I finally turn the spigot off and step out to wrap my hair in a towel. I wish I still had some extra clothes here. I'm not feeling up for my linen shorts again today, and I splattered a good amount of chili on my shirt last night.

Breath held, I press my ear to the door and listen for anyone stirring on the other side. I flick off the light and the fan to make sure the coast sounds clear, and when I'm convinced of it, I wrap a second towel around my body and clutch it at my chest. I head out for a quick sprint into my brother's room and his walk-in closet, and get a half step into the hallway before my face plants into Jensen's chest.

We back away from each other with loud and irrational screams.

"The light was off! I figured you were gone!" He points at me, his finger painting a line up and down the length of my body.

"I was being quiet!" I gripe back.

"Exactly. *Too* quiet!"

We stare each other in the eyes and then hear the sound of my brother's door popping open.

"Shit!" I say, reacting out of panic. I grab Jensen's arm, yank him into the bathroom with me, and close the door.

"Why would you bring me in here?" he growls.

"*Shh!*" I say, my finger to my lips. Not that he can see me because it's completely pitch black.

My hand is still wrapped around his bicep, and the steam left over from my shower has made the room humid as hell. His shirt feels damp within seconds. Or maybe I'm sweating because I'm fucking naked and touching his arm.

"Why are we hiding?" he whispers.

"I don't know." I let go of his arm and blink at the blackness, wondering why in the world I reacted that way. It's the damn face Billy made at me, his cautionary glare. I played out the scene one way and instantly decided I didn't want to hear him lecture me about walking around in front of my subject in a towel. He'd accuse me of flirting, which would be completely wrong but so very hard to defend.

"Why are you in a towel?" His voice is still close, and the fact I'm *only* in a towel carries an entirely different meaning in these close quarters.

"I was going to sneak into his room and steal some of his clothes," I whisper.

"Isn't your brother, like, twice your size?" he rationalizes.

"*Hmm,*" I respond, nodding to myself. It's one thing to wear Billy's giant T-shirts and his sweats around the apartment, but I'd probably fall out of them on my way down the walkway to my car.

"I've got some stuff," he says. My head flashes up, and even though it's devoid of light in this room, I somehow sense how close he is, sense his eyes on me. He smells of fabric softener and cotton, but also a spiced amber from whatever he washes his hair with. I cheated and smelled it when I showered, and I smell the faint fragrance on him now.

I pull my hand up and reach forward, flattening in on his chest to center myself. I could have turned to the side and flattened my palm on the door until I found the wall and then the light, a switch I know by heart after years of living here. But instead, I chose to do this. Because . . . no. No reason. I refuse to go down that thought string. Jensen is right in front of me and he's just a body in my way. That's all. Just a body—*a really fucking hot body.*

The pipes vibrate with the sound of running water, the signal that Billy's started his shower.

"I think we're good," I say, sliding my hand along Jensen's chest—because of course this is the best route—and eventually feeling the door behind him. As he moves to the side, I turn the knob and open the door slowly so it doesn't squeak. Once I'm sure the coast is clear, I literally sprint into Jensen's room across the hallway. He's hot on my trail, and when I turn around, his back is resting against his closed door and his hand is tugging nervously at the collar of his shirt.

"Now you have me doing it," he says, his expression

caught somewhere between amused and irritated.

We're both breathing too hard for a seven-foot jog across the hall, so I decide to push him to the less messy side of feelings by puckering my mouth into a barely contained laugh. He gives in completely, a raspy rumble escaping his chest as he shakes his head and moves across his room. I sit on the end of his bed, on the quilt he let me borrow the first night we met, while he pulls open the top drawer of his dresser.

"Who made this for you?" I ask, my hand running over the small threads that poke up like pieces of soft spring grass.

He glances over his shoulder and smiles.

"It was my nana's. She babysat me a lot when I was little, and that quilt was like the magic nap maker. I mean, I crawled under that sucker and was out, no matter how hard I fought it," he says.

He pulls some clothes into his hands and turns to face me, pushing the drawer closed with his hip.

"Here. I'm sure you're used to wearing Monsoon gear." He chuckles, holding out a familiar navy blue T-shirt and a pair of gray sweats.

I take the folded clothes and rest them on my lap to inspect.

"I'm pretty sure I own this exact shirt. Thanks," I say, smiling as I glance up at him. His gaze flicks up from my chest to meet my eyes, and I pull my towel a little tighter against my body, covering that hand with the one clutching the T-shirt and suddenly very aware that he was looking at my cleavage. I look down to check it for myself, pulling the shirt away from my chest to get a handle on his view. Not bad. They're ample-looking today.

"Yeah, uh. I'll just be in the shower," he says, his hand grabbing at the back of his neck as his eyes dart around me and his room.

"Relax. It's my fault for being in a towel," I say in an attempt to diffuse the situation.

"Ha, uh . . . yeah. I'll just . . ." Jensen points over his shoulder and trips over his feet while backing into his door.

I pull my lips into a tight smile and will away the burning sensation in my cheeks. I wave the shirt and hand at him.

"Off you go," I encourage.

He leaves me with one more wide-eyed expression tinged with that *I-might-throw-up* nervous edge. Once the door closes behind him, I fall flat on my back, onto Nana's quilt. I pull one side over my body, covering my face, and groan.

My brother is actually right. He's *soooooo* right. This is a bad idea.

I fling the quilt back into place then get to my feet, moving to the door so I can lock it. Once I know I'm safe from more awkward encounters, I drop my towel and quickly slip into his spare clothes. This should all be so simple, but damn, they smell just like him. Somehow, his clothes smell more like him than *he* does, which doesn't make sense since I've only really smelled him once. I've already etched the scent into my senses. This is a disaster.

Forcing myself to breathe and not overreact, I sit on the edge of his bed in his T-shirt and sweats, which I've rolled at the waist, and finger-comb the tangles in my hair. Once it's smooth enough, I pick up my towel and head for the door. But because I lack self-control and don't know any better, I stop before opening the door and spin around to take in his space.

The door is locked. This might be the only chance I get to spy on him without his eyes watching over me as I do. I won't go digging, at least not too deeply. But I want to see what makes him tick. Hints that might get me into his head a little without having to crack him open.

At first glance, his room is devoid of anything truly personal. I move to his night stand and unfurl the receipt from groceries along with a straw wrapper and thirty-two cents in change. There's a half-eaten pack of gum along with his wallet and his smartwatch, which isn't on the charger. Probably because he came home in a rush last night, routine interrupted thanks to *moi*.

I put it on the charger, then look over my shoulder on instinct before picking up his wallet and thumbing through the insides. There's a twenty in the main pocket, and despite my expectation, there isn't a condom to be found. I pull his license out and study the young boy looking back at me in the photo. I know this picture was only taken four years ago when he turned twenty-one, but still—he looks like a baby compared to the man showering across the hall.

The man who is naked across the hall.

I refold his wallet and drop it on the table, then move to his closet where I thumb through his shirts. One half of the hangers are taken up with jerseys—some his, some from favorite teams. The other end of the closet is occupied by two suits, a few button downs and a handful of casual dress shirts and pants.

I move to his drawers next, starting with the top drawer, which is filled with every sock type imaginable and about a dozen pair of black boxer briefs. I smirk and bite my tongue at the sight of them. Well, more at the visual in my head of Jensen *in* them.

"Okay," I hum quietly, closing that drawer.

The next drawer is more T-shirts and sweats, like the ones I'm wearing. And below that are jeans and shorts. He's incredibly basic. Six pairs of shoes of varying types are lined up under the window. He hasn't been here long, but how is there nothing meaningful in this space?

Then I turn to the bed—to the quilt.

"Oh," I breathe.

I'm an idiot.

The water turns off, both on his end of the hall and on my brother's, so I slip out of his room and rush into the living room so I can tuck the signed contract into my purse and make a last-ditch effort to make last night meaningful and result-driven.

"Sut," my brother says as he wanders into the kitchen in the same mint green robe he's worn since high school.

"Sut. Does that mean you forgive me?" I look over my shoulder as he pauses with the orange juice container pressed against his lips.

"What are you wearing?" He gestures toward me with the juice.

"Clothes. Am I forgiven?" *Shit. I didn't think the whole Jensen's clothes thing through.*

Billy keeps his eyes on me as he tilts his head back and takes a big gulp of the juice. He lets out an "Ahh" before putting the cap on and tucking it back in the door of the fridge. He moves to the edge of the counter, mouth in his famous judgmental straight line.

"Yeah, Sut. I forgive you," he says before turning and heading back into his room.

When he's gone, I let out the breath I was holding. The entire apartment smells like his fucking chili, which while delicious last night, is less appealing early in the morning. Especially when one's stomach is twisted into knots upon knots.

I shake everything off and focus on my phone, finding the website for *Sing for Your Dinner*. I scroll through until I find the clip from the first episode we watched last night, and I record it on my phone into the part where she closes her eyes and just sings with abandon.

When Jensen steps from the bathroom, this time the one in the towel, I follow him into his room.

"Uh, haven't we done this thing before?" he says, moving his finger to point between his towel and the spot where I stand.

"We have, which is why it's normal now. I need your phone."

He shakes his head but eventually walks out into the living room, bending down to pick it up from the floor where he must have left it last night.

"Here. And hurry. I'm going to need to charge it for a few minutes before I leave." He swipes his screen on and hands it to me.

"Yeah, okay, bossy," I respond.

Jensen rolls his eyes at me but hovers in my space as I swipe my screen awake then open my contact info and airdrop it to his device. Once it pops up on his phone, I shoot myself a quick text then hand him back his phone.

"There. Now I can reach you whenever I want," I say.

His mouth in a flat line, he simply pulls his phone from my grip and utters, "Goody."

Maybe a little for myself, but also to torture and tease

him for doing it to me, I let my eyes wander lazily down the deep line in the center of his chest as it cuts through his abs to a belly button and a smooth, rock-solid stomach. I swallow on purpose before moving my gaze back to his.

"You're going to do great today," I pronounce, spinning on my heels and marching into the bathroom to pick up my day-old clothes from the floor.

Jensen leans in his doorway as I leave, almost as if making sure I'm actually gone. I lock the door behind me as a little calling card for his benefit, and by the time I'm in the elevator, I get a text from him.

> JENSEN: Seriously, why do you have a key?

> ME: Because.

I smile at our brand-new text string, but quickly bury the glee. This isn't about flirting, or about a cute guy. Beneath the man is a self-centered prick. There always is. Nobody is good but my brother. And he only gets a pass because I say so.

I clear my throat and search for the clip I just made. Once I find it, I upload it to our chat with instructions.

> ME: Do not watch this until you get in the locker room. Put your earbuds in, too. Trust me. This is your first piece of homework.

I hit send then suck in my lip, eager to see his response now and again at the end of his day. I am under no assumption that Jensen Hawke will be easy to turn around. But I believe he can be. And I believe I'm the one to do it.

CHAPTER 8

Jensen

My phone buzzes while I'm changing, and unlike my sister's morning affirmation texts, I find I'm oddly eager to read more snarky bits from Sutter. This is a bad idea. But also, I was one towel away from making this worse. So close. *Too close.*

I pick up my phone once my shirt is on and sit on my bed to read it before slipping on my shoes. Sutter sent me some video clip with oddly specific instructions. I stare at the file for a few seconds, knocking around whether or not I should do as she asked when my phone buzzes in my hand.

> SUTTER: I said wait. You better follow directions.

I breathe out a laugh and begin to type.

> ME: How did you know? Let me guess. You snuck back in with your key and are hiding under my bed.

Before I send the text off, though, I second guess myself and decide Sutter and I are being a little too . . . much. I delete and fire off a different response.

ME: Fine.

I open the top drawer of my nightstand, where my sister's engagement party invitation still sits, the RSVP card un-RSVP'd. I snag my earbuds and sync them to my phone to make sure they're charged.

Once I finish getting dressed, I bolt out of the apartment before Billy has a chance to make me pancakes or waffles or whatever else he might try to whip up because he feels bad about his sister tricking me into dinner, or about whatever weirdness was going on between them, or about not feeding me more chili. I also feel strangely guilty for falling asleep on the couch next to his sister. Though there was an entire cushion between us—a wide expanse of thirty-six inches in upholstery—it still felt like maybe an overstep to dream next to her. And then there's the whole shower and towel situation. A recurring theme for us, it seems.

I make it to the elevator just as the doors close and reach forward to squeeze myself in, a little insurance that I won't accidentally run into Billy as he leaves. Once inside, it's instantly debatable which outcome would have been worse—stuck in the hall waiting for the next ride with Billy or stuck in here as I am now, with the old man who scowled at me in this elevator with Sutter a few days ago.

"Oh, it's you," he sneers.

"I'm afraid so," I say, offering a smile. I don't do small talk and chitchat well, and I'm not great at winning over strangers. When they've already formed an opinion of me, it's damn near impossible. But for some reason, I feel compelled to try.

"I'm Jensen. I play for the Monsoon." I glance down at the logo on my shirt before reaching out a hand.

"Is that so," the man says. He has a hint of an accent, maybe from Baltimore. My sister dated a lawyer from Baltimore right out of college and I always loved the way that guy talked. He had a natural way of sounding tough, kind of like this gentleman, who despite his years I feel could beat me down in seconds with his cane. Doubt he'd even have to take off his glasses.

He shakes my hand, albeit reluctantly, and coughs out a short laugh.

"Jensen, I'm Ernie. It's nice to meet you." He nods as our hands part.

"Same," I say, though I'm not exactly sure whether or not he was being sarcastic.

"What position are you?"

A half-mouthed smile stamps my face. "Pitcher." I hold up my left arm, as if somehow signaling I'm a lefty will earn his approval. It does not.

"Too bad," he responds.

"Ha, yeah. Probably," I say, pulling my gear bag up on my shoulder.

"Tell me, Jensen. Why do you ballplayers look more like ballerinas today? I mean, what's with the tights?" He knocks his cane against my compression-pant-covered calf. I look down at it.

"Theory is these things are better for muscle recovery, but honestly? I think some cool guy started wearing them and we all followed along because of peer pressure." I suck my mouth into a tight line and shrug. Ernie laughs hard enough that he has to hold his side and cough.

"Jensen, you said. All right. All right. You can stay." The elevator opens and out of precaution I hold the door and let him exit first.

"Have a good day, Ernie," I call after him. He holds up his cane and makes his way toward the bus stop.

I grin the entire way to the crosswalk. The thought that Ernie might be some angel from Christmas past or like that dude in *It's A Wonderful Life* waiting for his wings tickles my mind. Though he looks a lot more like the dude from that cartoon *Up*. It's been ages since I've bantered with a stranger like that. It felt good.

By the time I'm in the locker room, I'm almost buzzing with this crazy energy. I pull my shaker bottle from my bag and dump in my packet of protein, then pull out my phone and scroll to Sutter's message and the mystery file. I put my earbuds in again then hit play as I carry my bottle to the water dispenser and fill it nearly to the top. I mix my drink when last night's *Sing for Your Supper* winner begins singing in my ear. My steps stutter and I look around to check that I'm still alone. When I confirm I am, I press the replay icon to start the clip from the beginning so I can watch as well as listen.

It's weird how seeing it for a second time hits me. I'm not sure whether it's because I know what's coming or because I'm reliving the memories of watching Sutter gush. Whatever the reason, my arms tingle with chills when the girl on my screen sings. I instantly grin like a fool, and since I'm alone, I hum along with the melody. I have no clue what the words are, but I know I've heard this song a hundred times. It's one of those standards or something. Her voice is even more powerful directly in my ears. I can hear the small vibrations when her nerves strike. And then she gets to the middle part and just belts it out.

I'm nodding my head with the rhythm and I don't stop, even when I see a few of the other guys walk in from my periphery. When my second listen ends, I pull my earbuds out and tuck them in my bag with my phone before storing my stuff and heading out to the field. I catch myself whistling the damn song as I jog across the grass, and that sucker creeps in again while I'm stretching. It carries right through my arm care work by one of the practice field fences.

"Hawke!"

I peer over my shoulder to see who's calling my name by the bullpens. Coach Benson holds up a palm. I wave back and snag my stretching bands from the fence, giving my arm one final slow stretch across my chest.

"Like to take a look at that slider again. Not a full session, so let's keep it under fifteen pitches, yeah?" Coach Benson's holding the speed gun in his right hand. I know what he's looking for with that. They want me around eighty-four, and they want my fastball at ninety. That's right where I should be, or would be if I didn't take the whole Tommy John surgery detour.

"You ready?" He stirs me out of my thoughts.

"Yeah, sure," I say, my eyes scanning the field for Dalton. I drop my bands and tuck my glove under my arm before I pick up a ball to work it in my hands. Coach Mason is making his way in this direction, too, so I walk toward the rubber and draw in a slow breath to reset myself.

"Brad, you got this one?" Coach Benson says. I turn to see one of the new catchers pop up and grab his mask.

"Oh, I usually—" I stop myself before I get too far with my stupid protest. I was about to say I usually throw to Dalton, but that's not going to earn me any points. They don't care if I throw to a tire.

I clear my throat as the young dude across from me slides his mask down and pounds his mitt twice.

"What was that?" he says.

"Nothing. I'm good," I reply, tossing the ball to him for a few warm-ups.

Sutter's dad slips through the gate and moves to the space behind me where Coach Benson is set up with the speed gun. They're too far for me to clearly hear their muttered words, but I catch a few random phrases.

"This is it, right?"

"Yeah, I mean if there's nothing there, there's nothing there."

"It happens. They don't all come back."

Fuck. They're talking about me.

I shake my arm against my side and look up at the sky while I take a few steps around the mound. I pull the brim of my hat down low and adjust my glove on my hand. It suddenly feels strange against my skin, and my shirt feels too big on my body. I roll my shoulders and exhale in an effort to clear my mind of the noise and distractions, then throw my first pitch into the dirt.

"*Mmm*," Coach Benson hums behind me. I glance at the both of them after I catch the ball and walk back up the mound to the rubber. They're looking at the number on the gun, and their expression looks disappointed. Sutter's dad lifts his clipboard to cover the lower half of his face before leaning in close and saying something to Coach Benson that makes him laugh.

I clench my jaw with so much force it pops, sending a flash of pain down the side of my neck. *I won't be able to open my mouth wide enough to eat solid food for the rest of the day. Awesome.*

Digging my foot into the dirt by the rubber, I tuck my glove under my arm and work the ball in my palms again. My thoughts are racing around various points of failure. I can't even remember what a perfect slider looks like, and it's the entire reason I'm here.

I'm not sure what brings Sutter into my mind all of a sudden, but thinking about her is better than thinking about whatever my coaches found amusing a few seconds ago. I close my eyes for a second and force the *Sing for Your Supper* tune into my mind as a way to overwrite my thoughts. Mental coaching. My issues are in my head. That's what Sutter says.

I nod a few times before setting up to throw again. Even though my coaches and one of the other pitchers are now standing behind me muttering, I block them out. Nobody is in this except me. Time to sing for my supper.

Every movement I make matches the song in my head. I look in at the catcher to the low part at the beginning of the song. I stand tall and the singer's voice rises. She belts, and I begin my wind up, slider sailing from my hand to Brad's mitt with the perfect tail, and a final thought races through my head: *who gives a damn how fast that was?*

My mouth ticks up on one side, not an obnoxious smile, but a private one just for me. That felt good. *No. That felt fucking amazing.*

I take the toss from Brad with a little flick of my wrist

so the ball snaps in my glove. I work my jaw back and forth to test the soreness. It's still there, but I can whistle if I want to. And I almost do. I stop short of letting the sound escape my lips as I repeat everything and deliver another slider that feels even better than the first.

"All right," Brad says, popping up from his stance to throw the ball back. He pounds his glove, his excitement fueling mine. I chuckle softly under my breath but tuck it away before I face Coach again. My routine carries on through a dozen pitches, and I hit my spot like a sniper, throw after throw. I gear up for toss number fifteen when Coach Benson steps away from the back wall and holds out an open palm.

"That's good, Jensen. Good."

Damn right, that was good.

"Okay, thanks, Coach." I breathe out hard then pop my hat off and run a hand through my hair, eyes squinting as I look him in the eyes.

"Am I getting closer?" I ask.

That's all I need—growth. If this is moving in the right direction, if I'm getting better, I can build on things. If I'm floundering, though, I'm not sure where to go from there. That had to be better. I felt it. That had to be . . .

"Son, you throw like that, you're starting opening day," Sutter's dad says, his words coming from one side of his mouth, a wad of gum pushed into the other cheek.

I open my mouth to respond but quickly snap it shut and simply nod. *Okay.*

"Good work, Hawke," Coach Benson says, smacking my ass before he follows Coach Mason out of the dugout.

"Dude, those were wicked," Brad says as he comes up behind me.

"Yeah? Wicked, huh?" Kid must be from Boston.

"For real, man. That shit's fun to catch. Hard work, but fun. Ya know?" He flashes me a toothy grin before jogging out with his mask propped on his head.

I toss the ball in my hand a few times, catching it and spinning it in my palm before finally dumping it in the bucket by the bench. I earn a few nods from some of the other guys waiting their turn and head into the training room for my ice.

"Looks like someone had a good day," Shannon says as she works on my arm. Her sideways glance is full of suspicion.

"Felt like me today, is all. Like . . . the old me. Maybe better."

She nods, her mouth drawn in tight like she's still holding something back.

"What?" I question as she finishes up my wrap.

"I told you she was good," she says, patting the ice pack on my arm as she gathers her materials and moves to the next arm waiting for her attention.

A reluctant half smile touches my mouth and I chuckle as I slide from the table and adjust my sleeve.

"That's a pretty big leap. We haven't even done anything yet to work on my mental game. We had dinner, sort of."

"You were humming a song the entire time I wrapped your arm," she says, which catches the attention of a few other guys in the training room.

I laugh it off at first, but then cut it off when she raises a brow in challenge. *Shit. Was I really?*

"What did you have for dinner? Maybe she drugged you

into a good mood. Who knows," Shannon says with a raspy laugh.

I scowl. "I'm always in a good mood."

She laughs harder.

"Shannon—"

"No, stop. Seriously," she says, grabbing her side. "You're killing me."

She tries to form a serious face again, but it breaks into laughter when our eyes meet. I titter, but only because I'm super uncomfortable and now the guy getting his arm wrapped is laughing too. Fucker doesn't even know the full story.

Arm wrapped, I leave Shannon with her laughter at my expense and head back up to the field in time to watch Dalton run through some catching drills.

"You two work well together, you know," Coach says at my side. I didn't see him sitting in the dugout behind me.

"Dalton? Yeah, he's a great catch," I say.

Coach Mason pulls a handful of Double Bubble from his back pocket and holds it out for me in an open palm. I take it and stuff it into my pocket and unwrap one piece to chew.

"How many of these do you go through a day?" I motion toward his jaw, which hasn't stopped working since I arrived this morning.

"Fifty. Maybe sixty," he says. "Beats the other stuff I used to go through every practice."

He winces and I gather he means tobacco.

"Hard to quit?" I ask.

"Every damn day," he laughs out. "But . . . I promised Sutter and my wife."

I nod. My grandfather died when I was three, maybe

four, from cancer. I don't remember much about the man, but I do know he had an incredible laugh and arms long enough to lift me up to look over the fence and see the goats that lived in the yard next door. When he died, nobody ever lifted me up again. Cancer took that away from me, which is probably the main reason I never indulged in tobacco when everyone else on my college squad did.

"You looked real comfortable today, Hawke. At ease. You notice you weren't falling to the right like last time?" He walks to the back of the dugout to spit out one piece of gum only to start on another, and I consider my response while his back is to me.

"Maybe, yeah. I did work on feeling loose, which I think is what I was missing," I say, still not convinced about the whole falling to the right thing.

"Well, you sure changed something. You were a whole different arm out there. Rest up. You'll be throwing three innings on Saturday." He rolls up his practice sheet and taps my arm with it as he walks up the steps and out onto the field where I'm sure he'll get into some other player's head. I thought about asking him what was so funny back in the bullpen but decided a second before the question came out of my mouth that I didn't care.

I was good today. Damn good. I was loose. Which puts an entirely different question in my head.

Did Sutter actually help me?

The whistling keeps showing up, accompanying me on my walk home that morning, and again in the afternoon during my cardio and weight training. When I catch myself actually humming the song in the elevator, I switch to holding my breath for a few seconds in an effort to force it to stop.

I practically skip out of the elevator, my body doped up on serotonin, but make a hard stop when I notice someone pounding on my apartment door. Not *someone*. Corbin Forsythe.

"What the actual fu—" I mutter to myself.

This guy has no clue how we're connected, and I'm fine with him never having that insight. In fact, I'm fine with him being traded to the Yankees for hundreds of millions of dollars if it puts him on the opposite side of the country from me. Why the hell he's knocking on my apartment door right now beats the hell out of me.

"Can I help you?" I pull my keys from my pocket as I walk up and interrupt him. His brow furrows and his eyes dart from the keys to the door and back to me.

"You . . . live here?" He points to my door as I'm literally opening it.

"I do. Can I help you?" I lift a brow and step into the doorway, spinning around before he can follow. I can tell he wants to.

He studies me for a few seconds and slowly smiles as realization comes to him.

"Hey, I met you yesterday. You're new to Monsoon baseball. You're a rookie, right?" His half-mast smile pisses me off, as does the slight squint to his eye as if he knows some secret and feels special.

"Not really a rookie. I was drafted two years ago, but just had Tommy John, so—" I shrug.

"Class after me. Nice. Right. Well, congrats on that, man. I uh . . . I was looking for Sutter. She around?" He cranes his neck a pinch and looks over my shoulder. I close the door closer to my body.

"No Sutter here," I say, ending my information dump there. As far as I'm concerned, we're done here.

I start to close the door and he pushes back with a heavy palm. Our eyes meet and he breathes out a laugh.

"Sorry, just . . . I'm confused. Sutter doesn't live here?" His expression pulls in more. He obviously knows she *used* to live here. I have no idea what she would want Corbin Forsythe to know about her now, though, and frankly, this is more time than I ever intended on being in his presence. I decide to shrug instead of confirming or deny his question.

"Oh, I see. So, you're the new guy. Like, *her* new guy. Okay, yeah." He takes a step back, his laugh a little more ominous. Maybe I imagine the tone, but I don't think so.

"Not the new guy. But again, thanks for stopping by." I try to shut the door again, but he jams his toe against the bottom, stopping me.

I flash my eyes at him a bit wider this time, my smile a tight-lipped, teeth-grinding sort of grin.

"If you see her . . ."

"Yeah, sure. I'll tell her you're knocking on everyone's door looking for her. Have a good day." I push with extra force this time, twisting the lock on the door and holding my breath for a few seconds until I hear his steps moving away from my door.

"Thanks for that," Sutter says from behind me.

"Ah!" I leap to the side and spin to face her. She's walking out of her brother's room.

"Sorry." She flashes a tiny sheepish smile.

"You have got to stop popping up in my apartment. You. Don't. Live. Here." I hold her stare until she nods that she heard me.

"I know, but I have a key," she says as I turn to head into my room.

"Gah! That damn key. I'm going to find out how we change the locks. That's it," I grumble. She follows me into my room, stopping at the doorway and hanging half inside, half out.

"So, Corbin Forsythe knows where I live now." I change subjects. Pretty major subject. Bigger than she knows.

"To be fair, he doesn't really care that *you* live here," she offers, her lips twisted with indifference.

I roll my eyes as I kick my shoes off and toss my bag into the corner.

"He seems to care that you *don't* live here. Want to share why that's the case? Were you and him . . ." I lean my head to the side and lift a brow.

"It was nothing," she says, waving it off. "A total mistake."

Her cheeks blush, which makes me think that mistake or not, he's definitely seen under the towel. I push out my bottom lip and nod.

"Okay, so that's interesting." My stomach tightens a hair, probably because Corbin is the person in question. There's no reason this should bother me, other than him putting his stink somewhere else.

"It's not really interesting," Sutter interjects. I turn and hold up both palms to give in.

"Okay, it's not," I say. But it is. And that stomach knot is still there.

I pull out clean clothes from my drawer and move to the doorway, expecting Sutter to move. She doesn't, instead she puts her palm on my chest when I attempt to move through the doorway.

"Umm," I say as I freeze in place. I look down at her fingers and she curls them into a fist but keeps her hand on the center of my chest. She knocks on me lightly, and it urges my lips to curve with a hint of amusement.

"Yes?" I coax her to go on. She's staring at her hand, and the middle of my body, her mouth caught halfway open but wordless. Her eyes suddenly flicker up to mine and her lips break into a coy smile as the redness returns to her cheeks, like cotton candy stains on her skin.

"Billy's day went well. He has a date." Her fist is still firmly planted against my chest, so I lift my free hand and wrap it around her wrist.

"Good for Billy," I say, dragging her arm away so I can continue on to the shower. She tugs the back of my shirt before I can get in, though.

"You're stretching it," I chastise.

"I mean, it's a T-shirt. It'll bounce back, but . . . that's not important," she says, waving both hands in the air between us as if they're erasers. "Thing is, he's nervous. And it's really sweet. And I want this to go well for him, so I maybe sort of promised I would tag along."

I nod but the blank stare remains on my face. Not sure why I need to know this.

"Yeahhhhhhh, and my friend was coming with me, only, she has a date of her own. And well, my friend Kiki does not need anyone with her on her dates. And because it would be really weird to be a third wheel and look like I'm chaperoning my grown-ass brother, I thought . . ."

"Oh oh, ho ho no. Wait a minute." I waggle my finger and back further into the bathroom.

"Come on. We'll use it to work on things. It's just dinner. And horseshoes." She throws that last part in as if it's completely normal. Like dessert.

"Sorry, but . . . what shoes?" I tilt my head slightly.

Sutter straightens her spine, a quirk I'm beginning to recognize in her. It's something she does when she's rallying her confidence. It's like her bones become steel. *Shit.*

"Horseshoes. And I never lose. You're not chicken, are you?" She's literally daring me into going out tonight by playing on my fragile masculinity.

"I'm 'fraid so. I'm a total chicken. Yup. That's me. Buk buk buk, be-gawk," I say, accenting my response with a little flap of my pretend wing.

"Come on. It'll be fun." She reaches forward and pulls my clean shirt from my hand.

"I can just go get another one, you know," I defend, irritated that I'm also laughing a little.

"You'd have to get through me. And I think that process would get really hairy. I'm not above scratching," she says, forming a claw. I reach up and tap her fingertips.

"Not very threatening nubs," I tease.

"Dammit," she huffs, curling her nails into her fist to hide them.

I hold out my hand for my shirt and she relents, but doesn't immediately let go of her end, forcing a mini tug-o-war.

"Please, Jensen? We'll count it toward our sessions. Your second workshop," she proudly grins.

"Uh, we had a first session?" I question.

She falls back on her heels a little and pushes her tongue into her cheek.

"What do you think that little video motivation tool was this morning?" Her brows shift, one high, one low. "Little birdie told me you were on today when I called and asked. And yes, that little birdie was my father. And no, we did not talk long. We don't . . . talk. But he told me enough. You were finally relaxed. You threw and had fun. Nothing was forced. And your speed—"

"What was my speed?" I didn't ask on the field. I didn't want to push things since the feedback was so damn good.

"Twelve in a row at eighty-four. That's pretty much perfect."

I lean back against the bathroom sink as she leans against my bedroom door frame across the hall and we both simmer with arrogant grins on our lips.

"That's so?" I fish.

"Yes, sir. That is so," she says.

I bite my bottom lip and glance down, secretly also taking in the rest of her outfit. She's wearing Vans and black leggings and one of those cropped shirts that sits right above the waistline. She looks casual and dangerously cute.

And Corbin came to see her, but she wanted nothing to do with him.

"All right, but nothing late. I want to be well-rested for my workouts tomorrow. I don't throw again until Saturday, and I want to be in top form by then." I hold out a pinkie and she bites her tongue, half smiling. Eventually, she hooks her finger with mine and we shake like children. A pinky swear.

"You'll be in this apartment by ten. I promise," she

says, crossing her finger over her chest and finally leaving me alone to shower. I pop my head out in time to catch her walking away, her sassy sway of the hips on point. Nothing about this is a good idea, but at the moment, I don't care, because Corbin came to see her, but I'm the one taking her out.

I should have known better.

In this apartment by ten, she said. No—she *swore!*

There were pinkies!

I can't blame Sutter completely that it's past eleven and I'm standing in the middle of a sand pit about a block from the university, swinging a bright orange horseshoe from my side. My competitive nature exists. I simply thought I had better control over it. Turns out, having a girl repeatedly kick my ass in horseshoes is the key to obliterating my restraint.

Also, I haven't had more than three beers in a sitting in a long time, and I have no idea how many pitchers we've finished off, but I'm feeling good.

Fuck bedtime.

"All I know, Jensen, is you suck at horseshoes for a guy whose entire job is throwing things to the perfect spot," Billy jokes, finishing off our most recent pitcher and raising his glass in toast to me.

"Like I said, overhand is a totally different game," I respond.

I squint as I line up my throw, doing my best to block out Sutter's chants behind me. Where the hell she learned my *Jay Hawk* nickname I have no clue, but it's really annoying.

I let the horseshoe go, flinging it in a perfect line, and it manages to hook the top of the post and swirl around twice before flinging off into the grass.

"Ohhh!" Sutter chants, stepping up next to me with her bright pink horseshoe primed and ready to throw. "So. Close."

She hip checks me out of the way, and though I could hold my own if I wanted to, I fall to the side thanks to my buzz. And because I'm having a good time.

I'm having a good time.

I breathe in deeply and scan the entire outdoor patioscape. I haven't been in a place like this since before the draft. Definitely not since surgery. Maybe it wouldn't kill me to cut loose from time to time, get to know my teammates a little more.

I tip my head back, drain the last of my beer, and take the stool on the other side of the pub table from Billy and his date. Kendra seems nice, and the fact she gave as good as she got in our shit-talking game out here is a sign of a good woman. She's not very good at horseshoes, but she didn't care. Neither did Billy. Besides, apparently Sutter is a ringer and carried the girls' team all night.

To make it really sting, Sutter waves her fingers in front of her face then closes them and places her palm over her eyes. She swings and counts to three with each sway before letting the horseshoe fly, and unlike me, she rings that sucker dead to rights.

"Aw, maybe next time, Jay Hawk," she jokes.

I chuckle and shake my head but reach out my hand to shake hers and lose as gracefully as I know how. When our hands clasp, Sutter leans in close and lifts up on her toes, cupping her mouth to speak in my ear.

"I think Kendra likes him," she says, flashing me with smiling eyes that crinkle at the edges when she backs away.

I smile back, but my expression is pure façade. Internally, I'm thinking about how her breath felt at my ear, and how my other hand naturally reached around her waist as she lifted up on her toes. The way her bare back felt against my fingertips. That tight feeling creeps back into my stomach, but before I can categorize it, Sutter is tossing down cash on the bill and pulling me by the sleeve of my T-shirt toward the exit behind Billy and Kendra.

"We should totally watch that movie, the one you guys were talking about earlier," Sutter says, slapping her brother on the arm.

"That surf movie with Keanu?" I ask.

"Yesssss!" Sutter's got a good buzz going too. Different from last time when she accused me of being an attacker and maced me with hair spray. Or maybe it's just my own drunk goggles playing tricks on me. Whatever the case, I somehow let her take my hand, and she's pulling me into the back of a ride share SUV. She flips down the second row of seats so she and I can take the back and leave the easier ones for her brother and Kendra.

"This was easier when I was a kid," she grunts as she basically hurdles her right leg over the folded seat and crawls on all fours into the small bench seat in the back.

"I don't think I'm going to fit back there," I say. Honestly, it's doubtful. Kendra offers to trade me places but before she can get in, Sutter calls me a baby and hits me with a glare that says if I don't let her brother and

Kendra sit together she's going to rip my arm off and sew it on backward.

"No, it's okay. I'm limber," I lie. I mean, I can touch my toes, but I don't see how that helps in this situation.

In order to fit in the third row I have to sit sideways with one leg resting on the center of the bench and my knee nearly folded into my chest, but eventually we're all in. After the most uncomfortable five-mile drive ever, I manage to get out a lot smoother than I crawled into the vehicle.

Everyone piles inside our apartment, but as the three of them head into the living room where Sutter is already searching for *Point Break*, I excuse myself to my room.

"Party pooper! Come on," she pleads.

I shake my head and hold up my pinky to remind her. She hits me with a pouty face, but finally mouths, "Okay."

I linger a little longer than I should after she gives me permission to go, and Sutter keeps her eyes on me instead of the TV as she flips through the various options. For a second, I consider giving in and flopping onto the couch and pulling her down with me. Resting my arm on the back of the sofa the same way Billy is, with the intent of slowly working it down to her shoulder until I'm holding her close. Somehow I convince my feet to move toward my bedroom though, away from temptation.

This is going to be an incredibly long week.

CHAPTER 9
Sutter

I had a feeling the whole movie thing was a front for my brother. Honestly, it was a front for me, too. One bad idea piled on after the other.

We made it to the football scene on the beach when the whispering between my brother and Kendra picked up and eventually the two of them retreated to Billy's room, leaving me alone to watch the rest of the Keanu goodness on my own.

There was a small kernel in my mind that thought maybe I'd end up out here on the sofa with Jensen again, and maybe I could nuzzle next to him. It's a stupid thought. A foolish one. And completely not part of our agreement or my agreement with myself. But hearing Corbin at the door today was hard. I didn't say anything to Billy about it. Like I didn't let on that Corbin texted me during our fun evening out. He texted twice tonight, the most recent one coming in right after Billy and Kendra left me alone on the couch.

I press replay on the remote and let *Point Break* start

again just to let the sound keep me company. I slouch into the sofa and pick up my phone from the coffee table to read his texts again.

> CORBIN: I stopped by our apartment today to catch up. Seems you've moved. Or was that your new boyfriend guarding the fortress? Good for you.

Good for me? That one line is the part that dug at me for most of the night. Why is it good for me to have a replacement boyfriend? Why do I need a boyfriend to be whole or to be worthy of a *good for you?* I stewed about that for a good hour, and I maybe let it drive my need to win at horseshoes.

Then Corbin's second text came in.

> CORBIN: You know we never really got to talk. About things. I hope we can find some time. I leave on Tuesday afternoon for LA.

I thumb up through the hundreds of messages that remain between us. I never deleted him from my phone. A weakness on my part, I know. But the nights when I pretended my life was still on course were often spent revisiting those old messages. They were so affectionate. Some of them downright sexy.

I should have deleted them.

I should have blocked him.

He's . . . engaged. And truly? Jensen is right. Corbin's a real dick.

Letting my arm flop to the side, I click my screen off and chew at the inside of my cheek while long-haired surfers ride the waves on our big screen—correction, on Billy's big screen. I didn't pay for this TV, so I guess I don't have a right to resent that it lives here without me, but I kinda do.

A soft giggle travels down the hallway from behind the kitchen and I smirk. I hope she doesn't break Billy's heart. He's soft. A lot softer than me, despite what he might say.

I roll my head to the other side and stare at the dark hallway to my right. I lean forward and press mute on the remote, then rest my phone on the table next to it. Jensen doesn't seem to snore. Corbin was a major snore machine. I had to wear my earbuds to bed and play the wave sounds on repeat.

Kicking my shoes out of the way, I stand and toe my way into the hallway until my hand rests on his door. It's closed, but the knob turns, so he didn't lock me out. That isn't saying he wants me to come in. *I shouldn't go in.*

Yet . . .

I turn the knob slowly, careful not to make a sound, then inch the door open, willing the hinges to obey and remain quiet. I shut it just as softly once I'm inside, but the moment I turn to face the bed, the gravity of what I'm doing hits me.

No, Sutter!

My heart kicks like a rabbit in my chest, my arms tingling with the rush of panic. This was a terrible idea fueled by the bravery of way too many glasses of whatever was on tap. Still, I don't seem to be moving.

I'll leave after a minute of watching him. I just need to see him sleep for a few minutes to calm my mind. He's probably in such a deep sleep, he'll never even notice. In fact, I bet I could sit on the bed without him realizing.

I slide my feet toward the bed, first testing the mattress by pressing down with my palm and then giving in to the overwhelming desire to lay with him. He's on his side, his arms folded around a pillow at his chest, clutching it like a child with a teddy bear. His quilt is only half covering his body, one leg bent at the knee, his gray sweatpants visible and his white T-shirt tight around his biceps.

I breathe in, smelling the stale beer on his breath. *Or maybe that's mine?* Even through that fog I find the undertones of his cotton shirt, his favorite quilt, his shampoo, and as weird as it may seem, his day. It's something about being at a ballpark all day, about walking in the dirt and living with the velvet grass. I can smell the ballpark on people. I always could with my dad. Same with Corbin. Breathing in again, I find that same scent now. Only with Jensen, it's more.

We didn't get a chance to talk about how he did today. I didn't really plan to dive into my process with him until I wore down his guard more. But tonight, I was tempted. I wanted to brag about what I know is working. He's learning to relax, and by extension, he's able to perform. Everything in life needs balance. For Jensen, pitching is work. And he was pouring every ounce of his heart and soul into each throw. That's too much for one arm to bear. Too much for one man. He was weighing himself down, physically and mentally. And without him realizing it, in two days, we lightened his load. Simply by forcing him to slow down and live a little.

The pale light in his room is enough to let me study the contours of his face. I think of everyone I've ever watched sleep, he is my very favorite. And that is why come morning, I should probably say goodbye.

The pitfall of drinking too much and indulging in sleep-spying on a beautiful man is that one is eventually bound to be lulled into their own dreams. It happened to me sometime after three in the morning. And thanks to my mental cocktail of an ex, a hot guy, beers, and sharing a bed with said hot guy, naturally my dream did a number on me. It started with Corbin and a kiss in an elevator—this building's elevator, sort of. By the time it reached the ground level, however, I was definitely kissing Jensen and we were *definitely* naked.

The harsh reality of morning is far less appealing, and the way Jensen is jostling me by my shoulder might provoke me to vomit.

"Yeah, I'm up. I hear you," I gripe.

I crack open one eyelid and find him dressed for his training and standing at my side.

"Look, you gotta get out of here before your brother wakes up. I don't think either of us wants him making assumptions about anything." Jensen's eyes are wide and alert as they dart from me to his closed bedroom door.

My brain is still a little rattled from my dream and the faint memory that I promised myself I would cancel our deal when I woke up. Things feel like a jostled mess at the moment, plus Jensen is wearing all black, and something about his body in that color resonates with my overloaded libido thanks to my fucking dreams.

"I could just stay in here, you know. Sleep until you both are gone?" I stretch out, taking up the entire bed and pulling his abandoned quilt over my body. I'm exhausted.

Sadly, though, I also have work at the job that actually pays me. And since Jensen hasn't budged from the spot he lectured me from, or blinked for that matter, I get the hint that he'd prefer I leave *now*.

"Fine," I relent, grumbling my way to my feet.

My shirt is wrinkled, and my hair is a little wild, half of it curled into waves and the other side a series of zigzags from being slept on. I cup my mouth and fog my breath then recoil, repelled by myself.

"I'm gonna need toothpaste," I say. Jensen has moved his hands to his hips as his eyes follow my every movement like a teacher on recess duty who's trying to herd the kids back into class. "Come on. I am sure I still have a brush hidden in the bathroom drawer. One squeeze of toothpaste and then I'm out."

I step into him and clasp my hands into prayer. I let the pair of joined fists fall into his chest, a move definitely motivated by the leftover boldness still burning off from my dream. Jensen simply drops his chin and stares at my hands on his body.

God, I'm a sucker for a man in black. Even though it's just a black Monsoon workout shirt and black shorts and compression pants, it's still black, and it does something for him. *For me.*

"Just . . . get in the bathroom and don't come out until I'm gone. Then we can pretend you were never in here," he huffs, straightening his blanket over his bed as if to aid in erasing all evidence.

"Got it. Maybe I'll even floss to take extra long," I joke.

He grimaces then grabs my shoulders, spinning me toward the door and giving me a gentle shove.

"Jeeze, pushy," I say. I'm masking the buzz I feel from

having his hands on me, even in this totally innocuous way. It's amazing what damage one hot dream can do.

I open the door quietly and peek through the small crack with one eye to check whether the coast is clear. It seems safe, so I rush across the hall and into the bathroom, literally leaping the three feet of the hallway floor to not even make a toe print. I turn around at the last second and catch a flash of a smile on Jensen's lips. He deletes it as soon as his gaze meets mine. He's all business this morning. Maybe we can keep moving forward this way and I don't have to end things early. We can finish out the week for sure, and then get back on track.

"I have to go." His tone is curt.

My hands grab both sides of the door jamb and I lean out into the hallway with a "*Psst!*" Jensen glances over his shoulder, his eyes flared and jaw clenched. I think I'm frustrating him.

"Session three will have to be tonight, when I get off from work," I say.

Jensen twists his mouth, and I fear he's had the same train of thoughts I have, that we need to quit while we're ahead. Only, I've come full circle and I'm still in. I need to be in. My degree depends on this.

"We can meet at the field. I can be there by seven, and we'll work this around your workout schedule. No more breaking into your room and acting like I live here." I can't cross my fingers, so I cross my toes instead, mostly because I know myself and if I feel like barging in, I'm probably going to. It's how I operate. If something needs to get done, I bulldoze whatever is in the way. And if it's an apartment door? Well, I have a key.

"Seven. At the field," he rehashes.

I fling one arm out as I hang from the frame with the other and flash him what I think is a scout's honor sign. Or maybe it's the Vulcan hello from the old Star Treks my dad used to watch.

"Fine. I'll make sure I'm done in the gym." He nods and turns to leave but stops and makes a quick pivot, holding a finger up. "One thing, though."

"*Hmm?*" I lift my chin. My hand is starting to slip. I'm pretty close to face planting into his bedroom door.

"You said this will be our third session, but I kinda think it's our first."

He still doesn't see it.

I smirk and nod at him slowly. "I meant third. I'll explain tonight." I hold my hand up in the same gesture.

Jensen stares at it for a beat, then chuckles as he turns and leaves for his morning workouts. I step into the hall to catch my balance and consider the form of my hand for a few seconds. It's definitely the Vulcan thing.

In the bathroom, I tug open the row of drawers until I get to the plastic bin in the bottom one where most of my leftover shit lives. I have some mascara and lip gloss tucked away too which might help me whip up a decent fresh face, so I only have to rush home to change my clothes. I brush my teeth and do my best with the tools I find, untangling my hair with Jensen's blue plastic comb. Now when I get to my place, it should be easy to throw my hair up in a ponytail.

I leave the bathroom and stand silently in the dim hallway, listening to see if I hear Billy stirring yet. He and Kendra work at the same place, and I wonder if they have to keep their budding romance all hush hush or if they plan to drive in together. Regardless, I'm sure their morning conversation was a lot more amicable than the one I had with Jensen.

Turning to Jensen's door, I pause for a full second before grabbing the knob and heading back into his space. When I sifted through his things the other day I came up empty, but I had the realization this morning that I never pulled open the night table drawer. I move around his bed and slide the drawer open carefully, my pulse racing with my overactive imagination. I'm not sure what I expect to find, but an invitation to some girl named Amber's engagement party next weekend isn't exactly a secret stash of porn kind of bombshell.

I pick it up and read the details. Drinks and appetizers at 6 p.m. at The Costa in downtown LA. That's a pretty swanky spot for a party that's only purpose is to say *hey, he bought me a ring*. Of course, I guess the kind of people who want to throw that type of party are already fairly swanky. Corbin and I played pool at McGill's and posted a photo on social media. It took two weeks for either of us to tell my dad. Corbin was too afraid to ask him for permission without me. As if permission is necessary. Or my dad gets any say in anyone's relationships anywhere ever, what with his own stellar record and all.

I drop the invite back in the drawer and close it, then just to be a stink, I flip Jensen's quilt up and twist it in the middle of the bed, so it looks like wild shit went down. I leave his room and head to the living room for my shoes, keys, wallet, and phone, but halt the minute my toes leave the safety of the hallway. Billy's sitting on the arm of the sofa, dressed for work and blowing on his steaming cup of coffee.

I rock back on my heels but remember I didn't really do

anything for him to get all judgey about, so I move on to the more important conversation.

"You make a full pot? Or is that one of those pod things?" I flop my hand open and point at the cup he's cradling.

"This is a bad idea, Sutter. You're not thinking."

I circle around him and move to the other end of the sofa, working my feet into my shoes and pulling them up one at a time to slide the backs on with my fingers.

"I have always liked coffee, Billy. You know that. I'm thinking I would *love* a cup this morning." I know that's not what he means, but I'm also not the one in this apartment who spent the night banging a coworker.

"Sut."

"Bill." He hates to be called that.

We do the sibling death stare for a few minutes while I finish adjusting my shoes and gathering my things, but eventually he leans his head to the side, pulling out the wise big brother card. I fall into the couch cushion with a heavy breath.

"It's not anything like that, I swear," I say, rolling my head along the back of the sofa until I match him with my own know-it-all baby sister doe eyes.

"Maybe not," he says, taking a cautious sip of his coffee. "But it's still a bad idea. You're repeating a pattern, and you know more about this than I do."

I breathe in long and slow through my nose because damn, he's right. I am repeating a pattern. It's a fair assessment. But I'm not naive about the potential pitfalls. Yeah, last night was probably over the line. *It was definitely over the line.* But I recognize that.

"I was only snooping in his room," I fib. I can tell by the

way he glares at me that he knows I was in there most of the night, so I look away before my cheeks blush.

"Nothing happened. I swear."

Billy gets up from the sofa and makes his way into the kitchen without reacting, and I take the brief few seconds out of his view to let my shoulders drop along with my heart and various other organs inside my body. I'm screwing this up.

A few seconds later, my brother appears with a travel mug. He sits on the coffee table facing me and holds it out with a serious expression etched on his face. He doesn't release the tumbler immediately when I wrap my hand around the handle.

"You can have this coffee on one condition," he says.

I bunch my face into a sour expression and croak, "Okay."

"You have to promise me you won't make the same mistake you did with Corbin. You have to promise me that if this experiment starts to turn the wrong way, you'll see it coming. Because I know we joke about it a lot, you coming over here anytime you want to lament your ex-boyfriend—"

"Ex fiancé," I correct.

He mashes his lips into a hard line and his nostrils flare. Billy doesn't show his emotions often, but he's pretty clear about where he stands on Corbin.

"He hurt you, Sut. And that's not okay with me."

His hand releases the mug and I pull it toward my chest while holding on to his gaze. My brother sets a really high bar for men in general. I reach forward and take his tie in my free hand. I set my coffee gift on the side table then use both hands to straighten his nearly perfect Windsor knot and flatten out his collar.

"I really like her," I say, glancing toward his room, where I assume Kendra is hiding.

Billy's cheeks lift with his bashful smile.

"Me, too," he says.

I pat his tie flat against his chest and lean forward to kiss his cheek.

"I promise," I say.

He gives me a quick nod then moves back into the kitchen where he pours another cup to carry into his room and deliver to Kendra. I slip out the door before he has a chance to come back out and make me promise anything else. This one promise is already going to be tricky to navigate.

Traffic is on my side thankfully, and I make it home and to my office in record time, stepping foot in the district office building with exactly five minutes to spare. An enormous bouquet is blocking Julia, the receptionist, so I stop and lift up on my toes so I can smell the spring flowers and maybe get the scoop on who they're for.

"Is it your birthday?" I say to Julia, who is now standing with me and breathing in the sweet scent.

"I thought it was yours!" Her wide eyes set off a dozen alarms in my head that only get louder after I fumble to read the card poked in the center of the arrangement.

I rip it out of the tiny envelope and hold my breath.

Sutter,
I really hope we can find time to talk.
Corbs

Corbs. Mother-fucking *Corbs?*

My mouth hung open, I promptly walk around Julia's desk and toss the card and envelope into her trash.

"Would you like them?" I say to her.

Her brow furrows, but after a few trips of her gaze between me and the bouquet, I think she realizes that the only shot those flowers have at surviving is if she takes them home.

"Sure," she says, grasping the oversized glass orb vase in her hands. She carries them in the opposite direction, toward the break room, and I pledge not to enter that room once today.

Once in the safety of my cubicle, I fire up my computer and pull out my phone to shoot Kiki a text.

> ME: I fucked up.

It takes her maybe half a second to read my text and another half second to call.

"I'm going to need details," she says instead of hello.

I pop up to scan the office and make sure I'm decently secluded in the sea of cubicles. Satisfied that I am, I duck back down and wheel myself into the deepest corner by my computer where I proceed to tell my best friend every detail, from the flowers from the ex all the way to my sleep-stalker ways. Kiki, naturally, zeros in on the part most important to her.

"Wait, wait. Go back. I need to hear more about this sex dream," she says. I can hear the crunch of her snack break in her teeth. I let my head drop to the desk and look at my feet, and for the next thirty minutes I recall the best night of sleep I've had in nearly a year.

CHAPTER 10

Jensen

Sometimes I miss taking batting practice.

It was pretty clear by my senior year in high school that my talent on the mound was far more valuable than swinging a bat. I was an average hitter. Some might say below average. Doesn't mean it still isn't the best part about playing baseball. Every kid wants to hit, even the kids in their twenties.

"You ready for Saturday?" Coach Mason pulls a piece of gum from his back pocket and hands it to me. I take it as not to be rude, but the last piece he gave me was stale as shit.

"I think so," I say, unwrapping the hard-as-rock gum and popping it my mouth for a tooth-cracking experience.

"See if you can turn that *think* into a nice solid *yes* before then, 'kay? You're starting." He pats me on the back as he heads toward the batting shell on the field where his prized hitters are taking hacks.

I hold things together until he's far enough away for me to spit the gum into my palm and swear under my breath.

Why didn't I just say yes? Probably because I don't actually feel ready. I'm on my way, for sure. But I don't know how to find that feeling I had going for me the last time I threw. I worry it was a fluke.

I take a few steps down into the dugout to toss the gum in the trash, then check my smartwatch for the time. It's ten after seven, and Sutter is nowhere in sight. Maybe she had second thoughts about this. It wouldn't be the worst thing in the world if she didn't show up. In a way, it might take the elephant-sized weight off of my shoulders. My head has been a mess since she slipped into bed with me last night. Truthfully, it was a decent mess before then. It's not right to say but I think she's too pretty to be able to take away my distractions. She *is* the distraction. She's moved right into my head and set up a lease.

I hang around for one more batter, some kid named Chip who hasn't hit a single ball away from the third base-line in ten pitches. He's not going to make it. I can tell, and I wish I had the balls to find him later and let him know so it won't hurt so much when he gets bumped from the roster this weekend.

"Screw this," I mumble to myself, snagging my bag from the dugout bench and heading through the locker room to the side door closest to the street. I push the button for the WALK sign that leads toward my apartment when a white sedan squeals up to the curb. Sutter's laying on the horn as if I didn't notice she basically almost took out the traffic light.

"Hey, James Bond called. He wants his driving habits back," I say as she kicks open her door and jogs around the front of her car toward me.

"I'm so sorry I'm late. I just wanted to make sure I

caught you. Here, give me your bag," she says, hooking a few of her fingers in the strap hanging from my hand. I hold on tight and jerk back, pulling her from the street and up to the sidewalk.

"Uh uh. We said we would meet on the field," I protest.

Sutter rolls her neck and lets out a heavy sigh. "I know, but that was before I was late, and since I'm parked illegally and all, can you just get in the damn car?" She gestures toward the passenger side.

"I'm sure you understand my hesitation at getting in a car with you right now." I wave my hand around the scene she's created. At least six cars have honked as they passed the roadblock she created.

"Fine, you drive," she says, yanking open the passenger door and getting inside. She buckles up and crosses her arms over her chest to stare at me.

Great. Now it looks like I'm the one who parked the car like a jackass and is tying up traffic.

"Unbelievable," I say as I give in and move to the driver's side.

I toss my bag over the seat to the back and get in. I pull us away and start toward my apartment building, but Sutter reaches over and pushes the wheel straight when I try to turn.

"Change of plans," she says.

I glare at her at the stoplight.

"Unless you want to go to your bedroom again and make things all awkward," she zings back.

I suck in my lips as my chest tightens. As awkward as it was with her in my bedroom, it also wasn't completely her fault that it felt that way. I wasn't sad to see her there when I woke up. I wasn't sad to hear her open my door and put

147

her weight on my bed. The only thing I was upset about was that we never touched. And *that* is why things are awkward now.

"Okay then, where are we going?" I pull through the intersection as the light turns green but go slow, unsure if she's going to ask me to turn around at a moment's notice.

Sutter guides me down the street for a dozen blocks, eventually turning right toward the mountainside. We park in a cul-de-sac of some neighborhood.

"The trailhead is right over there. Let me swap out my shoes and we can go," she says. I look her body up and down, noting her nice blouse and rather short skirt.

"Are we hiking?" I quirk a brow.

"I mean, the mountain is right here." She shoots me a crooked grin as she slips out the door and pulls open her trunk.

I kill the engine, get out, and take note of the lack of people on the mountain and the fast-fading light of dusk.

"Sutter, I don't think we're gonna be able to see—"

I stop hard and swallow as I catch her slipping out of her blouse and tossing it into the back of her car. It's only a flash of a visual, but I'm pretty sure if the police needed me to give them a record account to draw, I could give them every detail of the white lacy bra I just memorized and the light pink nipples that showed through the delicate material.

Goddamn.

"One more sec," she says, unfazed by my presence.

I keep my eyes at the ground and roam the area as she shimmies out of her skirt, tight shorts already on underneath. She steps into her trail runners and flips her trunk shut before asking me to hold her keys.

"Uh, sure," I stammer, dropping them into my side pocket.

"Is this safe?" I call after her. She's already a dozen steps ahead of me and scaling the gravel trail that seems to cut in zigzags up the mountain.

"Sure." She laughs.

Her tone is convincing but the word itself is not. I follow her regardless as she turns on a mini flashlight and illuminates our path up the rocky hillside. We climb for about fifteen minutes before she stops at a large plateau that overlooks the city.

"Come here," she says, urging me to stand next to her on a large rock. She reaches out a hand and I take hold of her as I step up and turn to take in the lights twinkling across miles and miles of urban desert.

"This place can really get under your skin," she says, a soft smile playing at her lips as her eyes flicker around the horizon. The sun fully disappeared, the sky is a deep purple that fades to black as I glance straight above.

"So?" she prompts.

I drop my chin and look out at the view again, then to her.

"It's pretty spectacular," I admit.

"Right?" Her smile stretches as she blinks away from me and back out to the skyline. She flicks off the flashlight to give us the full effect of the city lights and stars. When she sits down on the rock, I squat to join her.

"So, when are you going to explain how climbing mountains is part of my mental coaching?" I place my palms at my sides and kick my feet out to sit comfortably.

"Well, I mean . . . you climbed a mountain. That's a

pretty good metaphor, don't you think?" She raises a brow and I let out a light laugh.

"Fair enough. But I've climbed mountains before."

"Ah, yes. You have," she says.

Sutter pulls her phone from her hip pocket and taps her screen, opening an app that looks like a chart. She taps on a few lines and brings up a series of numbers, then hands the phone to me.

"I went through your last twenty starts. You haven't really started on the mound in over a year because of the injury, but we needed a baseline."

I click around and try to make sense of the numbers she's plotted. I know what most of them mean, but the lack of a pattern doesn't make sense. Maybe that's the problem. I have no pattern.

"And the mountain fits in this . . ." I hand her phone back.

She slides her finger around and opens a new screen, one that's ready for more data.

"I can't say for certain, Jensen, but my gut tells me you have great days and not so great days. And I bet your great days come along when your mind isn't totally wrapped up in the stakes of the game." She pops her head up to meet my gaze as she chews at her lip.

"Maybe. I don't really know," I say, shaking my head.

"What did you think about when you threw for my dad last time? What was taking up space in your head?" She leans forward, cupping her phone in her hands, the light from her screen silhouetting her face.

"How I throw my slider, I guess? Maybe how I should stand straight and try not falling to my right like everyone says."

"Liar." Her response is immediate.

I shake my head and bunch my brow.

"What. Did. You. Think about?" She cocks her head to the side and widens her eyes.

I glance around us and try to remember my thoughts from then. Suddenly, Sutter starts to hum the song from the reality show we watched. I smirk and whistle along with her for a few notes.

"I mean, yeah. That song was stuck in my head, I guess."

"It was more than stuck in your head. I picked that episode on purpose, Jensen. It's two years old, and when I saw it the first time I knew it could be used to evoke emotion. And let's face it, you can't go wrong with Sinatra."

"Sinatra! That's it!" How I didn't realize it was one of his classics amazes me. Of course, that's why I know it. My nana loved Sinatra.

Sutter rocks back, holding her thighs as she laughs into the night air.

"See?" she exclaims.

"See what? Sinatra?" I shake my head.

"No. You think of something that feels good, even something small and silly like that, and you just . . . relax." She rocks forward and reaches out to place her hands on my shoulders. She pushes them down with a light pressure, and I give in, letting them drop.

"You're telling me watching some bad reality TV show was part of your therapy?" I'm skeptical, but Sutter nods.

"It's not all we're going to do, but I had to break your habits somehow. And you know as well as I do that *Sing for Your Supper* is great TV."

I twist my lips and lower my brow as I stare back at her, but eventually I nod and give in. She might be onto something.

"Okay then, so why the mountain?" I look around us. We're secluded, and even though I can see the city nearby we feel very much in the wild. I haven't asked, but I'm pretty sure I hear the vibration of a rattler nearby.

"How far do you think we went?"

I tilt my head with thought and crane my neck to gauge the distance between us and the edge of the neighborhood where we parked. It doesn't seem far, but also there were a lot of switchbacks involved. And we were going pretty fast.

"A mile maybe?"

"Two," she corrects.

"*Pfft*, no," I say, seriously doubting her.

She holds her phone out with a new app showing where we are in the trail system. Right at the two-mile mark.

"You know, most seasoned hikers can't get up here in that time. And you did it in just over twenty minutes."

I look at the map on her phone then turn around to study it again in real life. It's hard to make out the details in nothing but moonlight, but even without the sun, I know we're up fairly high.

"You didn't think. You just did," Sutter explains.

I just did.

I nod eventually, and after several quiet seconds I relent that Sutter has a point.

"Okay, so what do I do Saturday? Do I run this trail before every start? Do I blast Sinatra?" I scrunch up my shoulders because I honestly don't know how I achieve this relaxed state of mind on my own.

"Maybe. Though, I wouldn't climb the mountain. You're gonna feel this tomorrow." She laughs.

She gestures with her head for me to stand and follow her. Lighting up the trail with her flashlight, she guides me back down, our pace far more relaxed.

"You need to make pitching fun again, for you. Maybe make a list of the reasons you wanted to play this game in the first place," she suggests.

"To be a millionaire," I joke. I'm half serious.

"Okay, but success wasn't always based in dollars. When you were a kid and you picked up a ball and threw it as hard as you could, what drove you?"

Her question pulls me back to fourth grade, when I was picked last at recess for the pick-up game after lunch. I was never picked first before that day, but I was also never picked last. Tanner Blythe hated me because I took the last chocolate cupcake during the class party a week before, and he was one of the team captains at recess. He was the reason I got picked last, and since he was on the other team, I convinced the one who took me that I could pitch.

"This kid when I was little, Tanner—he was a bit of a bully. And I wanted to embarrass him," I admit.

Sutter glances to me over her shoulder and I shrug.

"Not a proud moment, but you need honesty, right?"

"I do," she says.

"Well, I chucked the ball so hard to our catcher that he had no shot at making contact. I'm pretty sure my throws weren't anywhere near the strike zone, but I threw so hard that it made him panic and he just swung and missed. Three times in a row."

I'm smiling at the memory, and when Sutter asks me how that day made me feel, I laugh out, "Fantastic."

My laughter dies quickly, though, and Sutter stops our descent, turning around and flashing the light up toward my face.

"What is it?" she asks.

I sigh, the rest of that day coming into focus along with my great revenge on Tanner Blythe.

"That was the first time I ever played baseball. I was athletic and tough so there was some natural talent there, but that stupid half-hour game on a dirt lot was different. I ran home from school that day and begged my dad to sign me up for Little League. You know what he said? Waste of his damn time and money."

I look to my side as the memory of his disgusted face plays in my mind. I flit my gaze back to Sutter, and her eyes are sloped with pity. I shake my head and move to walk past her. I don't like her looking at me that way.

"It's fine. My parents have always been that way."

"What way?" she questions.

"I don't know. Practical, I guess? Baseball wasn't useful. Math was practical. Schoolwork was practical, and having a paper route was practical. Saving money was smart. Playing games was a waste of time. Of course, now that my sister is marrying a famous ballplayer, all of that shit seems to have gone out the window."

Sutter tugs at the back of my shirt. I turn as I walk, not wanting to stop and make this more of a thing.

"Is that what the invite is for? The one in your drawer?"

I roll my head back toward the trail.

"You went through my drawers. I mean, why wouldn't you?" I snicker, but I'm not really amused. I'm a little pissed, but she's holding the flashlight and I'm not about to jog away into this snake-infested desert without it.

"I admit I have issues, and liking to watch people sleep is only the tip of the iceberg. But I wanted to get to know you better, so yeah, I snooped. I'm sorry," she says. I think she's purposely looking down at her feet when I glance her way. Maybe embarrassed, which, frankly, she should be. She snooped in my drawer after basically breaking into my room while I slept. Of course, I also didn't mind. And if I were alone with her drawers . . .

I try to pick up our pace, but when she seems to hang back, I slow.

"You could try asking me questions," I offer over my shoulder.

She doesn't respond right away. It's not until we've cleared at least a quarter of the switchbacks in silence that she finally levels me with an actual personal question.

"Who's Amber?"

I smile at my sister's name.

"My sister. Remember the one you swore you were nothing like?" I chuckle then glance over my shoulder to check her reaction and am surprised to see the timid look on her face. Sutter is always so confident. Downright pushy most of the time. Right now, though, she's holding back. Almost nervous.

Oh, my God!

"Did you think—"

"No!" She cuts me off before I can finish the question, but her insistent rejection is enough of an answer. Sutter thought Amber was my girlfriend. I laugh a little louder, maybe bragging and shoving it in her face more than I should because suddenly the trail goes dark. I stop where I am and flip around.

"Turn that back on, Sutter!"

"Are you afraid of the dark?" she teases.

"I'm not afraid of the dark. I'm afraid of tripping and breaking an ankle."

"*Mmmmmm*, I dunno." That timid, bashful version of this girl is gone. This is what I'm used to.

"Fine, I'm afraid of the dark. Now give me the flashlight," I ask, holding out my hand as we standoff in the middle of a dark mountain trail. I can't see her features clearly, but her posture seems completely at ease. I think she'd be fine walking down this mountain in complete darkness.

When the light clicks back on, a jolt of adrenaline and relief floods my chest. It's not the dark that scares me. It's the relentless rattling.

"Why am I like your sister?" she asks, the flashlight clutched to her chest and pointed to the ground. She's clearly not giving it up.

"You walk first," I say, stepping to the side for her to pass. She walks by me slowly, smirking. She flashes the light off and on to taunt me.

"You're annoying." I sigh.

"So you've said," she practically sings.

I follow along behind her, a little concerned that she'll click off the light and break into a sprint the next time I test her. I hold my tongue as I prepare to answer her last question.

"That little moment right there, with the light? That's how you're like my sister," I explain. Amber would applaud Sutter for most of the things she says to me. She'd even be on board with the whole snooping thing.

"Do you have your flight booked?" she asks.

"Ummm." I know what she means—for the engagement party. And the answer is *no, because I'm not going.*

When I don't answer with more than stalling mumbles, Sutter turns around and shines the light in my face. I squint and hold my arm over my eyes.

"Jensen Hawke, you have to go to your sister's celebration. Not going is unacceptable." She points at my chest and actually pokes it a few times to make her point.

"Why?" I ask, grabbing her finger. She jerks it away from my grasp.

"Because I am someone's sister, and if I am like her then I know how much it would hurt for her brother not to show up." Even in the dark I can tell there isn't a tinge of a humor in her right now.

"It's next weekend. It's probably too late." I actually feel guilty saying this to her, as though I am saying it to Amber herself. I put my response off so long there was no way I would be able to make it, and I did that on purpose. Because I don't want to have to pretend for the other people who will be there. Namely, my parents.

"I'm taking you," Sutter pronounces, breaking up my mental self-torture and igniting a very public one.

"No, that's not happening," I contend. Sutter's already started to walk away, and as I feared, she's jogging. I fumble in my pocket for my phone and light up the ground with my flashlight app as best I can and work to keep up with her.

"It is. I'll have it figured out by tomorrow. You won't even miss workouts or anything. I've always wanted to see The Costa." She says a few more things I don't quite hear as she jogs ahead. She's travel planning in her head.

"How much time did you spend with that invitation? You memorized it," I call after her.

"Oh, I took a photo," she says over her shoulder.

I stop and let her continue down the hill a few more steps without me. Eventually, she notices and stops, flipping around and beaming me with the light.

"I'm kidding, Jensen. That would be creepy."

"Ha!" There's nothing left to do but laugh at my predicament and her brazen moves, self-awareness, and painfully direct humor.

Oddly, though I was hellbent on not attending the hoity toity party for my sister's engagement, I'm suddenly more all right with going than not. My chest seems to have loosened, the knot that's been lingering just under my pecs and taunting me as I try to concentrate on *my* things is gone. And as I travel the rest of the way down the hill, I think about the things Sutter said at the top—about how I don't know how to relax. How I overthink. How I stack the pressure up so high it nearly crushes me.

When we clear the trailhead and hit the sidewalk, Sutter asks for her keys and I hand them over. I turn my flashlight app off and tuck my phone back in my pocket, then stop a few feet from the car while she pops open her trunk and switches out her trail runners for a pair of slides. When she shuts it, her gaze meets mine. I was waiting for her to catch me looking. I think I need to get caught to be pushed to speak. I need to be pushed to make decisions. And apparently, I need to be dragged up a mountain at night to be made to listen.

"Thanks," I say, shrugging one shoulder.

Sutter shifts her stance, her palm on her trunk. She

seems a little surprised at my response, which means I probably need to work on being grateful too.

"I didn't do anything, Jensen. You did," she says, her gaze hanging on for an extra second before she makes a move toward the driver's seat.

I tug open the passenger side and fall in, my legs primed with the blood that rose to the surface during the climb. I may have been flexing more than normal during the scale down, too, thanks to the constant rattle stream. Sutter's right; I'm probably going to feel this tomorrow. I can't wait to be sore. New sore is the best kind, and it's been a while since I changed up my routine. Turns out, that applies to a lot of things in my life.

It takes us less than five minutes to get to the apartment. This mountain has been here, a handful of blocks away from me, this whole time. I can probably see the peaks from the field. I've never even looked.

Sutter pulls into the roundabout, and I check my watch, surprised she's following my boundaries and that we're already done with my supposed third session.

"Somewhere you need to be?" She glances to my wrist.

"Not really. It's just, you've acclimated me to ridiculously late nights in the span of a few days, and the thought of heading upstairs right now and turning in for bed feels absurd."

Sutter smirks.

Maybe I was expecting her to somehow invite herself up because that's what she does. She invades. But now that I'm faced with getting out of her car and going up to my apartment alone, which believe me I've been praying for, for days, I'm a little bummed out about it.

I chuckle and shake my head before reaching over the seat to grab my bag.

"What's so funny?" she asks.

"Nothing." I swallow my amusement, but it must still be present in my expression because Sutter leans in and touches my arm, forcing my gaze back to hers.

"Tell me," she pleads.

I swallow down my laugh and whatever that other feeling is that's tightening my airway. I twist enough to grab the door handle, but I don't open it. My face is tingling. My neck is too. I think . . . I might be embarrassed? Nervous? I grab my neck and laugh uneasily.

"You're good company." I give in, turning back to her. Her lips tighten and curl in at the sides with a touch of smugness, but also I think she's flattered.

"Shit, it's starting to feel like junior high in this car. I gotta go," I say, my nervous laughter more pervasive, infecting every word I utter.

"Wait," Sutter says, reaching over and grabbing my wrist. I look down at her delicate hand and chewed-down nails, then up to her face. Her smile is a bit easier than before.

"I like talking to you, too," she says.

A pleased breath leaves my nostrils, and my muscles relax, but only a little. I want to ask her things, see what's hidden in her night table drawers, learn what mountains she's trying to climb. And I want to know why Corbin Forsythe was banging on my door looking for her.

"Hey, can I ask one thing?" I ask.

Her eyes slit as she studies me, maybe a tad unsure whether she wants to allow this role reversal.

"Shoot," she finally gives in.

"That case study you showed me, the one of the lefty who made such killer progress when you worked with him?"

She swallows, which is answer enough, but I ask anyway.

"That Corbin?"

She blinks but doesn't break our hold. A few seconds pass and I use them to count the various ways she confirms my suspicion without actually speaking. Her nostrils flare. Her right eye twitches slightly. And her lips are trembling. The movements are so slight they should go unnoticed. But I'm looking for them.

"I'm not allowed to disclose who Subject A is. Part of the contract," she says.

My eyes narrow. I should probably read the one I signed with her, not that I care who knows I tried some crazy talk therapy to help with my pitching. Hell, I've done yoga and even two sessions of jazz dance to try and limber up. I'm not against experimenting. I was against accepting help. But Sutter forced her way in and didn't give me a choice. And I guess I'm glad she did.

"I throw Saturday. You coming?" I switch gears from the Corbin topic, her answer good enough.

"Wouldn't miss it," she says.

I nod and exit her car, and she drives away almost immediately. It looks like tonight I'll be sleeping intruder free. It kinda sucks.

CHAPTER 11
Sutter

It's been a while since I've come to a Monsoon game and sat in one of these seats like a fan. I used to love this place. When I was a kid, going to work with Dad was the greatest perk in the world. Before things between him and Mom bittered, we would make family events out of weekend game days. Everyone had their favorite player for the season, but I only had one jersey—double-zero for Mason. My dad.

I still have that jersey somewhere in a box, though it's about seventy sizes too small. I never really thought about it but I'm pretty sure my dad had it specially made. They don't sell coach gear at the team shop. They barely sell the big names that come through. Nobody sticks around this place for long. That's not the purpose of this team. It's for growing up or aging out. In a way, a minor league team is like a library, where players get checked out and checked back in until their spines are so worn out they need to be replaced.

Sad and beautiful at the same time.

"Girl, why can't we sit right down front behind the plate? Those seats aren't sold out," Kiki says, nudging me with her elbow while her giant tub of popcorn rests on her lap.

"This is my favorite view," I remind her. She's heard me say those words a hundred times. Kiki went to a lot of Corbin's games with me, and we always sat in the same seats.

"Yeah, I know. But one of these days I'm gonna leave your ass to sit here alone so I can see what it's like to be rich," she says, shoveling a palmful of popcorn into her mouth.

I look at her and laugh.

"Keeks, those seats cost forty bucks. They aren't rich seats. And you're a lawyer," I remind her.

"A lawyer with fucking student loans, clerking with the county, which means I'm poor." She purses her lips. I grab a handful of popcorn from her and pop a piece in my mouth with a shrug. She could go the law firm route and earn more, but my bestie has always been about nonprofit and justice. She's trying to get in with the county attorney's office to help clean up some of the sketchy politics that seem to be pervasive around here.

"At least you have your degree," I remind her.

"And isn't that why we're here? So you can get yours?" She nods toward the field where Jensen is throwing long-toss in the outfield with the catcher.

"I sense a double entendre in those words," I snipe.

Kiki laughs out a bite of popcorn, kernel flakes falling on her chest as she coughs.

"It wasn't intentional, but that's funny. And now that you say it . . ."

I push her arm, annoyed. I shouldn't have told her about my sex dream. She's going to be relentless, and I'm already struggling with where to draw the line with Jensen.

I glance in his direction but only for a few seconds. I don't want him catching me looking. I want him thinking about nothing but mountains and dumb reality shows, and flashlights versus rattle snakes.

"So, is starting a big deal? I mean, opening game and all?" Kiki takes a long sip of her beer and I follow suit to settle my own nerves. My empathy is in overdrive, as if I'm taking the mound.

"My dad doesn't put that ball in someone's hand unless he has expectations," I say.

"Well, that's not stressful at all." Kiki laughs.

I join her, then take a bigger gulp of beer.

"Not in the least."

We both prop our feet on the seat backs in front of us. I'm glad nobody is sitting there yet. It's early in the minor season and it's a little warm out for an April day in the desert. Night games will start soon, and that's when people really turn out.

The pregame people have been the same voices since I was a preteen. It's two guys who have lived in Tucson for years. They started this when they were in their late forties, and now they're in their early sixties and still trying to pull off the same campy jokes. It's awkward to watch as they dance in hotdog costumes, and at least one of them is busting out of the backside.

Jensen is pacing in the bullpen. They'll announce the players any second, and the pitcher is always last. The slow jog out to the mound is a tradition for the Monsoon. My dad doesn't like the other team to see his guys' tricks. He wants to show them nothing but fastballs when they take the mound for warmups. I hope Jensen got his slider locked down behind the scenes.

The announcements start for the opposing team, and the crowd gathered for the Dubuque Bulldogs goes nuts when the clean-up hitter is called. Enrique Montez won't be in Iowa long. He was a top-ten draft pick, and he can hit. I just hope he can't hit sliders.

When the music fires up for the Monsoon player announcements, we all get to our feet. The stadium screens are a little dated, but the lightning bolts and slow rolling clouds over the desert still get to me. I rub the goose bumps on my arms and Kiki rolls her eyes.

"You're corny," she adds.

"Probably," I admit. I still love it. The thunder roars as AC/DC's famous intro growls from the speakers and the Monsoon players step onto the field one at a time with their names. It's opening day, so everyone gets an intro. It's only the starters for the rest of the season. Today's lengthy pregame, though, means Jensen has more time to grow anxious.

I start to hum Sinatra in my head, willing him to do the same. It's all I can do from here. The rest of today is all him, and I hope he kills it. My job is easier if he starts on good footing, sure, but even if he were to fail I could find something to help turn his thinking around. I want him to win for him today. The man needs it.

"And taking the mound for your hometown Arizona Monsoon—Jensen Hawke!"

Jensen begins his jog across the outfield toward the mound and I flop my sunglasses down from atop my head to shield my eyes, then clap with the continued roar of thunder blaring from the sound system. It's a pathetic crowd size, but the couple thousand people are clapping in rhythm, and it feels like enough as Jensen makes it to the dirt and digs his cleat into the soft ground by the rubber.

"I might start having sex dreams about that man," Kiki mutters at my side.

"Oh, my God," I grumble. Internally, my stomach knots with an odd pang. I ignore it at first, but as I glance around us and take note of the five or six other women my age all staring at Jensen and likely having the same thoughts Kiki just admitted to, I realize what's making me so ill.

Fuck. I'm jealous.

Jensen throws seven or eight pitches to continue his warmup. All fastballs. All right down the pipe. The other team is salivating, ready to hit. They've been properly fooled—I hope.

Everything pauses for the national anthem, then the two men in hotdog uniforms drag a kid up to the top of the dugout in front of me and Kiki and they let the boy shout, "Play ball!"

Kiki pulls her ball cap down to shade her face and we both sit back with our feet up, ready for the show.

"I hope you know I love you," Kiki says.

"I do." She still finds this game boring. I get her here because of the men and their pants. It's a pretty basic and reverse-sexist objectification, but until it fully grows out of fashion to gawk at pretty women, I'm going to keep using it to drag my best friend to baseball games.

Jensen looks at ease on the mound, his arm loose at his side as he kicks at the ground, waiting for the first batter to get in the box. I hunch down in my seat, suddenly feeling too caught in his line of sight. I don't want anything pulling him out of his headspace, assuming he's built a good one today. We didn't talk yesterday, other than me sending him a text to get rest and play some Sinatra. I probably should have stopped by after work, but my head wasn't in a healthy place. Seemed odd to try and help make someone else's right.

I hold my breath as Jensen starts his windup, but when the first pitch clips the top corner of the strike zone and catches the hitter stunned, nearly buckling his knees, I exhale into a smile.

"That's good, right?" Kiki leans into me as she chews popcorn through her words.

"Yeah, Keeks. That's good." I chuckle.

Jensen finishes the inning with two strikeouts and one pop up to the first baseman. He hasn't thrown anything but fastballs yet, which means he's got a lot left in his tank to surprise them with. It also means that despite my dad telling him he's only throwing three innings today, he might luck into more.

His hat sitting low and hiding his face as he walks back to the dugout, Jensen doesn't glance up once. It's good that he's locked in, but also . . . I don't know. I shouldn't *want* him to look for me. I also want him to look for me.

"He's all moody. I like it. It's sexy," Kiki says. I sigh.

"I'm going to quit dragging you to games. You're annoying." I huff.

She puffs out a laugh and twists in her seat.

"And here I was just getting into this game." She glares at me for a few seconds, giving up when she realizes I'm not going to give in and look back. I'm also not going to explain my sudden sulking. It's childish, and it means I'm more attracted to Jensen than I want to admit. More than that, I care about his attention more than I should. My brother told me to look for those signs and walk away. Well, here they are. Bold and flashing with skipping heart-beats and sweaty palms and pits. I fucking like this boy, and working with him is going to mess me up.

Time's up. Walk away, Sutter.

Only . . . I can't.

My phone buzzes at my side, so I slip it from the pocket of my leggings and cringe when I realize who it's from. I'm too slow to shut the screen off and Kiki, who is the only person nosier than me, manages to catch a glimpse of Corbin's text.

"Damn, he's getting pushy. You think he wants to propose again? Like, now that he has so much practice and all?" She's joking, and maybe a week ago I would have laughed at her humor, but now it only amps up my discomfort.

"Keeks, be less right now. Okay?" I turn my head and give her a hard glare that she seems to get immediately, tilting her popcorn in my direction and lifting a brow.

"Eat your troubles away?" she suggests.

I breathe out a soft laugh and reach in for another helping of popcorn.

"He wants to meet for coffee before he leaves. It feels weird. And it's just going to be a big PR move for him, like everything else has been since we broke up. He's going to remind me not to talk about us and blah, blah, blah." *And he's engaged, again.*

"Blow him off," Kiki advises. She's probably right, but there's also this nagging sensation in my gut that I need to power through and meet with him. Like I have to prove to myself that I can or something.

"Oh, hey, our guy is back," Kiki says, nudging me more with her elbow. I'm going to have a light bruise there before today is done.

"So, he's our guy, huh?" I say, settling in because this next batter is going to be his true test.

"Until he's officially *your guy?* Yeah, he's ours," Kiki says. The tight sensation creeps back into my belly. I don't want to share.

The other side of the stadium cheers when Enrique Montez is announced. His family is from Mexico, and I am pretty sure they all came up for his debut game since Tucson is so close. It must be nice having family like that— big, loud, and together. Neither Jensen nor I have anything close to that.

At least four major sports stations are here too, the camera guys all primed and ready in the photographer's pen. Normally, I'd love to see Enrique knock one into the desert behind the right field wall for his first at-bat since the draft. But today, I need him to choke. I need him fooled and sloppy. And if he could do it in three pitches, even better.

Jensen settles in, his chin and the sharp angles of his jaw the only thing I can see clearly from under the shadow of his hat. He's serious. And that amps up my nerves. I should have dropped in last night, maybe brought my Uno cards or Battleship. Anything to make him breathe. I wonder if he actually took my advice at all.

My head is dizzy with worry that I failed him when, in the middle of staring down the hitter, Jensen's mouth ticks up on the side closest to me. His lips move slightly. So do mine. To anyone else close enough to see, I'm sure it looks like he's muttering swearwords. But I know better. That motherfucker is singing. And he's about to send Enrique Montez back to the bench on three straight sliders.

The first one dives late, sucking Montez in for a swing, and pissing him off that he wasn't even close. The whiff draws out some boos from half of the stadium and rowdy cheers from our side. I get to my feet and stuff my fingers in my mouth to whistle. Kiki plops her bucket of popcorn down by her feet and tries to whistle with me. She's basically spitting, but the gesture is meaningful. She's not just cheering for Jensen. She's cheering for me.

Jensen catches the ball from his catcher and walks back up the mound, glove tucked under his arm as he works the ball with his hands. His lips are still moving with the lyrics, and because I know what song he's singing, I join in.

"Regrets, I've had a few," I say, my voice soft but loud enough for my friend to hear and turn to me.

"Huh?"

"He's doing a thing I taught him," I explain before continuing on to the next verse as Jensen stares at his catcher and rolls the ball behind his back, searching for the perfect grip—the right threads.

"But then again, too much to mention," I hum.

"Are you singing *'My Way?'*" Kiki's brow draws in and her face twists like she's about to laugh.

"I am. And so is he." I nod toward the mound where Jensen levels another perfect slider that hooks Montez with another swing and miss.

The small but mighty crowd grows louder, both fan bases rivaling in volume. I haven't felt this excitement from a pitcher/hitter duel in so long. By the end, Corbin was so dominant it didn't make my stomach drop and soar the same way. What's playing out now is the purest of drama.

It's the reason butts sit in seats at this ballpark—at every ballpark. It's only the second inning and already a rivalry is born. I feel it in my gut. Jensen and Enrique are going to be foes for a long, long time. They'll probably become drinking buddies off the field, and one day, they might even be teammates. But like this? When Jensen is on the mound and Montez is holding his Louisville Slugger, tensions will rise. A man will sing a Sinatra song. And an anointed giant will go down swinging.

As the third strike lands in the dirt and Montez tries to run to first on the drop, the catcher swipes his leg, tagging him out.

"Yeahhhhh!" I leap from my seat, fist in air. And after Jensen snaps his glove at the ball from his catcher, he marches back up the hill and pops his head in my direction, and he smiles.

CHAPTER 12

Jensen

Five full innings.

Fifty-two pitches.

Goddamn, was that fun.

Coach takes a seat on the bench across from my cubby as I organize my cleats, various compression sleeves, and glove into my equipment bag. It's hard to move easily when one of my shoulders is wrapped in plastic and pinned to my side under five pounds of ice.

"How's the arm?" Coach asks.

I do my best to move it with my limited range in the ice pack.

"Honestly? It feels better than it did before the injury," I say. I've heard from several guys that Tommy John has come so far that it's almost like a tune up for pitchers. I couldn't see it at the time, when I was staring down sixteen months away from the sport, but now that I'm on the other side, I can see the positives. I'm stronger.

"Good. You looked comfortable out there. The slider's working," Coach says.

"I was really glad Enrique didn't line that ball back down my throat." I laugh.

Coach grabs the bench on either side of where he sits and rocks back with mutual laughter.

"I'm just glad he didn't line one into the dugout," he coughs out.

"I bet. Those screens are shit."

"No doubt!" he agrees. The Monsoon field is iconic, and I get how it's special to him and his daughter and the city, but it's in desperate need of safety upgrades. I'm pretty sure I saw a piece of the concrete rafter fall onto the concourse the other night on my way home from lifting.

"Hey, Jensen. Can I ask you something?" He leans forward and lifts a brow.

I nod, then zip my bag and take a seat across from him, clasping my hands together as I lean forward and rest my arms on my legs. I'm suddenly nervous.

"Do you really believe in this cockamamie head shrinking business my daughter's roped you into?"

I lean back at first, breathing in deeply and studying his expression to get a better read on his intent. He doesn't seem angry, and I don't get a sense that he's warning me to avoid his daughter the way a dad gets protective over his little girl. I think he really wants to understand her business. His old-school ways are being challenged by her in a way.

"At first, honestly, I thought it was bullshit," I admit.

He laughs out hard then crosses his arms over his chest, refocusing on my face with even more interest in my answer.

"At first, you say. So that means you've changed your opinion," he prompts.

"*Hmmm,*" I ponder. "Do I think I would have thrown as well as I did tonight if I hadn't had a few strange conversations with Sutter? I don't know. That's hard to answer, though I'm sure your daughter has quantified it differently."

"Oh, no doubt!" he busts out.

We commiserate for a few minutes over Sutter's insistence and persistence, but eventually the conversation comes back to his original question. Do I believe in her concept? Do I think people can be mentally coached to have an edge?

"Sir, I'm a pretty hard-headed pessimist. I've been counted out a lot in my young baseball career, and I know . . ." I hold up a hand before he can tell me that's part of the game. I've heard that part. I know it is. And I know I'll be on the bottom again one day, or in the middle, or taste the top then get knocked on my ass. "What I can say for certain is tonight, when I was throwing the ball, I was having the time of my fucking life.

"Before your daughter started putting ideas in my head, it was work. Going out there and overthinking every placement of my hand on the ball, wondering about the thoughts in your head, in Coach Bensen's head—it was work. But tonight? It was nothing but fun. And if baseball can be like that—if all I need to do is keep an open mind to Sutter's theory, and maybe let her get songs stuck in my head—then what do I have to lose?"

Coach Mason stares into my eyes for a full breath before nodding. I'm not sure he *really* understands what I'm saying, but he seems satisfied enough not to question it further.

"Welp," he grunts as he stands. He pulls his hat from

his head and runs his fingers through his thinning hair before putting it back on. "You keep throwing like that, I don't care what song is stuck in your head."

His heavy hand pats my shoulder as he passes. I linger behind, enjoying being the last in the locker room. I pick up my phone to message Dalton my thanks for catching a great game since he took off already, but before I get to his contact info, a message comes in from Sutter.

> SUTTER: You have groupies.

My brow puzzles, and I send back a question mark.

I shoot a quick note to Dalton as I grab my bag, then hold my phone in my palm and head down the corridor that leads to the back exit, where Sutter said she'd wait after the game. Before I get there, she sends me a photo of a group of five or six women all wearing tight jeans and tall heels hovering around the exit.

> ME: Uhhh. WTF?

I'm not used to that kind of attention. I mean, in college I played the game. I hooked up with my share of girls my freshman year, before I got into a long-term relationship. But these women aren't sorority girls. They're . . . just wow. Beautiful, sure. But I think they might also eat me up and spit me out. I don't think there are enough Sinatra songs in the universe to un-fuck my head after they were through with me.

> SUTTER: Change of plans. I'm coming in. Meet me at the team shop.

I reverse course when I read her message and make my way to the other end of the stadium where a man is running a vacuum around the storeroom floor. He has huge headphones on, so I wave until he spots me. He shuts the machine off and pushes his headphones down around his neck as he jogs over and pushes open the door.

"Hey, man! Nice game today," he says. He looks about my age, maybe a year or two younger. He's wearing a Wildcat hat with his Monsoon staff shirt.

"Thanks," I say, shaking his outstretched hand. It's weird to be recognized, though I guess he works here and probably saw the entire game. "You play?"

I motion to his hat.

He tips the bill down a bit.

"Nah, I suck. I just like to watch. I go to school there, though. Sports management. Hey! Maybe I can represent you one day!" He seems genuine about the idea, so rather than deflate him by explaining my long-term contract with a huge firm based in LA, I simply say, "Maybe."

When Sutter and her friend press their faces to the glass on the other side of the store, I nod toward them, redirecting his attention.

"They're with me," I say, using my sudden small-time fame to get them in.

He chuckles as he walks over to the door.

"I'm pretty sure we're all with her. Sutter's basically royalty around here," he says. *Okay, so not that famous yet.*

Sutter slips in and hugs my new friend.

"You're the best, Matt," she says.

Matt. Fuck, I didn't even ask him his name.

"Seriously, you saved me," I add, a strange sense of wanting to be in his good graces gripping me.

I glance behind Sutter to where her friend—the one who picked her up outside the stadium a week ago—is grinning and bouncing on her toes.

"Hi." I smile.

"I'm Kiki. You pitched really good." She steps in front of Sutter and doesn't bother to wait for me to extend my hand. Instead she grabs mine, and clutching it between both of hers, she shakes it. My eyes pop to the right to meet Sutter's gaze, but she simply rolls her eyes.

"Kiki thinks you're hot," she says.

My face ignites and my eyes widen at her bluntness. How I'm still surprised by the things that come out of her mouth, I have no idea.

"I do. She's right," Kiki doubles down.

"Oh, wow. I maybe should have exited with the groupies," I say through nervous laughter.

Kiki is still shaking my hand and both Sutter and I are staring at it as she says *probably*.

Eventually, Sutter grabs her friend's wrist along with mine and pries us apart.

"So hot," Kiki whispers under her breath.

"I feel so objectified," I joke, but only half. I feel really aware of the face I'm making, and I don't think I want Kiki walking behind me and staring at my ass.

"Come on, Ace." Sutter takes over, looping her arm through mine and pulling me back through the door. Kiki trails behind us—*behind me*.

"I don't know if Ace is fitting yet," I say. She halts us with a jerk and pushes my bicep before relinking her arm with mine.

"If I call you Ace, you accept it. Tonight, we work on you accepting positive feedback." She winks at me and leads me toward her car. Rather than getting inside, though, she opens her trunk and tugs my bag from my shoulder. I grab the strap before she completely takes hold of it.

"Sutter, I don't need a ride. I live, like, right there. You know, where *you* used to live," I say with a touch of sarcasm. She looks at me flatly, her mouth a tight line.

"We're going to celebrate. Put your shit in the trunk," she orders.

"Oh." I blink. I haven't had much to celebrate lately, and my social outings have only extended as long as I've known Sutter and she's forced me out of my cave.

I drop my bag next to her hiking gear and she pushes the trunk closed with her palm. Rather than get in the car, the three of us walk to the end of the block, then across the street behind the stadium toward a bar named McGill's. A lot of the guys come here. I've been invited, but naturally I don't show.

I glance behind me, where my fan group had been, and note that the gate area is now devoid of people.

"Oh, they'll be at McGill's. Don't you worry," Sutter pipes in.

"Awesome," I deadpan, which makes her laugh hard.

"Jensen Hawke, you are the only man I've ever met who purposely hides from female attention."

I'm not really hiding. I simply don't want attention from that group of women. The trouble is, I like the attention I'm currently getting. From Sutter. My coach's daughter. Who had a *fling*, apparently, with Corbin Forsythe. The man I hated without actually meeting him and whom I dislike even more now that I have.

Sutter and Kiki move to the front of the line waiting to

get in, and after Sutter leans in and has a short laugh with the bouncer working the door, he steps to the side and waves the three of us in. He puts his hand on my arm as I pass, and I jolt to a stop, not in the mood to be harassed.

"Nice game, Ace," he says.

"Oh, uh . . . thanks," I stammer, forming a sloppy smile as I look ahead to Sutter, who holds a fist to her mouth to hide her snickering.

"Oh, I get it. You told him to say that." I nod. The bouncer laughs with her, then pats my shoulder twice.

"She's always pulling shit like that, pal. It means she likes you. Seriously, though. I heard you threw a good game. Congrats."

He forms a fist and I pound it.

She likes you.

I follow an amused Sutter and suddenly dancing Kiki into the middle of McGill's. The space is very much an Irish sports pub with music blaring from a jukebox and a line of TVs hanging from the back wall. A group of teammates surround a few pool tables to the right, and others are fully into playing the hookup game with women at the bar. It seems the ones who were waiting for me moved on.

"Welcome to Monsoon home base," Sutter says, holding her arms out at her sides as she turns in a slow spin, showing off the grungy yet perfect joint.

"When you go pro? This will always be your home. Okay?" she prompts.

I laugh off her suggestion but when I'm met with her serious face, I swallow down my low self-esteem and garble out an, "Okay."

"Pitcher of your finest, Trev," Sutter says, patting her palm on the bar.

"Good to see you, Sut," the bartender says, serving her up and cutting off the rest of the thirsty patrons waiting for attention. Nobody seems to make a stink, however. She must be a known fixture here. I would not be shocked if she pulled out a key to the damn city.

Pitcher and mugs in hand, Sutter leads me toward a pub table in the center of the room with a clear view of every TV in the place. She pours three pints and glances around the back of the bar until she spots Kiki and waves her over.

Sutter hands each of us a beer and holds hers up to toast.

"May this be the first of many toasts in honor of the next great pitcher to come out of Monsoon baseball," she utters, pushing her mug toward mine. Kiki moves her beer to touch both of ours and before anyone can utter cheers, Sutter adds in, "To me, and my very lucky client."

Bringing her mug to her mouth, she tips her head back and downs a big gulp while I stare at her with pursed lips. She winks at me sideways as Kiki laughs at my expense.

"You can't even give me an ounce of credit, can you?" I chastise. My smirk breaks through despite how hard I want to play the grump.

"Nope. This game was all me. I saw those lips move." She sets her mug down then moves her fingertip to my bottom lip. I cross my eyes looking at it. My body rushes with adrenaline and my dick flexes.

"Whatever." I scoff, my words a distraction for the shifting of my legs underneath the table.

"Let's dance," Sutter says, taking another big gulp, then tugging on my shirt sleeve. She urges me to follow her and her friend out to the open area, where only women seem to be dancing to some electronic version of a song I used to think was great but now, like this? Not so much.

"Oh, no. I'm not much of a dancer," I protest. It's no use. Sutter grabs both of my wrists, forcing my beer down and literally towing me step by step toward the dance area.

"Everyone is a dancer. Just relax," she says, shaking my arms at my sides to loosen me up. I give in and sway, moving only enough for her to feel satisfied and quit forcing me. We move out here—me awkwardly and Sutter and Kiki with the skill of NBA dance team members—for two songs before Brad, the young catcher I worked with a few days ago, rescues me.

"Hey, nice work today!" He has to shout over the music, so I urge him to follow me back to the table. We talk about the game and the clutch he had as the designated hitter. A few of the other guys join our table, rehashing the game and swapping stories about weird shit we've seen in some of the minor league towns. Inevitably, the conversation turns to the topic of women. One of the guys brags about his two girlfriends in two different cities, but when the rest of us don't pile on and high five him, he backtracks and starts in with the excuses. I've heard them all uttered before.

It's not like she doesn't step out too.

It's a casual thing.

As long as they don't know then nobody gets hurt.

It's all bullshit, and it makes me wary of my sister marrying a guy with a World Series ring. I hold on to the fact he's retired and hope that means he's mature and ready to be settled down because Amber? She's desperate to start a family and have that happily ever after. Me on the other hand? I'm not so sure I'm the guy who gets the girl, at least not for keeps.

"Hey, what about that?" Brad says, leaning in close and pointing to the makeshift dance floor. Sutter is moving in sync with her best friend, her arms above her head, her cropped shirt showing her belly, and her curvy, muscular hips and legs moving in the kind of way that has a knack for putting men like Brad—*and me*—into a stupid trance. Stupid, because it *makes us stupid*.

"I think she's Coach's daughter, that's what I think," I say, taking a slow sip of beer while eyeing Sutter over the top of my glass.

"Yeah, true. You guys hang out a lot, though, don't you?" He eyes me sideways while drinking his beer, and I sense suspicion in his prolonged stare.

"She's my mental coach," I answer flatly.

Brad flinches at my response.

"That's a thing? Like, we have that on the team?" he asks.

"Not exactly," I say, and rather than sticking around to get into the details of how Sutter and I fell into this strange arrangement, I down the rest of my beer then leave Brad behind to rejoin Sutter and her friend on the dance floor—which suddenly feels like a much safer space.

Over the course of the next hour, McGill's quiets as locals head home for dinner and most of the team turns in. Kiki ends up ditching us for one of our outfielders, a guy named Chris Marte who is here on a rehab assignment like me. Well, not exactly like me. Chris will be here for two weeks, three at the most. He's nursing a sprain, and heading to Texas where he'll pick right back up with his all-star track record in no time.

"You think she knows he's kind of a big deal?" I ask Sutter as we make our way back to the bar.

"Absolutely no clue whatsoever," she answers through a laugh. She's holding out a credit card to settle the tab, but I flick it from her hand and offer mine to the bartender instead.

"That was dirty," she rebukes, eyeing me sideways as she searches for her card somewhere on the floor. I chuckle, glad I refused to let her pay.

I sign for the bill then slide a chair out of the way, revealing Sutter's card under a table. She squats and picks it up while giving me the middle finger.

"I've never had someone get so mad about free beer before," I say, shoving my wallet in the back pocket of my jeans.

"You drank *a* beer. You basically paid for me and Kiki to get tipsy," she argues as we leave the bar.

"What can I say? I'm a gentleman."

Sutter stops in the middle of the sidewalk and tilts her head back, laughing at my statement.

"Hey, I am gentlemanly," I retort.

She continues to snicker as we cross the street. As we approach her car, she fishes her keys from her pocket and tosses them at my chest. I catch them against my body.

"Okay, gentleman. Drive me home."

I smirk but get in gladly. I'd planned on refusing to let her drive.

I turn over the engine as she buckles, giving me basic directions to her place. I had wondered how she could afford a place on her own with part-time work, but as we drift to the outskirts of the city and pull up in front of a single-story brick building lined with doors, I get a better understanding.

"I got it from here. I don't have work tomorrow so maybe just text me and you can bring my car back and I'll take you home." She's halfway out the door before I sort through her logistics. I scan the area, which is basically completely devoid of life—no people, no cars, not even a dog barking in the distance.

"It's not even dinnertime yet. Let me get you in safely and I can call an Uber," I insist.

"*Psshh*, I'm really okay. Sleepy maybe, but it's fine." But the way her gaze sticks to me, her eyes drooping with a hint of *please*, says she'd prefer I walk her to the door.

I don't give her the option, meeting her halfway up her walkway. She unlocks her door and pushes it open, welcoming me inside. I step into a narrow hallway that leads to a narrow living room, followed by a galley kitchen and then what I assume is a bathroom and bedroom in the back.

"Nice space," I lie. It's bright and clean, but the rooms are stiflingly small. "Why did you move out of your brother's pad again?"

I stretch my arms in either direction to test whether I can touch both walls at once. Sutter slaps one of them down and glares at me.

"It's not that small."

I follow her toward the kitchen, where I drop her keys on the counter. She pulls a pitcher of water with a built-in filter from her fridge, then two glasses from a cabinet. She pours me a glass, which I take before wandering around her home.

"It used to be military. There were four buildings, but

this is the only one left. Some old Tucson family owns it, and it's really not as bad as it seems." She says it a bit like she's convincing herself instead of me.

"Yeah, but your view . . ." I move into her bedroom and pull back the curtain on the back window that reveals a rocky alleyway and nearly toppled block wall.

"I can't argue there," she admits. She leans against her doorway clutching her water in both hands. She brings it to her mouth and sips slowly, staring at me from over the glass.

"You sang Sinatra today," she recalls, bringing it up for a second time.

I chuckle and take a drink of my water before nodding to her.

"I did. It helped." I shrug and our eyes tangle for a few long seconds. Her expression seems proud, but the way our gazes fight to stay in the moment also feels like something heavier is happening between us.

She nods over her shoulder.

"Want to catch some of the playoffs?" It's the first round of NBA games, and she's already established her fever for her hometown Suns. They aren't playing today, but the Lakers are, and I grew up watching them.

"This morning, your brother invited me to join him and Kendra for dinner at the apartment, as in a third wheel, as in he was secretly telling me to find something else to do for the night, so I'm yours," I say, holding out a palm as I shrug.

Sutter bites at her lip and I replay my words—*I'm yours.*

"I mean, I can stay. If I'm not overstepping." I clear my throat as I move past her. The tight space forces my chest to brush against hers as I pass through the door and move into the living room where I plop down on the far end of her couch and pretend we didn't touch at all.

"Make yourself at home. Kick your shoes off, and if you're hungry, I might have some Ritz crackers and mustard packets," she hollers, shutting her bedroom door.

I cringe and shout back, "No thanks."

I push my shoes off and rest my feet on the small coffee table covered in notebooks, index cards and random folders. The two on top are labeled RECEIPTS and CONTRACTS, the latter piquing my interest. I lean forward and look toward her room to make sure the door is still closed. I rest my finger on the contract folder and drag it close enough to thumb it open slightly and spy inside. Unfortunately, the name on the top page is mine. No big secret there.

When her door creaks down the hall, I sit back and thread my hands behind my neck.

"That's better," she says, her hair tied into a bun on top of her head. She's kept on the oversized crop T-shirt but changed into baggy sweats that she's rolled at her hips. I assume they're a pair she snagged from Corbin at some point, which makes me hate them.

Plopping down on the other end of the couch, Sutter sits to the side and stretches her legs out, her pink painted toes nearly touching my thigh. I glance down and she wiggles her toes.

"Head or feet. You're gonna be stuck with one," she asserts.

I scrunch my face and look at my own feet, which are crossed on the coffee table. I'm pretty sure she could sit like I am, but it is a bit of a tight fit, and then we'd have to be side by side. I suppose her feet are the safest option.

"Fine." I sigh.

Sutter waves her toes at me one more time. Even her feet taunt me. She reaches out toward the table and snags the remote, clicking on the television, which seems auto-programmed directly to the game. It's already the end of the first quarter, and the Lakers are up by eight.

I give a fist pump and Sutter slides down enough to actually kick my hip.

"Hey!" I protest, rubbing the spot that doesn't really hurt.

"You cannot be a Laker fan!" she admonishes.

I chuckle and hold my palms out in apology.

"I don't know what to tell you, but I am," I admit.

"Grrrr," she growls, actually sneering her teeth and wrinkling her nose. "Sworn enemy. How did I let you into my house?"

Our eyes meet again for a few long seconds, half smiles on the verge of laughter teasing our lips. We've crossed a line, and I'm not sure when, but it's long gone. This is flirt-ing, and neither of us seems anxious to knock it off.

"I could go," I say in a soft voice, no intention of leaving at all.

Her chest rises and falls with a long, slow breath.

"No, you can stay. But only because it's really awkward to watch my brother make moves on Kendra. Trust me; I was the third wheel the other night."

She shakes her head, as if she's trying to shake off the memory, then turns her attention back to the TV. She hasn't moved from her new spot, and her feet basically rest on my lap. I'm not really a foot guy, but Sutter could convince me to get into it. Her second toe has a thin silver ring around it, and after a few minutes, I grow brave enough to tap it with my finger. Her head jerks in my direction and she pushes herself up and stretches to touch her toes, turning the silver ring until it reveals a dolphin.

"It's kind of childish, I guess. I got it in San Diego last summer with Kiki. We took a girls' trip." Her eyes linger on the ring, and I can't tell from her barely parted lips if she's reliving something fondly.

"You go there a lot?" I ask.

"*Hmm?*" Her gaze shifts to my face. There's still a bit of distance behind her eyes, but the longer I hold on to her stare, the more she comes back to me.

"You and your family, did you go to San Diego a lot when you were little? I hear that's where every Arizonan goes for vacation." Before this trade, I had no idea what to expect of the desert. My only impression was classic Bugs Bunny cartoons I saw on cable growing up—mountains, cacti, and coyotes everywhere. It's not like that at all, though those things exist. This place is actually kind of majestic, especially the mountains and the starscapes at night.

"My family had a timeshare for a while," Sutter says, drawing me in. She leans back on her elbows and looks up at her ceiling as if pulling her memories from up there. "Dad always booked us two solid weeks after playoffs. It was the one time the four of us were like a family. The rest of the year, my parents were never in the same room. Sometimes, not even the same house."

"Are they still together?" I already figured they weren't, but it felt like a natural segue to confirmation.

"Not for eight years now. They split when I was in high school. It was *amicable*," she says, her tone sharp-tongued.

"You say that like it wasn't," I point out.

She falls back to lay on the sofa, her legs fully on my lap. I lower my arms over them, aware of how intimate this small move is.

"No. I mean, it was. Dad was never around, and my mom had all of these ambitions and life plans she'd put off. And Billy was in college. I was in high school. We didn't really need that type of co-parenting support anymore," she explains.

"They still get along? I mean, do they have dinner and stuff, or . . . ?" I'm not sure what I'd rather have, my house where my parents are always on the same page only that page is against me and my choices, or Sutter's case, where her parents aren't together but seem to be on board with her. Of course, Billy said Sutter and her dad don't talk much now, so maybe I don't have it so bad. Or less bad.

"My mom . . ." She pauses, chewing at the inside of her mouth as her head rolls to the side and she lets her gaze get lost on the commercial on TV. "She was diagnosed with young-onset dementia right after the split. I always suspected she had gotten the news before then and maybe that's why she decided to fill the last few years with the things *she* wanted, but I don't know."

"I'm sorry," I croak. I'm guessing her mom is around the same age as her dad, which doesn't seem old enough for such ailments.

Sutter shrugs, picking up a pillow from the floor and hugging it to her chest.

"It is what it is. I only wish my dad would man up and visit her before it's too late. She's in a memory campus, which she picked for herself. Of course."

Sutter must get her planning habits from her mom.

Though, I don't know where the messy disarray of research on her table fits into the gene pool.

"Sometimes, as men, we don't know what's good for us until it's too late." My words draw her attention, and she lets the pillow fall back to the floor so she can look at me.

"You mean like the way I'm turning you into an amazing pitcher?" She quirks a brow and I laugh.

"Yeah, a little like that."

I move my hands along her shins, squeezing lightly, mostly to test whether they're as muscular to the touch as they seem. They live up to the visual. I'm finally getting comfortable with this new level of intimacy, rationalizing it internally as friendship, when Sutter suddenly flips around so her head is on my thigh, closing the distance in our gaze. I tilt my head in caution as I look down at her, half waiting for her to punch me in the dick, the other half worrying about my swelling, well, dick.

"Tell me something personal," she demands.

I laugh out but when I look down into her eyes I realize she isn't joking. If I've learned one thing when it comes to Sutter Mason, it's that she is not going to let her teeth out of my skin until I cough up what she wants.

"Well, we talked about my sister. And you basically bullied me into going to her engagement party." I sigh.

"Yes, I did," she says, her tone smug.

I look down and shake my head, still not convinced she'll be able to pull off a flight. I'm sort of banking on her not coming through.

"Well, you may as well be prepared. My sister is marrying Ryan Fairleigh," I reveal.

Sutter's eyes splash wide. Most people know who Ryan Fairleigh is, thanks in part to his shoe sponsorship and

World Series run three years ago. To someone like Sutter, though, Fairleigh is like meeting royalty, or a president.

"Shut. Up." She sits up and twists so our eyes meet. I'd laugh but her reaction is exactly why I don't want to go.

"I'm sure he's a nice guy," I concede. "My sister wouldn't accept anything but the highest in integrity. It's just that I'm going to show up to a party being hosted by people who think my life plan is a joke only to celebrate someone else who made similar choices. And a sister who is *marrying* that kind of life. I'll have to smile through speeches and play nice with my mom and dad. I'm not sure I'm capable. There's a lot of resentment brewing in my belly, and I don't think you have enough time to rid me of all that."

She blinks at me a few times and purses her lips, her expression challenged yet serious.

"I'm gonna try," she finally says before snuggling back into my lap.

I breathe out and stare ahead at the TV, every part of my body aware of her lying on me. I don't know what to do with my hands. My left is glued to the arm rest, but my right is uncomfortably stranded along her sofa back.

"The Lakers are losing," I say in a hushed tone. I caught the score out of the corner of my eye, and I use it to return her attention to the TV. She turns to her side, her cheek resting on my thigh with one hand tucked under her chin. The other is holding my knee. Every muscle in my lower half is rigid and paralyzed. I commit to remaining this frozen for as long as it takes for her to fall asleep. I could leave now except I don't want to.

I don't want to.

Eventually, I relax enough to get invested in the game,

and by the time halftime rolls around, I've allowed myself to slowly stroke Sutter's arm, from the curve of her shoulder down to the middle of her bicep. It's hard to be certain from this angle, but I think her eyes are closed. Her breathing remains steady as I shift in my seat to adjust my legs and sink deeper into the couch. If I'm going to end up sleeping here like this, I need to support my neck.

I pause tickling her arm long enough to reach to the side and grab a small yellow pillow. I stuff it behind my head then return my attention to her arm. Only, Sutter has moved. Her hand that was on my knee has moved across her head, resting along her ear, the soft underside of her arm exposed. And that's not the only thing.

Sutter's not wearing a bra. It's something I realized when she came out of her bedroom thanks to the chill of her air conditioning. It's something I haven't stopped thinking about as she's rested in my lap. But now that her arm is stretched over her head, her cropped shirt has risen enough to offer an unbridled peek at her pebbled nipple.

Fucking dick is so hard now.

I shift slightly to adjust myself enough to avoid the sharp edge of my zipper. Sutter's eyelashes flutter when I move, her gaze still locked on the TV. I move my right hand to the back of my neck and peel my eyes away from the torn cotton edge of her shirt, and when I glance down at her face, she shifts her eyes to the side to meet my gaze.

"Hey, you, uh," I say, flitting my focus to her perfect round tit. My voice quakes with soft, nervous laughter.

Sutter, however, only blinks at me slowly. I wonder if she's not fully awake. Or if she had more to drink than I thought. It's been an hour or more since we left the bar.

But she seems to have zero interest in adjusting her shirt. She must not be aware.

I move my right hand to tug the fabric down her body, and I'm able to cover her . . . mostly. Her shirt remains in place for seconds, then she rolls onto her back and lifts both of her arms over her head, tempting me with two hard, pink buds and perfect palm-sized breasts.

"Sutter," I breathe out.

Her eyes blink slowly, luring me. Fucking hell, my cock is so hard. Her tits are so hard. She's right fucking there.

"How drunk are you?" I ask, my head falling to the side as my fingertips graze their way up her rib cage. I draw a mental line on her body that I forbid myself from passing, but I break the rule over and over, inch by inch.

"I'm fully present," she hums, her heavy lids sweeping shut as her mouth forms a soft, closed-lip smile. The hum of someone eating delectable chocolate escapes her as she reaches toward the arm of the couch, arching her back over my thigh. Her shoulder blade presses into my hard on, and I fight my desire to push against the pressure. I fantasize about moving her out of the way and pulling out my cock for her to squeeze between her breasts. For her to lick up and down. For her to suck and then straddle and sink down on while I flick her tits raw with my tongue.

My dick flexes and my hand inches upward toward the point of no return. A straight man's ultimate test lies in that tempting bottom curve of a breast, and right now I am scoring a resounding F in self-control. Sutter's eyes flicker open, her lips parting to let out a soft moan. I need to extricate myself. We shouldn't do this. But I want to please her so fucking bad. I want her to feel something because of me.

I want to see how far I can take her without letting myself completely feel, without giving in and losing total control.

Her back arches with a deep breath, pushing her nipple up to taunt me and beg for my touch. My thumb circles the curve of her breast, each trip around moving me closer to the hard center until I let my palm graze over the raw tip.

"Ahh," she whimpers.

Hearing her pleasure tests my self-control even more. I've already obliterated so many lines, I may as well give her a release.

A soft cry leaves her lips as I take her nipple between my finger and thumb, at first squeezing with light pressure but pinching harder as her moans increase. I roll the hard pink bud, my tongue growing numb with the want to taste it. She is so fucking hot, and as she pulls her knees up and clenches her thighs together my mind races to how wet she probably is. I can smell her need, and if I stay here any longer, we're going to fuck.

"I'm sorry," I blurt out, lifting her from my lap and escaping the couch. I adjust my dick enough to walk across the room, ignoring the exasperated breath that leaves Sutter's body in my wake.

Fuck. Fuck. Fuck.

"Don't go—" she begins.

"It's okay. It's my fault, and we've been drinking. I . . . it wouldn't be right. I can get home fine. Really, this is all me. It's so not you." I turn to face her one last time as my hand scrambles to find the doorknob. Her hair is messy and wild, the tie that was holding it up long gone. Her eyes are hazed, and while I know she's buzzed, I think she was probably honest about being fully aware of what she's doing—what *I* was doing. To her.

"We don't have to . . ." she tries again.

I wave my hand. If I give in, I will ruin this. I won't be able to control myself. Sutter is too much. She's too perfect. Too sexy and smart and funny. She's exactly what I thought didn't exist. She's a tornado cutting through my path, destroying my blueprint. Just like I would be for hers.

There's a contract. This is all business. I'm her case study, and she's my confidence whisperer. I'm too fucked up to let feelings into the mix. And she's too perfect to give in to sex without feelings. That wouldn't be possible. One taste of her and I would be doomed.

"I'll see you tomorrow. Maybe we can hike or something. Or, heck, day off. Let's take a day off. I just . . . I gotta go." I fumble my way backward through her front door. I pull it closed behind me and stride across the gravel front, cutting across the length of the building until I make it to the intersection. I don't bother for a walk sign. Nobody is on the roadway out here, out on the fringes, to the place where Sutter escaped, to probably get away from guys like me. Guys like Corbin.

I don't even bother calling for a ride. This walk is necessary to get my head on straight. And the late Arizona sun isn't hot enough to burn away my mistake.

CHAPTER 13

Sutter

I meant what I said yesterday—I was fully present and aware with Jensen. More than that, I was in control. I was manipulating.

And now I feel stupid and desperate.

I can't even tell Kiki what I did. I played that situation like the cheer captain in one of those books I read in high school. Only, in those books, the heroine gets what she wants. All I was left with was seven minutes with my Rocket in the bedroom.

I've driven by my brother's apartment a dozen times. This is the first time since I moved out that I haven't felt welcome, or more exactly that I was too intimidated to use my key and barge right in.

With my thirteenth loop past visitor parking, I happen to pass Ernie on his way out, probably heading to the casino. He has his routine. I slow down and pull into the drop-off area and roll down my window, whistling.

Ernie points his cane at me and winks before shuffling closer.

"What are you up to this fine Sunday, Miss Sutter?" Ernie always makes me feel special. He was my third favorite thing about this building, just behind Corbin and my brother. Now, he's probably number one. He's definitely the only person in this building who still welcomes me in.

Maybe because I didn't try to force my tits on him. What the hell, Sutter!

"Nothing much, just trying to work up the right story to trick my brother into helping me with something. You know, same old, same old."

Ernie leans back and belts out a laugh, then taps my windowsill.

"I'm sure you'll think of something. You always do," he encourages before heading toward his bus stop.

"Hey, you want to maybe take in a game with me this week? New kid has some stuff," I shout, blushing at the mention of Jensen. Thank God I'm out of view and hiding under my enormous sunglasses.

"Eh, we'll see," Ernie hollers with the wave of his cane.

I can't remember the last time I watched a game at the ballpark with him. It was definitely when I was in high school, and I think my parents were even still together. People have no idea what an icon he is, and he's just fine keeping the secret to himself. I'm in on the secret because of family. Ernie was the first coach in Monsoon history, and before that, he played for the Kansas City Royals. My dad keeps a lot of his things up in his office, yet none of the guys ever seem to notice. Corbin did. Ernie hated Corbin.

Ernie Chester, number seven.

Emboldened by my senior friend's belief in me, I park and stride into my old building, holding my shoulders high.

I panic a little when the elevator opens, but sigh with relief when it's empty. The process repeats when I exit on the third floor, but by the time I get to my old apartment door, I'm primed with my key and ready to march in like I own the joint. Or at least like I still live there.

The scent of bacon hits me right out of the gate, and when I hear the clank of pans in the kitchen, I smirk and wonder what strange thing my brother is trying to apologize to Jensen for.

"There better be extra," I announce.

"Tell me, did you smell the bacon all the way from your apartment and float here like in the cartoons?" My brother's back is to me as he flips a pancake in a pan. I take a seat at the table and await the food I know he'll feed me.

"That's exactly how it happened," I answer.

My brother chuckles, then turns to slide the cake onto a plate. He drops it on the counter behind him and I leap to my feet to add strips of bacon and syrup to the mix.

"Soooooo," I lead. "What are we trying to make up for?"

My brother pours the last of his pancake batter into the pan and glances at me over his shoulder.

"Sometimes, Sutter, I simply want breakfast."

I narrow my eyes on him, and eventually he breaks.

"Fine, I felt bad because I made dinner for Kendra last night and I sort of pushed Jensen out of the apartment. But he must have left early. I haven't seen him all morning, and bacon is a pretty tough scent to ignore."

I, of course, already know this, but since the mere mention of yesterday sends beads of sweat down my spine, I opt to simply nod.

"Hey, want to make it up to him even more?" It's a

natural segue.

"Maybe," my brother grumps. He finishes flipping his pancake and turns his attention to me.

"I need your travel connections to book a last-minute trip to LA. Literally fly in and fly out," I say, stuffing my mouth with a bite of half pancake-half bacon, partly as a move to not have to answer his incoming question.

"Sure, LA is always easy. But how is getting *you* a flight going to help Jensen?" My brother turns back to the stove and checks his pancake before sliding it onto a plate.

"Because Jensen is coming with me." I follow my words with another big bite followed by a big gulp of orange juice. Maybe I can drown them.

"You and Jensen are going to LA," my brother sums up.

"Umm," I hold my forkful of pancake near my mouth and glance to the side as if I have to think about it. "Yep. That's it."

"Sut." He abandons his plate on one side of the kitchen and leans against the opposite counter so he can properly stare at me.

"Bill." We're at this point again.

"I don't think I can help with this," he says, breaking our gaze and carrying his plate to the table where he sits across from me. He eats without looking up once. It's not like Billy to not savor every bite. He's a really great cook, even for the simple things, and for him not to indulge and enjoy his own effort is petty.

"Look, I appreciate your concern. I promise you, Billy, that Jensen and I are simply friends, and we are barely that. He's helping me finish my thesis by being my test subject, and this is the one favor he asked of me."

Most of that is a lie. *Okay, basically all of that is a lie.*

"Why does Jensen need to go to LA?" Billy glances up, but he keeps shoveling food into his mouth, not possibly enjoying a single bite. I feel guiltier about that than I do about lying to him.

"His family is having an engagement party for his sister, and he didn't think he would be able to make it with the season, but he's not scheduled for bullpens next Saturday, and it's a day of rest for him."

"Ha." Billy sets his fork on his now empty plate and pushes back from the table, crossing his legs and threading his hands behind his neck. "You have his schedule memorized?"

"For my charting, Billy. Yes, I have the schedule written down." *I have the next three weeks memorized.*

Billy leans forward, propping his elbows on the table and rubbing his hands together. He studies me for a few seconds, his mouth hinting at a smile, the kind of gotcha grin he always gets when we have game night and he's about to win.

"And why are you going with him?"

Fucker.

I sigh and turn my attention to the final few bites on my plate, pushing them around with the fork. My mouth in a tight, irritated line, I basically mash what's left of my pancake until it's inedible, then take my plate to the kitchen and scrape what's left into the trash. I drop my plate into the sink with a clank and take over the spot he stood in when he was leaning against the counter. Arms crossing my chest, I look him in the eyes.

"Because I need a break from things and LA sounded fun. Because he needs a plus-one, and I thought 'sure, why not.'"

Damn, my lies are getting deep.

He chews at the inside of his mouth for a beat, trying to read my face and call my bluff, but I'm too tough to crack now that we're adults. I don't break my serious expression once, and I control my blinking so I don't look nervous. Eventually, my brother breathes out and shrugs before carrying his own plate into the kitchen.

"Okay, fine. I will find you some flights to pick from today. I'll need you to reimburse me for the resort costs, but it shouldn't be too bad," he says.

I touch his arm and he freezes in front of the sink, his eyes remaining down but moving toward me.

"Thanks, Billy. I really appreciate it."

He glances up to meet my stare fully and pulls his mouth into a forced, tight-lipped smile. He's still not totally convinced, which means he's gotten better at reading me as an adult. He knows I'm not being completely truthful, but he also doesn't like to let me down. One day I am going to make things up to him. All of these times I've used him, relied on him, stolen his food, overstayed my welcome—the list goes on.

I grab my glass from the table and guzzle the last of my orange juice, then hand it to my brother to put into the dishwasher.

"You said Jensen left early?" I question, moving toward his side of the apartment. I listen near his door and don't hear a thing, not even the soft buzz of the fan.

"I'm pretty sure he took off, yeah. I'll tell him you stopped by," my brother says.

I wave him off.

"Nah, it's fine. I'll see him eventually." I want to play up my ambivalence to the man who is literally single-handedly dominating my dreams.

I give my brother a quick nod goodbye and flee the apartment, having taken care of step one in my make-things-right-with-Jensen plan. Now to erase my horndog behavior and pretend he did not in fact reject me last night. This next part, I fear, is going to be much harder.

I climb into my car and stare at the light posts poking out from the stadium. Now that the season is underway, workouts are more regimented. Since Jensen threw yesterday, he'll be due for some light cardio and maybe recovery work today. I'm sure my dad will also have video for him to review with the pitching coach, which means I'll get my first set of numbers to plot. I'm eager to match Jensen up against Corbin. Maybe too eager, and maybe I'm matching him up in the wrong ways. There's just something about him that has dug under my skin.

It's too early for Jensen to be at the stadium for any of his work. And on foot, there aren't many places he could go, so I drive to the most obvious place first. I park in my usual spot at the trailhead at the end of the cul-de-sac and duck in my back seat to swap out my jeans for my spare joggers that I keep in my workout bag. I tie up my trail runners and start my way up the mountain. My competitive spirit is determined to catch up to him before he makes it all the way up and back, but my practical side has me sending him a quick text to make sure I'm not zigging while he is zagging.

ME: You on the mountain? So am I!

I watch the message app while I flip my earbud case open and shut, my feet dragging slowly at the start of the trail. I feel like an ass sending him such a nonchalant message, as if last night didn't go the way it did. Man, though, what I wouldn't give for him to simply respond with a simple *yes* or a *meet you after.*

I shuffle along with no response for several minutes, and eventually I reach the point where the trail is too steep for me to navigate while staring at my phone. I pop my earbuds in and drop the case and car key fob in one pocket and my phone in the other. Immediately, though, things feel strange. My phone feels as though it's banging against my ass, and my fob is definitely rubbing awkwardly against my hip. Not to mention, my thong feels extra thong-like, and my waistband is riding awfully high.

I halt my steps and glance down. I stretch out the front of my pants, looking for the drawstring that's usually there and instead find the tag. My pants are on backward. I huff out a laugh at my own ridiculousness and do my best to make the best of the discomfort, rolling the front down a little. There isn't much to be done with the tight seam jamming up my ass, though, and after spending the first mile of my hike with my hand basically plucking cotton from between my butt cheeks, I give in and decide *what's a little public nudity in exchange for a major comfort upgrade?*

I hike up a few more steps to where the brush gets taller, and find a decent plateau with boulders blocking my view from anyone who might be glancing up from the back yards near my car. I know I'm far away, but if I lived in one of those houses, I'd have the binoculars on standby twenty-four-seven. There's good shit to see on this mountain.

The mountain is exceptionally dry, our winter rain season having been dismal, so I keep my shoes on, not wanting to pick up any jumping cactus needles or other thorns that blend into the golden ground. When I'm sure the trail is clear, I push my pants down my thighs and balance on one leg while I work the elastic bottoms over one shoe at a time. I finally free one foot when something rustles the brush about a dozen yards away.

My heart jolts as I hop frantically, my hand gripping at the sharp edge of a nearby rock for balance. Whatever is moving through the area is bigger than a rabbit, and it's definitely not a snake.

"Hey!" I call out sharply, hoping to scare off whatever it is, when I'm greeted by the equally startled bray of a wild burro.

"Oh, hey, buddy. No, *shh shh shh,*" I repeat, hopping with every word I utter.

He kicks at the ground and lowers his head, and as I survey the land behind him I see the skinny foal standing a few feet behind, well, her. I am the intruder. Also, she's going to knock me right off this mountain.

"Shit, shit, shit," I utter between panicked breaths as I hop haphazardly in the opposite direction. I'm working my way backward, out of the burro's sightline, when my feet get tangled with the loose pant leg swinging around my foot. I feel myself falling backward and swing my arms wildly in a hail Mary effort at somehow staying upright. I fail, landing on my bare ass in the dead center of the widest part of the trail.

Right in Jensen's path.

"Jesus, Sutter! Are you okay?" He rushes down the hill about twenty steps then swoops his hands under my armpits to stand me upright. Harsh, piping hot gravel is stuck to my bare ass cheeks and my pants are knotted around my legs, binding them together at the ankles like I've been kidnapped by resourceful mountain pirates.

"There's a burro up there, with her baby. She was about to attack," I rattle off bits and pieces between panting breaths. Jensen holds me steady on my feet as I clutch his forearms and will the feeling back into my legs.

"I don't even know how to react to this," he says. I blink wildly, my heart still going a million beats per second. When I settle on his face and catch his smirk, I realize that for the second time in less than twenty-four hours, I have stripped in some way or another for Jensen Hawke and made a complete ass hat out of myself.

"Oh, my God," I say, squeezing my eyes shut. I let go of his arms and flail my hands at him.

"Turn around!" I plea.

He chuckles, but I hear the ground shuffle with his feet.

"Okay, I'm turned around. There's another group behind me, so you better hurry," he says.

"Shit!" I squat and unravel my now-filthy pants from my leg, no longer giving a shit that my pants are still backward on my right leg.

"I need to lean on you. Oh, my God, I'm so sorry," I stammer. My body thrums with anxious nerves. My muscles feel like jelly as I internally will myself to stay on my feet. My knees shake as Jensen scoots backward enough for me to lean against his back. I plant my forehead on his shoulder blade for balance and focus on one task at a time without vomiting or passing out. I work my hands into the free pant leg first, rolling it up to make my step easier. Once I guide the elastic bottom over my shoe, I shimmy the waistband up my body and back over my hips.

"I think I'm good," I breathe out.

I'm brushing away pieces of nature when Jensen reaches toward my hip and pulls a cactus needle from the material.

"I bet there are dozens of those." I sigh, searching for more near the one he found.

"Probably, and I hate to tell you this, but your pants? They're on backward."

I freeze for a moment then pop my gaze up to meet his, my mouth a hard straight line.

"Really," I say in a peeved, flat tone.

"So, that's what that was? You figured the middle of a mountain trail was the place to do a quick wardrobe change?" he teases.

"No, that's not—" I hush as the steps of the group Jensen mentioned grow near. It's a group of four senior women, all dressed in matching bright green shirts that read Tucson Hikers or something similar. I'm having a hard time focusing at the moment, and it's all I can do to smile courteously and utter *good morning* as they pass, let alone read. They're dressed like pros with large sunhats and fanny packs with water bottles hung at their hips. The last in their group, the tallest with long platinum hair slung over either shoulder in fat braids, stops between Jensen and me, a devilish smirk on her face as if she somehow knows everything that's transpired over the last day.

"Well, aren't you two cute," she says, turning her attention to Jensen and giving his bicep an actual squeeze. She giggles, then picks up her pace to catch up to the rest of the women.

Both of our gazes chase the women down the trail until they make a turn around one of the outcroppings and dip out of sight. I look to Jensen, and his mouth is hanging open. He blinks his gaze to mine and laughs out a breath.

"Did that really just happen?"

"All I can say is that lady has bold moves and confidence up the ass," I say through an amused, crooked smile.

He shakes his head and lets out a heavy breath, his cheeks a touch red. I don't think it's because of the sun or the exertion of the hike. I'm about to poke fun at him having a new fan club when he reminds me why I have no right to make fun of anyone right now.

"Speaking of ass . . ." He leans into me and peers over my shoulder toward my backside.

I rub my rear end, the raspberry on my skin already burning and the first sign of a bruise definitely forming.

"I have no excuse. I thought I could be all smooth and flip my pants around without missing a step. And then you showed up, which . . . after last night—"

"Hey," he interjects. His heavy palm lands on my shoulder and my entire body melts from his touch. I wish I wore my tank top today instead of a T-shirt so I could feel him on my bare skin like I did last night. When he teased my breast, and . . .

"I'm so embarrassed by my behavior," I continue.

"No, don't be. It was . . . we were—" He cuts himself off, laughing nervously as he removes his hand from my shoulder to pinch the bridge of his nose. It's a small comfort to see he's as uncomfortable as I am, but a comfort nevertheless.

"It was a really long day, and we were simply riding the high of emotions," I blurt out. I don't necessarily buy my excuse, but I have to say something for both of our sakes. We need to move past last night without crap getting in the way of our plans.

"It was," Jensen agrees.

"And I'm sorry I mooned you just now," I add, my eyes

fluttering back behind my lids. My face grows hot as I mentally relive donkey-gate.

Jensen chuckles.

"I can't imagine donkeys are that fierce, but you get a pass. Besides, I can't lie—you've got a great ass." His mouth tightens into a sheepish grin and he shrugs one shoulder. My chest warms at the compliment, but rather than bask in that feeling too dangerously long, I flip the script and send his attention to the brush just beyond him.

"Hey," I whisper, pointing to the area I narrowly escaped.

Jensen turns to follow my direction, and hunches to match my height until a sharp breath leaves his mouth.

"Oh, holy cow! That's a donkey!" he whisper shouts.

"Burro, to be exact."

"Whatever," he mutters, totally captivated by the animals slowly plodding their way back into the thick overgrowth.

The mom nuzzles her foal, moving the baby along and out of danger. Kind of like Billy tries to do with me. And that reminds me . . .

"I should have flight information ready for you tomorrow. I'll get it to you when we meet at the field. How about we stick with five o'clock, since the game should be done? We can look at your numbers, maybe talk out a few things, see where your head is for your next start." My voice has shifted into business mode, and Jensen must hear the change in tone because his brow dents and his head turns slightly to the side.

He looks at me sideways for a few seconds, and I know why but pretend not to have a clue.

"What's up?" I ask.

"You're still coming to LA, right?"

"Oh, umm," I stall. I turn to hike back down the mountain, an excuse to hide my face from his view. I truly didn't think Jensen wanted me to tag along. I forced my way into his reluctant plans to begin with. In fact, I forced his reluctant plans on him.

"Sut," he says, my name shortened. It sits heavy in my gut, and it stings a bit because I like him saying it that way.

I glance up at him as we walk, our pace slowing until eventually, we both stop. My body quivers as I look at him again. My mouth feels dry, and my head swirls with too many thoughts to sort through. I want to go to LA with him but Billy is right; I shouldn't. I want him to kiss me right now, but that's a bad idea. I want to erase what happened last night, yet I wish it had turned into something more. And the way he said my name . . . That suddenly he seems all right with me going with him to a party he was hellbent against is a plot twist I'm not ready for. I swallow down the gritty sensation gobbling up my tongue and throat.

"I don't think I've been very . . . normal around you," I say, a pathetic categorization for my behavior. I squint and wince, but Jensen laughs off my response, shaking his head.

"I assumed your normal was chaotic," he responds. His eyes warm with the soft smile that plays at his lips. It's a little bit like empathy, and normally I might feel patronized, but I think Jensen is trying to give me a lifeline out of this hole I've dug.

"I had a bad breakup last year," I add.

He nods. "Corbin." He says his name so matter-of-factly, but also a little clipped. I remember his opinion of my ex and suddenly his tone matches the "real dick" stamp he put on Corbin's file.

I nod and begin to walk again. I'm relieved when he steps up beside me and matches my gait.

"Would it make you feel better if I told you my last relationship ended in a pretty bitter breakup too?" He squints one eye and looks at me sideways.

"Your fault? Or hers?"

"Oh, wow. Well, I mean, definitely her decision. She left me after the injury, right before I had surgery, and for a while I thought it was only because of that," he explains.

"Ouch," I say, gritting my teeth. I've seen that same kind of breakup play out a lot in this business. Hell, I've seen my kind of breakup happen a few times too. Nothing surprises me anymore when it comes to people and fickle hearts.

"Yeah. But now that I've gotten some space from it, I'm not so sure that's what really did us in. I think that's a bit unfair of me, laying it all on her like that," he admits. "We were young and had very little in common. She liked baseball players, and I was one. And maybe our breakup was less about me getting hurt and more about me not being the person she wanted to be with all the time. And looking back? Those feelings are mutual."

I lift my brows high as I meet his gaze, and he flinches a little, surprised by my response.

"What? Too mature for you?"

I shake my head.

"No, just . . . that's a very self-aware thing to say. I don't think I'm even close to you in the self-growth department. I'm pretty sure everything was Corbin's fault, and not a single thing was mine."

Jensen barks out a sharp laugh, grabbing his stomach, but holds his palm out to dissuade me from getting defensive. He must have seen my muscles twitch, ready to fight.

"No, I mean, when it comes to that guy, I think you're right. Fuck him," he adds.

I grin, my mouth tight and cheeks pushed into hard, apple-like circles on my skin.

"Anyhow, my ex has moved on. And I am finally focused on my goals, making my dream come true. And thanks to you"—he dips his head a little in deference to me—"I'm ready to put in the mental work it takes to play at this level."

My mouth tugs up on the right, happy to hear him so willing to give my methods real effort. Yet my gut still feels heavy, as if something is missing, something left unsaid. Unresolved. It's the attraction part that's still fire hot between us, or more exactly, that he doesn't seem to want to address it. Maybe it's one-sided, and that's why. And that stings because I haven't felt a pull like this to another person ever. Not even with Corbin.

"You know, Corbin and I . . ." I hold my tongue, not sure I'm ready to spill everything to Jensen. If we're going to build a friendship, though, and work together to get to both of our ultimate goals, then putting my raw history out in the open can only help. He'll better understand me, better get why I'm suddenly a bit guarded about over-inviting myself to someone's engagement celebration.

But then there's the non-disclosure agreement, and the payout—or rather, *bribe*—that I still refuse to cash. When Corbin came to collect his ring, he also leveled me with some legal leverage that locked away revealing his identity in my thesis as well as speaking publicly about our engagement. That second part was an add-on thanks to his new publicist, and I shouldn't have signed it. But I wanted him to leave, and I was hurt and angry. And for a brief moment, fifty grand didn't feel like a bribe, but more like something I deserved—something I earned.

Then the check came. I haven't even opened the envelope. And until a dozen days ago when Jensen handed it to me in my old apartment, I couldn't even recall where I put it.

"You can tell me. What about you and Corbin?" Jensen asks, pulling my attention back to him.

I shake my head and clear my lungs with a heavy exhale.

"You know what? It's nothing. Like you said, we get to move on. And I'm moved on."

Weird thing is, I think I finally am.

"How about this?" I present, pausing at the trailhead, steps away from my car. "I'll accompany you to LA and help you survive family drama if we can talk for the entire flight there and back?"

"As in *talk* talk? About . . . my issues?" He squints and I laugh out. I did say he had issues when we first started this exercise. He kinda does, but I probably should have put it less . . . ahh, hell no. He's got issues.

"Yes, Jensen. We're going to talk about your issues."

He holds out his hand after a few seconds, and we shake on it. Same page. Roles defined. Business, and no benefits. That should simply be that. Except his middle finger drags along the inside of my palm, grazing my wrist as our hands part, and suddenly, after a literal mountain of coming to terms with what we are and where we stand, I'm right back where I started, full of butterflies for a fucking left-handed pitcher.

CHAPTER 14

Jensen

"Jay Hawk! Jay Hawk!"

It's been a while since I forced myself to watch that dreadful game. It's something to be part of history. It's one of those things a lot of athletes strive for, to be in a record book, to be there for a big moment, to win a big game. Nobody thinks about the losers in those stories.

I think about them.

I am one.

I will forever be the guy whose college no-hitter was spoiled by the great Kendall Simpson. It couldn't have been a regular game, maybe a few runs on the board with me coming in for the fifth inning in relief. No—this was my best start. It was fastball mastery and slider grit. I was doing everything right, and it was about to be my moment. Then one swing rewrote the whole damn story.

Nobody knows my name, but they sure know Kendall's. Not that they wouldn't have someday anyhow. He's destined to be one of the special ones, like a Bo Jackson or a Tony Gwynn.

Sutter and I spent the entire week talking about this game. A few times, I was not very nice about it. More than a few times. I guess that's why she thinks it's something I need to talk about. Incessantly.

She has a theory that I lose control of my slider when I get stressed because somewhere in my psyche I've rooted a deeply damaged ego. She says my confidence took a turn after I hung the ball out over the plate and Kendall knocked it out of the park. My response is continually, "No shit."

Apparently, that's not the right answer.

And now we're on a plane, sitting side-by-side in a two-seat row, watching my worst baseball moment on an iPad. Thank God she has earbuds so the rest of the passengers aren't forced to listen to the commentary along with us.

We're on our third replay of the video, and my leg is starting to bob out in the aisle. At least twice the flight attendant has tapped my kneecap with her pen in a subtle suggestion to slide my leg back in place. I don't fit, though. And if she taps me again, I'm going to grab the pen and use it to stab Sutter's iPad screen.

I might be a little high strung.

My chest is tightening, so I reach forward and tap the screen, pausing the video right before *the* pitch. I pull the earbud from my ear and toss it onto the tray table, then rub my eyes with the butts of my hands.

"I'm sorry, but I think I need a break. I'm not a great flyer, and two-seat rows really squeeze me in. I'm just—" I pause as the attendant passes and gently taps her fingertips on my knee this time.

I growl out a sigh, do my best to shove my foot under the seat in front of me, and take over as much of Sutter's space as she'll allow.

"That's fair," Sutter says, closing her iPad and slipping it into the backpack at her feet. "I wanted to desensitize you to it some, but I don't think analyzing your stressors while in one of your stressors is great therapy."

"Ha, yeah. No." I shake my head.

I think Sutter has been all work to prove she's all right with moving on from our awkward night together. I also don't believe she's put that evening behind us at all. And as much as I told myself I have, I definitely have not.

We met on the field at five every day this week. She hung out with me during my recovery exercises, then we either finished up in the training room or out by the field where we talked. And talked. *And talked.*

But things were different. Two weeks ago, I would have paid good money for her to leave me alone. Days ago, I would have paid double for her to lay off the personal questions. The Sutter I have now, though, is a pale version. And damn if I don't want the old Sutter back.

She's almost clinical. She jokes, but not like usual. I miss it. All of it. The invasive prodding, the random visits. The flirting. I miss her perfect smile! She was this annoying distraction that I couldn't shake, and I was starting to enjoy.

That's the cold hard truth. I was afraid of how happy I was when she pushed me out of my comfort zone. Afraid of the little thrill I got from those brief—and not so brief—physical slips. I was terrified to care about her, to like her company. *Because what if I let her down?*

I lean back the two inches my seat allows for and close my eyes, willing those thoughts away. That's the thing about being inside your head, though. You can tell yourself not to think about something, but all you're doing is thinking, giving that person or idea more of you.

Sutter sat in her usual spot for my Thursday game. I threw well, only gave up a run. Walked one hitter. I was proud, but I wasn't as loose as I was the time before. She noticed it, and I blamed it on this trip, on having to see my parents and pretend to be thrilled for my sister. But that's not what had me tight.

I was off because of Sutter. Rather than thinking about how to get rid of her, I was hyper focused on how to draw her back in. Those thoughts led to ideas about us, about how maybe she's different for a reason, or how maybe the universe wanted me traded here, to this place, like fate or some shit. And then I started to think about losing it all— getting hurt, not living up to expectations, being a nobody rather than a ballplayer. Sutter wouldn't stick around for that.

"Do you want to give me some speaking points or something, so I can help deflect your parents for you?" Sutter asks.

Somehow she got us on this flight that lands with enough time to change clothes at the airport and zip over to The Costa for cocktails. We take a red eye back to Tucson, and Sutter calculated the whole thing should cost about seven bucks in parking at the airport. The plane tickets, however, were closer to four hunny. I wonder if I can convince Amber to accept my presence for this party as her wedding gift. Not that she needs any gifts. Hell, last time I read a bio on her fiancé, they estimated his net worth to be somewhere around six hundred million.

No wonder my parents are throwing a party. They've hit the in-law lottery.

"It's hard to predict. They're going to wonder who you are, so be prepared for that," I say.

She nods.

"All right. Well, I can explain if you want," she says. Her answer formal, like a contract. *Why did I leave her apartment that night? We would be here in a totally different context, as a couple. Instead, we're business partners.*

"No, the details will only bring out their critical side. You think your dad finds mental coaching to be a joke, wait until you meet Lyle Hawke. My father thinks the answer to any of life's problems is to suck it up and quit crying." I can imagine him now, saying those words when I was a kid.

"I see. So we're friends. And I like LA and wanted to come, and—"

I reach over and rest my hand on hers as she's jotting down notes on a sticky pad on her tray table. She flattens her pen and her hand collapses under my pressure, not that I'm holding down hard. I think because this is the first physical contact we've had since . . . well, the hike. And of course, before the hike.

"You can say whatever you want to them. Or tell them nothing and leave it a mystery. I don't care." Her knuckles roll under my palm, and I should let go, but I can't. I want to rest my hand here a little longer. Eventually, though, she slides her hand out from where it's sandwiched 'between me and the tray. My chest tightens with guilt, and I glance down at the aisle, where the guy across from me is stretching his long leg. *Fucking cheater.*

We land a few minutes later. I swear the entire flight was twenty minutes of climbing and then instantaneous descent. My suit is in a garment bag in the overhead bin along with a small carry-on with Sutter's change of clothes.

I carry our things off the plane for us, then let her roll her bag toward the ladies' room on the ground level while I head into the men's room.

Dressing in a place like this takes me back to college, when coaches made us wear nice clothes to away games where we often had to change into our uniforms on the bus or in a McDonald's off the Interstate. Despite the small stall, I manage to get myself together and nearly straighten my tie before escaping the scent of urinal cakes and bus stations.

Sutter's bathroom visit lasts a little longer, and when I realize I've watched an entire episode of Sports Center on my phone in the time I've been waiting for her by baggage claim, I worry she's either been kidnapped or realized what a nightmare a conversation with my dad is going to be and slipped back onto a plane heading home.

I stand, tug my jacket straight, and iron out the wrinkles on my legs with my palms before striding toward the women's restroom. I'm nearly halfway there when Sutter steps out in a black dress that hugs every goddamn sensual curve of her body and stops along the sexiest part of her upper thigh. It's strapless, which, *shit*—it's strapless. Her bronzed shoulders, kissed by the Arizona sun, shine under the unflattering glare of LAX lights. She stands in the middle of the concourse brushing invisible flaws from the hem of her dress, and at least a dozen men ranging from pre-teen to late sixties do doubletakes as they pass.

I can't help it. I whistle. It's a loud wolf whistle, and Sutter's head jerks up, her eyes wide on me. With blushed cheeks, she looks around, as if that compliment could be for anyone else. I stroll toward her and take the rolling suitcase handle out of her grasp. Nothing should impede her being able to walk through this busy airport like it's a fashion runway.

"I'm not used to wearing stuff like this. It's Kiki's, and it's a little snug," She grabs the bodice at her armpits and shimmies the dress up. It doesn't budge, but she thinks it does.

"It looks like it was made for you. Sutter, my sister is going to hate you."

Her brow pinches and she breathes out a *why?*

I smirk.

"Because this is supposed to be her day, and absolutely nobody is going to give a shit about some engagement ring when you walk in the room."

Sutter's lips pull in for a tight smile and her chin drops, causing her to look up at me through her lashes. She's wearing more makeup than she normally does, for the look, and while it's normally not my thing, *this* woman standing here in award-ready everything is making me rethink all of *my things.*

"Shall we?" I swallow down the lump in my throat left in the wake of Sutter's big reveal, then hold out my arm to escort her out to the rideshare area, where I'm sure we'll get picked up by some economy car driven by a college kid trying to pay rent.

"You know, you clean up pretty well yourself there, *Jay Hawk,*" she teases, leaning into my shoulder. Her breath sends a dose of shivers around my throat and down my chest. If I was confused about what we should and shouldn't be before this moment, I'm definitely off the map now.

"The last time I wore this was to the reading of my nana's will."

Her eyes flit up to me and I glance at her with a grimace.

"Sexy," she says in a flat tone.

I chuckle as we make our way through the baggage area and out to the street.

Sutter's hair is pulled high, but a few wispy tendrils cascade down her bare neck and tickle against her shoulders. Without restraint, I brush them against her skin as we stand curbside and wait for our rideshare to arrive. Her skin beads from my touch but she keeps her eyes locked on her phone screen, ignoring me. She's much better at keeping the line in place tonight.

We luck out with a minivan picking us up, making it easier for Sutter to step into the back in her dress. I still guard her protectively, shielding any undeserving view of the inches of skin revealed when that dress hikes up her thighs. When I take my seat next to her, those new inches are all I can think about. Her toned legs pressed together, hugged by the unforgiving black satin. I bet her panties are black too.

Fuck me.

I shift in my seat, my movement catching Sutter's attention and pulling it from her phone screen. She smirks but I pretend not to see. It's going to be a really long night.

We arrive at The Costa about half an hour late. Sutter keeps reminding me that it's fashionably acceptable in LA, but as an extremely punctual person who prefers to show up early for everything, her insistence doesn't help much.

We get to the lobby downstairs and Sutter talks to the concierge about storing our baggage for the next few hours. I take the few minutes on my own to regulate my breathing, which is border-lining on panic-attack levels. I move toward the large glass window that overlooks an empty garden. How I wish that was the party I was about to attend. I'd be happier sitting on that concrete bench with Sutter talking about my fear of failure for hours rather than enduring the next thirty minutes upstairs at the rooftop club while my parents pretend to be people they're not.

I tug at the knot on my tie, gaining myself a millimeter of breathing room to alleviate the choking sensation. Sutter walks up behind me, the vision of her in the reflection pulling me back to happier thoughts. She runs her hand along my back and steps in close, and I can't help but imagine that the people in the windowpane are actually us.

"You ready, champ?" She reaches to my neck and adjusts my tie, taking away the slack I created. My body grows hot, and swallowing feels impossible.

"Not in the least," I laugh out.

She joins me, her signature smile slightly easing my pounding heart.

Sutter slides her hand down my arm until it finds mine and she threads our fingers together, our fit natural and easy. I shoot her a tight smile as we walk toward the elevator, but what I really want to do is kiss her. I'm not sure if I feel that urge as a distraction or a need. Maybe both.

We're joined in the elevator by an older couple, probably someone on Ryan's side since our family circle is pretty minimal. I'm sure my Aunt Char will be there. She's an alcoholic, so that should make for an interesting night. There has always been this weird competitive thing between my mom and her, my aunt showing off her forever-single party-woman status while my mom brags about her steady home life with two kids and a yard. I bet she's shoving this party in my aunt's face, but I'm sure my aunt will get her vengeance by drinking the joint out of the most expensive top-shelf liquor being served.

The elevator doors open and the older couple steps out and moves toward the cluster of tables filled with more people I don't know. Sutter and I stop just outside the doors and she squeezes my hand as I scan the area in search of Amber and then anyone else I might recognize.

"I hate this, you know," I utter.

"I know. Come on," Sutter says, tugging me toward the bar. We wait in a short line for two themed drinks—the Amberyan, cleverly titled after my sister and her fiancé's names. It's a pinkish orange color, probably made of mostly vodka and orange juice, but it's spiked enough to ease my pulse as we navigate the crowded area.

"I don't know what your sister looks like, but I found Ryan," Sutter says, tugging my jacket sleeve with her free hand, then pointing to the plush seats overlooking the Hollywood Hills and city lights.

I'm secure enough to admit that Ryan Fairleigh is a damn good-looking man. He looks like one of those models in watch ads or on cologne displays at department stores. *Fuck, he probably is one of those models.* As handsome as he might be, he's nothing compared to the brightness and joy that literally blossoms from my sister. It's been a while since I've seen her, and looking upon her now, her mouth in the widest smile I have ever seen, I'm suddenly thankful Sutter made me come.

"Come on. Let's introduce you to Amber so you can become best friends then plot to destroy me."

I lead Sutter to the middle of the action. My sister spots me as we approach, and slaps Ryan's arm with excitement. He nearly chokes on his drink during her flailing but helps her step over a small cocktail table so she can sprint at me and leap into my arms.

"You came!" She's crying at my neck, and it instantly makes me feel both happy and terrible. *I wasn't going to come. What an asshole.*

"Wouldn't miss it," I choke out, hugging her to me as we spin in a slow circle.

"Liar," she jokes.

Amber slips from my arms after a full rotation, adjusting her long dress pants as she stands in front of me.

"Jensen, nice to meet you. I'm Ryan." The hall-of-famer extends his hand and offers me a warm smile. I'm temporarily star-struck and a short nervous laugh falls out of my mouth.

"Yeah, you are. I mean, I'm a fan. But also, you better be good to my sister." As if my threats mean a damn thing. He's Ryan *fucking* Fairleigh.

He pats the back of my palm with his other hand, truly embracing our shake, and tucks his chin.

"I'll be the best to your sister."

I hold his gaze for a short breath, and in that time I can tell he means it.

Sutter clears her throat at my side, so I quickly let go of Ryan's grip and move my hand to her back, coaxing her forward into our small party.

"I'm sorry. Amber, this is Sutter. You two are basically twins. I promise." Amber's eyes light with a mix of shock and hope, which I don't have the heart to diffuse.

My sister instantly takes Sutter's hand, pulling her to stand at her side instead of mine.

"Sutter, you have no idea how nice it is to meet you." Awestruck, my sister's gaze bounces between Sutter and me, her eyes filled with all of that big-sister hope that her brother isn't a broken hermit after all.

"It's really nice to meet you, too. Jensen tells me we're alike. Apparently, we both excel at putting him in his place."

My sister grabs Sutter's shoulders and jets her focus to me with her mouth wide open.

"I love her," she says, embracing Sutter in a full-body hug. Sutter's only choice is to laugh and hug my sister back.

"See?" I meet Sutter's eyes. "I told you."

We hold our stare for a few long seconds and a certain comfort settles in. Maybe this isn't a mistake—being here, feeling things, *us*.

"So, I hear you're down in Tucson, rehabbing. You know, I went through that same recovery. I would have killed to rehab in Arizona instead of Mississippi," Ryan says.

"Yeah, you can't beat the weather. Sutter's dad is actually the coach. It's how we met—"

"Now, see, Jensen. This is what it looks like when you do it right," my dad interrupts. I didn't see him coming; otherwise, I likely would have found a reason to leave the conversation.

"How's that drink, Dad? Stiff?" I drop my hands in my jacket pockets and bob my head at the amber liquid swirling in my father's tumbler. He's not a total drunk. That would be wasteful, and Lloyd Hawke doesn't believe in wasting a thing—time, money, resources. Well, that's not entirely true. He does believe in wasting away your life. He's good at that. Both of my parents are.

My dad grumbles and puts on his typical half-mast

smile that pulls up his jowls and forces his eyes into a squint for a brief second.

"Didn't think you'd be able to make it to this, what with your busy ball schedule and all." He's not being sincere, but only those of us in the know get the slight change in his inflection with certain words. The emphasis was on *busy* this time.

My sister, knowing the pattern that is my father and me, urges Ryan to mingle with more of their guests. She encourages Sutter to tag along, but she shakes off my sister's invite, instead inserting herself right in the center of the war.

"Mr. Hawke. It's nice to meet you. I'm Sutter Mason." In her heels, Sutter is about at eye-level with my dad, which amuses me. And since she's a beautiful girl, my father is instantly off his game.

"Well, this is news," he says, taking her hand and bringing it to his mouth to peck the back. It's gross. Sutter doesn't flinch, though. She should gag.

"You plan on making it out to a game soon? Your son threw an incredible five innings last weekend." My chest warms at her pride in me. She's selling things a bit, but still. Having someone on my side so fervently feels nice.

"Wow. Five whole innings."

My dad's torpedo is right on time. I don't think Sutter quite knew what to expect, and the pained weight that dims her eyes hurts me to see. I'm used to the dismissals from my family. Her? Not so much.

"It's early, Dad. I'll get more games, and then who knows . . . maybe I'll be wearing Armani like Ryan over there." I glance to my sister's fiancé while my father chuckles.

"What a nice surprise." My mom's voice sends a chill up my spine. How someone can be equal parts comfort and poison confounds me. My parents are classic co-dependents. Two miserable people who refuse to accept their resentment for holding each other back and instead take it out on their youngest child.

"Hi, Mom." I take her in my arms, hugging her thin body. She doesn't eat because she's constantly trying some diet. She has always looked ten years older than she actually is because of malnourishment, but there's no getting through to her about that. I tried when I was in high school, and that was the start of our frayed relationship. She only wants to be enabled. Not challenged. It's the same with my dad. He wants a son who is hard at the grind, like he always was. Dreams are foolish.

"Can you believe your sister is getting married?" My mother's eyes glisten with happy tears that I can't tell are real or not.

"Yep. Our girl is leaving the nest." It seems like the kind of thing people say, and that's the only reason I say it. But it's not what my dad wants to hear.

"Ha, nests. You know, sure would like you to get your act together so we can finally quit holding your nest open for you when you need a place to live." My dad finishes his drink and hands the empty glass to a server who walks by.

"I'm never coming back to that house, Dad. You can turn it into a man cave or sell the place. I don't care." I stop short of adding that I'd rather be homeless on the streets than live under his roof ever again.

"Sutter, I hope you aren't planning on this guy taking care of you. My son doesn't seem to have his roots in reality. And I'm afraid his sister's marriage is only going to make him think he can live in Fantasy Land longer." My dad laughs at what he considers a joke, but no one else does. My mom, as is her pattern, fusses with my tie and tries to distract me as she turns the conversation to gossip about people I don't know.

"Margaret is getting divorced," she tacks on at the end. Margaret is a meaningless name to me, but that word— divorce. That's a good transition.

"Mom, when are you getting divorced?" The words come out of my mouth louder than I wanted, and colder as well. My chest seizes but it's too late to put them back. My mom clutches the neckline of her deep green dress and the fake pearls I'm sure she's pretending are real for the night.

"That's enough," my dad pipes in.

Heat climbs my neck, and my fist balls in my right pocket. Before I make things worse, though, Sutter steps into the center of us all.

"It is. I'm sorry this is how we had to meet, Mr. Hawke. Your son is phenomenal, though. And maybe one day he'll invite you to his penthouse when he's pitching for the Mets. Now, if you'll excuse us." Sutter places her palm on the center of my chest, covering my raging heart as she not-so-gently shoves me backward until I have no choice but to turn around and walk straight to the lookout point at the other end of the rooftop.

"Wow, you were not kidding. In fact, you held back," she says, reaching up to my tie. I cover her hand with mine and she freezes.

"If you tighten that any more my face will turn blue."

Her face softens and her hand drops. I loosen my tie completely, letting it sag inches under my Adam's apple. I unbutton the top two shirt buttons while I'm at it, then thread my hands behind my head as I turn to face the glistening hills.

"I'm really sorry." Sutter's hand hesitantly lands on my back, and she cautiously moves it in circles. My urge is to fight it, to shirk her off and storm out of this place, but for some reason, her presence coaxes me to act differently. I match my breathing with her movement, in through my nose and out through my mouth. My pulse slows to something more human, and I let out a laugh.

"What?" Sutter's hand stops at her question.

I glance to her. "The Mets?"

Our eyes lock and after a short moment of silence we both crack up.

"I don't know, they're like the least problematic team. Nobody hates the Mets."

"I mean, Yankee fans do."

She purses her lips and pops her hip out, putting her hand on it in a defiant pose. Her sassiness has this magic quality, like a nucleus drawing me in.

"I wish I had half your confidence," I admit. I turn so I'm square with her and tentatively reach my hand forward, brushing away one of the loose waves that's fallen over her face. I run the back of my knuckles along her cheek next, and step in closer. My mouth feels numb, my pulse once again racing, though for a completely different reason. Tongue poised at the edge of my lips, gently held between my front teeth as I fight against my nervous smile. I'm nearly all in when Sutter steps to the side with wide, panicked eyes.

"Corbin is here." Her voice is flat, or more accurately, deflated. And my racing heart veers into entirely different territory, because if Corbin is here, that means so is my ex.

I squeeze my eyes shut, then turn toward the entrance where Ryan is jogging up the few steps to shake Corbin's hand. All the goodwill I had toward Ryan leaves my body the second they meet. I'm sure he's simply being welcoming, but someone had to invite that asshole. And I'm guessing it was him because there's no way in hell my sister would have.

"Let's go." I reach for Sutter's hand, but she curls her fingers into her palm and strides across the club toward trouble.

I linger behind a few steps, frozen at this pivotal point. I could walk out of here on my own and wait for her downstairs, maybe even head to the airport and wait there. Or, I can suck it up and face my past and failures with the confidence Sutter insists I have deep inside.

"Oh, fuck," I mumble under my breath. I start to follow behind her when Meghan steps out from behind Corbin and our eyes meet. I veer to my right and head straight for the bar.

I do my best to force my way in between two groups, hoping for cover as I order a Jack and Coke. But there aren't enough people in the world to hide me from this moment. And within a minute's time, Meghan is standing next to me, shoulder-to-shoulder, ordering a drink of her own.

"It's good to see you." She doesn't look my way when she speaks. Probably for good reason. I might have called her a few awful things when we broke up. That haunts me a bit. I'm better than that. Or I should be.

"Yeah. I didn't expect to see you here." *I didn't expect to be here myself.*

"I was hoping I'd see you," she responds.

I catch her eyes in my periphery, so I turn to face her head on. She does the same, and that awkward electricity between two people who burned hot then burned out fizzles in the air between us. I breathe out a short laugh through my nose and lift the right side of my mouth in apology. So many things I should apologize for.

"I wanted to talk to you. Or I was hoping to get the chance."

I widen my eyes, not expecting this from her.

"Hey, congratulations," I say, addressing the obvious. She lifts her hand and wiggles her fingers, flashing the big diamond.

"Yeah. I know, it seems fast. But it felt right. We're very excited." Her gaze lifts from her ring to meet my eyes, and she lets her hand slip back below the bar and out of view.

"I'm really glad for you." I'm not even sure I'm lying as I say these words. I held on to bitterness for so long I got bored with it. Maybe I matured more than I expected, or the late bloomer inside of me finally grew some balls. Whatever the reason, that hostility I had feels so much less relevant now.

"I wanted to say I'm sorry, Jensen. For all of it. The way I left. When I chose to."

"*Shh*," I say, leaning in and pecking her cheek. My pulse thumps in my head as I pull back. This entire interaction is out-of-body. I wonder if I'll be able to recall it later and understand what it all means. But for now, it feels right.

"We grew apart. Or maybe we weren't ever really right together." We both laugh, probably remembering some of the same moments, like fighting over watching or not watching *The Bachelor*.

"I really am happy for you." Our eyes settle onto one

another for a soft, silent truce. I'm tempted to talk longer, to ask her when they plan to wed, see if she's traveling with the team for all of their games or setting up her business. Meghan's an artist. A potter, actually. She's always wanted to have a studio, and Corbin, dick that he still is, can make that happen. But now is not the time to catch up. It's my sister's party, and Sutter is . . . wait, where is Sutter?

"Excuse me," I say, squeezing Meghan's shoulder lightly as I take my drink and slip back through the crowd in search of the girl I came here with. She was on a beeline toward Corbin, which means she's probably landed herself in jail at this point, judging by the way she marched toward him. Of the two of us, I didn't expect me to be the one to handle running into my ex with grace. Sutter has even seen the guy recently, so the shock of not having laid eyes on him in a while shouldn't be so jolting.

I see Corbin's back weaving through the crowd, probably looking for Meghan, so I scan the room looking for a hot-headed blonde with a knife. Instead, I see Sutter slip through the main doors and head toward the elevators. I deposit my drink on a nearby table and jog to the exit, catching her just as the elevator door is opening.

"Where are you going?"

She spins around and quickly runs her arm across her eyes.

"We should probably get to the airport. I . . . I was going to get our things and text you. I'm sorry . . . I should have told you." Her bottom lip quivers with her lie.

I step into the elevator and pull her into me, wrapping my arms around her and letting her cry for the entire trip down to the ground floor. She forces her tears back when the doors open, and by the time we're on the curb waiting for our ride, the hardness in her features is back. She doesn't speak until the car pulls up, and before we get inside, she looks up at me.

"Corbin and Ryan have the same agent. What luck, huh?" Her eyes are blank, devoid of any tells. She would be killer at poker. But the agent thing explains Meghan's presence too. She and Corbin weren't invited by my sister. It was Ryan. A kind gesture probably, especially with the team in town. Ryan played for Texas, too. He and Corbin will always have that baseball bond, shared agent, and shared team.

I wait until we're in the back seat and the car rolls forward before responding.

"I should have said something." My hands are shaking, so I tuck them under my thighs as Sutter's gaze moves to me. "Corbin's fiancé? Meghan?"

I glance to her, and her head falls slightly to the side.

"She's my ex."

Sutter blinks, and for a moment I think that's going to be her only response. Then, out of nowhere, she bursts out laughing. It's a bit maniacal, and definitely beyond her control. I join her with zero understanding of what is funny but simply not wanting her to be in this alone. When she finally composes herself, I glance into the rear-view mirror to catch the confused amusement crinkling our driver's eyes. The woman is probably praying we're not drunk and about to throw up in her car.

"What's so funny?" I whisper.

Sutter's eyes flutter shut, and she shakes her head, her lips puckering in an effort to keep the laughing at bay.

When they open on mine, they're clear, the blue like daylight.

"That ring on her finger? It was mine a year ago."

Her mouth struggles to stay straight, the smile breaking through as she spittles out more laughter. I join her again so as not to leave her on her own, but inside, my gut weighs me down to the road we're driving on. The fact I'm falling for this girl feels even more wrong than it did before. As though the universe is giving me a million Corbin-shaped signs to stay away.

CHAPTER 15

Sutter

It's been two days since we got home from LA. I knew enough not to spend that night of all nights at my brother's place—at Jensen's place.

My head is a wreck, and I'm embarrassed that I cried over that fucking loser. I didn't stick around long enough to meet Meghan, but when I was rational enough to have grown-up talk with Jensen on the plane, he took me through his whole story. And here I thought he was the one with baggage and issues. Turns out, Corbin did a number on my trust. I mean, I knew he did, but the brazen way he was just there. *He was there!* Who comes to someone's engagement party when they don't even know the couple? *Well, besides me.*

Thing is, before that minor distraction, I was finally willing to give in to these feelings. And I think Jensen was too. There's a cone of silence that comes over two people right before they kiss, and I swear I felt it when we stood on the lookout at The Costa. I couldn't breathe because of the damn dress, but I was also soaring. I felt it from my fingertips to my toes. The tingling, the rush, the ache.

"That man has the most kissable lips, I swear," Kiki says as she hangs her dress back up in the depths of her closet.

"Thanks again for letting me borrow it." I don't indulge her on her lip comment. I've told her enough.

"Maybe you need to make the move?" This is not the first time my best friend has suggested this when it comes to Jensen. Or any man I've been remotely interested in during our years-long friendship. And normally, yeah. I'm the move maker.

"I don't know. I have to pick how I want this to go. Either I get to finish my thesis and Jensen becomes the next great—"

"Don't you dare say Corbin Forsythe," Kiki steps in.

I laugh.

"I wasn't going to, but yeah. Maybe he does. Or we go atomic and both completely give in to our basic cravings and feelings."

"Feelings?" Shit, that's the thread she pulls out of our conversation. *Not cravings?*

"I don't know, maybe." No maybes. I have feelings. And they crept in fast. Unwanted. Unexpected. But so fucking present.

"You know, Jensen doesn't seem like Corbin."

"Keeks, you've met him twice." Granted, she didn't meet Corbin many times before I jumped full in with him. And she never once used a complimentary word when talking about him, besides maybe talking about his hair. Corbin's got that beach punk vibe about him. How the hell he cultivated that from a small town outside Little Rock, Arkansas beats me, but he sells it.

"You're different since he's been here, though."

"Different how?"

My friend shrugs and turns her attention to her closet, sifting through shirts until she stops on the cute flowery wrap top I've always coveted. She pulls it from the hanger and tosses it to me.

"Take it. It's better on you anyway. Goes with your glow." She rolls her eyes while I glee and hug the shirt to my chest.

My phone buzzes in my back pocket so I pull it out, expecting a reminder from Jensen about our meeting in an hour. I pushed him off yesterday, but he starts tonight. And after the weekend he had—that I sort of forced on him—I feel obligated to undo that damage his parents did in the span of half an hour.

> CORBIN: Five minutes. That's all I'm asking.

I'm so stunned seeing his name and his brazen effort to needle at me that I freeze with my phone in my palm, blinking as I stare at it. Kiki steps in behind me and grabs it from my hand.

"What the ever-loving fuck is that?"

She shows me my screen as if I don't know whose text is displayed. I've kept her up on things, mostly. She doesn't know how hard he's been badgering me to talk, though. And after I lost my shit for him daring to be at The Costa at the same time I was, I can't imagine why in the world he still wants to talk.

"I promise you it has everything to do with him and nothing to do with me." I snag my phone out of her grasp before she gets the idea to send him a response on my behalf. But before I can open his contact info and finally follow through with blocking him, my phone rings in my hand.

"Oh, shit." I lift my head and make wide eyes at Kiki.

"No. Are you serious?" She paws at me to give her back my phone, but I give her a stiff arm and stare at Corbin's name for another two rings before finally answering. Only way this is going to end is for me to literally end it.

"Why are you calling me?" Blunt rudeness seems the best entry into this.

"You answered, at least."

"*Hmm*," I grunt, regretting that fact.

Kiki is still grabbing at my arm, so I slap at her and make my way into her bathroom where I barricade myself and sit on the edge of her tub.

"What do you want, Corbin?" His heavy sigh into the phone prods at my edgy nerves. "Oh, I'm sorry. Am I trying your patience? Would you prefer maybe I planned your wedding for you? And, I don't know, maybe go pick out some more jewelry I'd like you to buy for another woman?" Okay, that was petty. Still felt fucking great to say.

"Sut, listen."

"Don't call me that."

There's dead air for several seconds, and I consider hanging up.

"It's been a year, Sutter. I'm not worth pining over, I promise."

I laugh out at his attempt at . . . I guess an apology. Or maybe that was his version of therapy. Whatever it was, it definitely quashed any remaining pleasant thoughts I might have had for him.

"Noted," I say. "So, goodbye, then?"

Kiki is asking me for details from the other side of the door. She can only hear my side of the conversation, but she seems pleased with my responses based on her *hell, yeahs.*

"Actually. I'm coming to you with a business opportunity."

My stomach tightens as my inner voice threatens to punch me in the face for indulging him. I do it anyway, because opportunity is one of my weaknesses. And because I only now realize I was more hurt by all of my hard work Corbin took away with him than I was hurt by him leaving me romantically.

"I assume the silence means I can go on," he says.

"I haven't hung up yet." Though I should.

His heavy breath in the phone clues me in that he must be out walking somewhere.

"You on a hike?" He never wanted to hike with me.

"Oh, heck no. I'm back in Texas. Just finished getting my work in and getting ready to head home. I finally got that Beamer."

My face falls at his new car brag. When we were dating, he was saving his signing bonus and driving a six-year-old Toyota.

"Good for you. I've gotta go—"

"Wait. Sutter, I want you to work for me. Or . . . with me. Not for me. I know you don't like that term."

Uh, he's right. I have no desire to be his employee. I'm not property.

"You seem to be doing fine without me."

My phone buzzes in my hand, so I pull it away from my face and see a text from Jensen. I slide it out of the way and try to get out of this conversation with Corbin.

"I'm doing all right. I know I could be better, though. Sutter, I'm talking a hundred thousand a year. You would be on staff. A consultant. Whatever you want to call yourself. I talked to Meghan, and she's all right with it."

I suck in a hard breath.

"You told Meghan about me." I'm a little shocked since not sharing our past was a big part of his non-disclosure agreement.

"She knows we dated. Yeah."

"Ha, dated. But not that you proposed."

The phone goes silent again.

I shake my head, mad that I've let this conversation go on this long.

"I can double that," he says before I can get the word *no* out of my mouth. I'm not proud that money moves my internal needle, but two hundred thousand dollars doing something I love and building a portfolio that would include Corbin's name is tempting.

"And I would be allowed to talk about it? Share that I'm your mental coach?" This was a huge sticking point with him before.

"Yes. Absolutely."

My mouth hangs open at how easily he agrees. Kiki pounds on the door, growing impatient and probably not liking the hesitation she hears on my end of the conversation.

"I'll think about it," I finally say, and before he has a chance to upsell me anymore, I end the call and leave Kiki's bathroom.

"What are you thinking about?" She's on me fast.

"I'm thinking about . . . not killing him," I respond.

"She's joking. FBI secretly listening to this, my friend was joking." Kiki has always done this after I make pointless threats, ever since one of her ex-boyfriends in college got mugged about a day after I wished it upon him.

"It's nothing. And I'm probably going to say no." I gather my bag and slip on my shoes by Kiki's door so I can get to the ballpark before Jensen has to start his warmups.

"You're definitely saying no to whatever it is."

"It's two hundred thousand dollars," I toss over my shoulder as I step outside. Kiki hooks her finger in my bag strap and spins me around.

Her wide eyes search mine to see if I'm kidding, and when she gleans that I'm not, she licks her lips and crosses her arms over her chest, falling back on her heels and shifting her weight from side to side.

"Maybe thinking about it isn't so bad."

I laugh at her quick flip-flop and give her a hug.

"I'll see you tonight, after the game." She gives me a little nod before I skip down her walkway to my car.

Kiki has a little thing going with Chris Marte, the player she hooked up with the other night. I hope she's figured out he's a little bigger than the Monsoon and likely headed back to Texas in another week or two. Regardless, it's fun to see her smitten for once. And it makes it a lot easier to get her to games and afterparties at McGill's.

I get in my car and drop my phone in the cup holder, the notification for Jensen's text catching my eye.

"Shit." I grab my phone while my engine idles and quickly realize that text he sent was only the most recent of maybe six or seven notes explaining that he needed to talk to me a lot earlier than we originally planned, as in right now. His last text asked if I was there, anywhere.

I press dial and leave my phone on my lap while I peel away from Kiki's apartment and rush toward the stadium. My call goes right to voicemail, so I try again only to get the same result. I call four more times, giving up when my tires hit the Monsoon parking lot. I flash my badge, the one perk I will never give up no matter how much my dad pisses me off. The parking attendant waves me through to the VIP area and I park in one of the last spots near the training door.

My purse strap gets caught in my car door, so I fumble with the key fob and end up tearing my blouse in the process. I roll up the sleeve to hide it as I blunder my way up the hill and through the back gate.

I get inside the training room just as Shannon is done looking over Jensen's arm. He glances in my direction and our eyes meet briefly, just long enough for him to flit his gaze away and turn a slight shade of red.

"What's up?" I look to Shannon as I walk past her and chase after Jensen.

"He's fine. Needs you more than me," she says, putting away the muscle stimulator.

"Is he hurt?" I mouth.

She shakes her head and grumbles, "He's fine. Physically."

Physically. But mentally, maybe not. And here I am, his mental coach—running late.

"Jensen, wait up!" I rush down the tunnel to catch up to him, my bag sliding from one shoulder and sleeve falling off the other.

"Where were you, in a cage fight?" He nods toward my

torn shirt, and I think that was his attempt at a joke despite his clearly unamused tone.

"I didn't see your text. I'm so sorry."

I pivot to keep up with him as he seems to be pacing now. He's usually a lot more collected than this. Even when he's in his own head, he's not manic. Irritable, maybe. Hard-headed, for certain. But he looks like a trapped kitten in a pit full of angry dogs.

"Meghan called today. Hasn't called me in months, but today, she called." He stops walking and leans his back against the wall, his arm wrapped in what Shannon always calls magic pretend tape. She doesn't call it that to the people she puts it on, just to people like me, behind the scenes.

"She did, huh? What did she want? And what's with . . ." I tap my finger on the small section of wrap poking out from under his left jersey sleeve.

"I felt a pinch," he says, moving his arm. Shannon seemed to think he's fine, but maybe he's not. If he felt something, maybe he should let my dad know.

"Do you think you should have them pull you?" I lean my head to the side, trying to get his eyes to connect. If he truly feels something, he shouldn't throw. My dad would never want him to force himself, and I know from seeing it happen over and over again that powering through only leads to long-term injuries. The career-ending kind.

His head falls back against the brick wall and his hat tips up in front as he twists to look at me.

"Meghan said Corbin was trying to track you down. He find you?" His eyes are flat, and dare I say jealous?

I blink and nod my head, my pause a little too long.

"What did he want?"

"It doesn't matter. Jensen, tell me about your arm." I reach for his sleeve and tenderly pull it up to see Shannon's equivalent of a grown-up Band-Aid made out of KT tape. My eyes flicker to Jensen's.

"What hurts?" I run my fingertip along the curve of the tape, around his bicep and toward his shoulder, my hand under his sleeve.

"My parents are here tonight. With Amber. A whole big family affair. Her idea, of course." He blinks slowly.

And there it is.

"Jensen, you didn't feel a pinch."

His eyes dim and his mouth grows into a hard straight line. I can't back down and baby him. It won't do him any good. He's feeling the pressure of the need to prove himself. And I hate his sister a little for dragging his parents to see him. I wonder if Ryan came with her, too. If so, I hope Jensen doesn't know that part. It will only make things worse.

"I'll be fine." He pushes away from the wall and swings his arms in wide circles, working them out. Game time is still far off, and I can fix this. He just needs the right thoughts in his head.

"You know you're leading the league in strikeouts." I don't have a lot of his numbers at the top of my mind, but that's one little tidbit I locked away last night during my research. I was excited to share it with him because I know he's not searching for things like that. Jensen isn't about the accolades. He's about the growing and getting there—to the big time.

"I've thrown two games. Big deal." He shakes his head and puts his hand on the locker room door.

"It is a big deal. It's something you did. Because you are talented, and—"

"You can stop, Sutter. I know my parents being here is putting the pressure on and I should sing Sinatra and blah, blah, blah."

I blink away the quick sting from his dismissal of my work.

"That's good. You know it so you can ignore it. Nothing different between today's game and your last outing."

"Except that Albuquerque is the reigning champs and they're loaded with guys who like to hit the long ball. Except that." His tone is clipped.

I wish I had time to dissect all of this with him, but while the game is still a while off, there's not a big enough window for me to talk to him the way I want.

"So are you saying Corbin didn't get in touch with you?"

"We spoke." I shrug, wondering why he's circling back to this.

"Great." He nods once and pulls his mouth into a tight smile that's about as childish as anything I've ever seen. I know I shouldn't put negative feelings out there before his game, but this cold-shoulder thing isn't fair.

"Jensen, are you mad that I spoke to him on the phone? Because it was nothing. He wants me to work for him, and that's it."

His immediate laughter is off-putting.

"Oh, that's just perfect." He claps his hands together slowly, repetitively. It's like ragey applause and it pisses me off.

"He offered me a ridiculous salary to be his mental coach. I said I'd think about it."

I'm turning him down, but for whatever reason, I don't want to say that to Jensen right now. Because I want to piss him off like he's pissing me off. Because he's acting like a jealous boyfriend even though he's the one who walked out of my apartment. And our whole thing was never supposed to be complicated. He's getting my magic for free. Corbin will have to pay for it.

"You can't work for that asshole."

He's right. I can't.

But fuck him for thinking he gets to decide.

"You're right that he's an asshole, but why can't I work for him if I want to?"

Jensen swivels his head and lets out a *pfft* in disbelief. He tilts his head and narrows his eyes.

"You're not serious."

I suck my lips in and hold back any words I might regret. I'm fucking his head up right now, but he's messing with mine. There's no way he's going out there relaxed tonight. And if we keep this up . . .

"Sutter, he stole my girl. The man's a piece of shit."

I swallow hard, emotional razorblades slicing down my throat.

"Your girl." I echo the part that really brings all of this home. A painful, amused chuckle hits my chest and I look down at my feet and nod.

"That's not what I meant."

I laugh a little louder, still not the happy kind, then look up to meet his eyes. That fire that was fueling him a moment ago seems to be extinguished. That's what happens when you get irrationally jealous and angry over things that aren't in your control, only to stick your foot in your mouth. Which Jensen did. Just now.

"You know, we can talk until midnight every night, then wake up again at six in the morning and talk until I run out of words, until you run out of air. But none of that is going to matter with the shit going on in your head, Jensen, unless you learn to let go of things. You're still holding on to *your girl*."

"I'm not," he interjects. I look at him flatly, challenging his stare.

"Maybe not in that way, but the jilted ex way? You've got that in droves, and it's eating you up inside. I recognize it because so do I. But I see it now. And maybe only because I don't like the way it looks on you. But Jensen, I'm done carrying that stuff around. You need to go out there and throw that ball for you. Damn your dad and his regrets for not living his own life. Screw Meghan and her fickle heart. Fuck Corbin. You throw for you. And if you do that, and maybe let yourself enjoy it a little, goddamn, are you going to be great."

My chest hurts from my heart beating against it so hard. Jensen's nostrils flare with his breath, and I mentally fast-forward to the part where he's kissing me. That's not how reality plays out, though.

"Sut." My dad steps up just as the air between Jensen and me is at its very thickest. It's a wonder he can pass between us at all rather than drown in the tension.

"Hi, Dad. Good luck," I say, leaving them both and heading for my car, where I plan to put Sinatra on repeat until it's time to take my seat next to Kiki and chew off what's left of my nails.

CHAPTER 16

Jensen

I'm in the Bermuda Triangle of baseball purgatory. Of intimacy hell. Of dad issues and family drama. From where I stand on the mound, a glance to my left gives me a clear shot of my father, who is flanked on either side by my guilt-ridden mom and ever-hopeful sister. To my right, Sutter studies my every move. She is sunk down in her seat and wearing a hat so low on her head she may as well cut holes in the front to see.

Still, she showed up. After that dressing-down outside the locker room, she's here. I was so unfair to her. And there isn't a single thing she said that was off the mark. Did I tell her that? No. Not me. Because I've gotten so used to that pit searing a hole in my stomach that when it starts to dissolve, I scrape and claw my way through all things good to make sure I get it back.

And I did.

It's sitting heavy in my gut right now. Torturing me, along with the runners on first and third while I navigate my way through a two-two ballgame and a somehow

255

miraculous outing for myself despite the fact nothing about this game has been fun.

That's what Sutter said was my missing piece. Fun.

There is no fun in sight out here. I should be losing my mind with excitement because I haven't gone seven innings in years. Not since college. My pitch count is getting up there, though, so I know this is it. I'll finish the seventh and then hand the ball over to the closers. I'll probably check out, too, because as great as this game is for every-body else, it's absolute torture for me.

Our infield has saved my ass this inning. I need one more out and I can walk off this mound holding my head high, or at least knowing my father can't pick me apart completely.

I size up the batter as he steps into the box. He's young. Fresh out of college. Dan Mullen, like the tat on his arm says. You don't get your name tatted on yourself unless you're a stud. Or you have chronic amnesia and are apt to forget your own name.

Coach gave me the rundown on everyone in the lineup, and this guy eats lefties up. So far, I've sat him down twice with my slider but now he's looking for it. Third time through is always the hardest.

My arm feels loose at my side, and I work the ball in my palm against my hip as I dig my foot in then bend down to stare at Dalton's glove. Everyone wants the slider, but I shake them off—Dalton, Coach. I can't. He's going to take those and then take his base, and fuck if I'm going to leave this game with bases loaded.

Dalton looks off to the side, probably swearing under his breath, but he comes back and sets up for my fastball. I'll hook him high. He won't be able to touch it.

My fingers feel around for the perfect spot, but nothing seems to hit right. The threads are too thick. The ball is slick. My fingertips are dry. My arm is fine, but the rest of me is tight and rigid. I'm going to have to resort to bad habits to get through this batter. Just once. He's young, though, and I can fool him.

I come set and work the ball in my glove one more time. Maybe I'll find it. I've got seconds, but that's enough. *Find the feel, Jensen. Find it.*

Someone is shouting *Jay Hawk* in the stands. It's not coming from Sutter's direction, and my family isn't the kind that cheers. I used to love that nickname, but now all I see is that damn home run. My clock is running. I have to throw.

I'm off from the very first twitch of my leg, my kick half its usual height as I glide forward and release later than I want to. The ball is out of my control and my leg is falling off to the right. I get my glove up fast, just in case. I've hung the ball in the center. This kid—Mullen with the name tattoo—has big eyes. Cartoon eyes. Like he's dreaming of a hamburger.

I don't even watch his swing. I hear it. The ball practically clicks off the bat, the sweetest of sweet spots. Rather than watch it sail over the right field wall, I turn to face the dugout, where Coach Mason has held up a hand to the bullpen and started that slow, mortifying stroll out toward me. My mouth is dry, but when he gets to me I still try to speak.

"I'm sorry, Coach. I blew it," I croak.

"Nonsense. I'm in charge. I left you in one too long. It happens," he says, slapping my ass and sending me to the dugout.

My eyes scan the line of fans just above it, to Sutter and Kiki. Her friend is clapping and wearing that face I imagine other people's parents make when their kids don't win. I didn't win. I lost. Hard. And when my gaze shifts to Sutter, I see how much of what happened is my fault reflected in her eyes.

I fight the urge to tell her I'm sorry for letting her down. Everything about right now sucks. And mental coaching? Snake oil. Unless Sutter plans on giving me an earpiece that she can talk into nonstop to combat the other voices in my head, I'm a lost cause.

I take a seat on the end of the bench, slipping on my jacket to keep my muscles warm until I head down to the training room for ice. I fold my hands together and hold them to my mouth, elbows on my knees as I stare out at the young right-hander throwing more heat out on the mound. That's my inning out there. My business that I left unfinished.

"Fuck!" I shove the stack of cups from the top of the cooler next to me and a few of the guys look over their shoulders.

"Sorry." I hold up my hand and get to my feet to pick up my mess. *So embarrassing.*

I restack the cups and pull one off the top to fill for myself. I guzzle the water and refill my cup to carry it around and sip my way through the rest of this inning. My replacement gets the third out with two pitches, getting a little dribbler of a grounder to the first baseman. It's hard to watch something like that and not think if only I was still in, that could have been me.

Of course, it's *my* fault we're down by three now, so maybe it's better it's him.

The score doesn't change for the final two innings, and I take the loss on my stats. It was bound to happen, but it still hurts. Shannon doesn't bother trying to cheer me up. She does give me a fair amount of shit.

"You think maybe I didn't put a big enough booboo strip on you?"

I level her with a hard glare that she laughs off, then tosses me a role of KT tape to take home. I clutch it against my chest with my right hand since she's got my left arm on ice-pack lockdown.

I keep looking toward the door, and Shannon knows I'm looking for Sutter. She's not coming, though. I wouldn't either if I were her. Not after my absolute temper tantrum and self-pity party. As much as I don't want to admit it, all of this was because of that one phone call and Corbin's name. But she was wrong about the *my girl* part. It's not Meghan I was mad about this time. It was her. As if I have any right to her whatsoever. As if Sutter is somehow mine.

I gather my things and head out behind Dalton, who has been around long enough to know better than to try and cheer me up. Sometimes a pitcher needs a good sulk. He gives me a head nod as we hit the parking lot, and while the rest of the team heads toward McGill's, he loads his gear into the back of his Jeep and climbs in to drive home to his life. To things that matter. A wife. Kids. A home.

"Hey, Jensen!" My sister's voice reverberates off of the concrete walls leading out of the home plate gates of the stadium.

I shut my eyes before turning around, knowing I'm going to have to plaster a smile on my face, not only for her but for our parents.

"You stuck around." My grin is forced and tight, and I get a feeling my sister sees right through it by the way her own smile drops a notch.

"Yeah, we did, silly!" She slings her arms around me, and I hug her with my free arm.

"Oh, I'm silly, all right," I hum.

She bunches her face and gives me the *I'm sorry* expression when we part.

"Tough loss." My dad sticks his hand out with the rigidity of a robot. It's as if someone had to tell him what to say and do. I shake it and nod.

"Yeah. Thanks."

My attention flips to my mom, who is smiling and looking around the stadium like she's on a casino tour in Vegas.

"Where are you staying?" I'm trying to get my mom to answer, but she's not interested in any of this. She's on a vacation.

"Hilton. The one with the golf course?" My sister turns and points toward the Catalina Mountains.

"I don't know which one that is, but my roommate manages a resort around there. I hear it's nice. Ryan come?" I lift a brow, already knowing he didn't. I made sure when I scoped my family out in their seats.

"He had meetings." My sister's soft smile is her sort of apology. I don't really care that her fiancé didn't come watch me lose a game.

"I wanted to see what this was all about." My dad's voice is a little louder than everyone else's, which makes sense because he likes things to be all about him.

"Yeah? What'd you think?" I stare at him as he looks

around. I'm not asking about the visit, and he damn well knows it.

He eventually shrugs. "It's nice. I see why you like it here."

I wait for him to say more, but when he doesn't I chuckle and run my palm over my face.

"Right, well. It's a nice town. Pretty building. You summed it up. But I'm beat, so how about we catch up later. Maybe Thanksgiving. Maybe not." I salute my dad and back away, but not fast enough.

"Jensen, hold on." My sister rushes to my side to walk with me toward my apartment.

"Amber, I don't know why you brought them here." God, how I wish she didn't.

"Dad seriously wanted to come. I know he's bad at showing it, but he's actually proud of you in his own way. He's just . . ."

"He's just an asshole, Amber. That's what." I halt our walk and pivot to gesture back at the man who is cupping his face to light his cigarette. My mom is touching the brick façade of the stadium, I guess testing to see if it's real.

"Are they like this with Ryan?" I quirk a brow when I look her in the eyes.

"We don't really talk about family stuff, and they aren't personal with him."

"Smart move on both of your parts." I point at her.

"Jensen, I'm really sorry. I didn't mean to ambush you and just show up. But I'm getting married, and I want you to be involved. And I'd love it if you and Dad could at least be civil at my wedding." She flutters her eyes at me and grits her teeth through her smile as guilt coats my insides. I sigh.

"I'll be fine for your wedding, Amber. I promise. I'll be a perfect son, even if I have to drug myself. I won't ruin this for you, and I'll make sure he doesn't, either. Even if I have to run away from him whenever he talks."

"That's going to be hard when he gives a speech." She twists her lips as if she's trumped me, but I laugh that off.

"Oh no, I'm sticking around for his speech for sure. That's gonna be gold."

She pushes me. For a little break in my life, we're back to being kids again. She was always the boss, and I was always the pesky little brother, and even now certain truths hold.

"We're not leaving until tomorrow evening. Maybe we could have breakfast, or lunch? I've got Ryan's credit card and our resort does have some fancy five-star restaurant." She waggles her brows and I take in a deep breath.

"We'll see." I glance beyond her to meet my dad's eyes, and he lifts his hand. I do the same.

"I'm gonna leave on that high note," I say to my sister. She nods then slings her arms around me one more time for good measure. Probably because she knows the odds of me actually showing up for breakfast tomorrow are really slim. About as high as Sutter and I ever having another serious talk about my issues.

CHAPTER 17
Sutter

I've been waiting here for an hour. I shouldn't have come at all, but I feel responsible. I feel committed. And if I'm being honest with myself, I care. Probably too much.

The apartment is dark but for the stadium lights in the distance that cast a blue glow through the open balcony window. It's quiet like this. I used to love this time of night, sitting on my own staring at the lights until they finally turned off. It's different now. It's too quiet. It's not the peaceful kind but instead the sort of silence that comes before a big storm. I anticipated it, and now I feel it brewing in Jensen's chest as he slams the door shut behind him and tosses his bag toward the hallway leading to his room. His hands clutch his neck then work up his jaw until his fingers dig into his sweaty hair.

"Sutter. . ." His eyes close then open during his massive exhale. "I don't know what magical shit you *think* you have to say right now, but you don't actually need to. Go home. We're done with this little experiment." He drops his hands to his sides and briefly flashes his palms, the ice pack wrapped around his shoulder crinkling. I wait for him to storm into his room, but he seems committed to his spot in the foyer.

"You don't seem done," I say, pulling my lips into a defiant tight line.

He breathes out a laugh and rolls his neck before tugging on the already-unraveling sports wrap dangling from his bicep.

"You should leave that on longer," I admonish.

He scoffs. "It's fucking melting. I'm fine."

I leave the safety of the couch and move toward him. He glances up at me and I catch a view of his pursed lips. He lightly slaps my hand away when I try to help him with the ice, but when he sees I'm undeterred, he gives in and turns to the side so I can unwrap his arm for him. I feel his eyes on me the entire time, and like before, I feel the quiet too. It's thick, no breath, no beating hearts. We're like ghosts.

"You quit too easily," I finally say as the last piece of wrap unfurls and I take the ice pack from his arm. I head into the kitchen and drop the soaking plastic bag in the sink.

"I'm not quitting. I'm just shit, that's all," he fires back.

It's a childish statement, and I laugh at it. Still, he doesn't walk away. Instead, he moves into the kitchen, feet away from me. I've never seen a man more in need of a taste of success. It's in him. If only he'd let me coax it out.

"Is that what you think this is, Jensen? That what happened tonight is it for you? That your whole life is defined by five minutes? Five seconds? Someone else's good day? Because it's not." I level him with a heavy stare he can't ignore, but it's obvious by his drawn brow and rigid jaw that he's not ready to listen.

"You're so fucking stubborn, but you don't listen. Not only to me, but to anyone. You've got this hard head that refuses to accept that you don't know everything, or that someone else might be able to make you better. You don't know how to rely on people. You can't. Something always gets in your way, and you know what that something is? It's you, Jensen. It's fucking *you!*"

I stop my words as he flinches and takes in a quick breath. His eyes hold on to mine and flicker, but before I can inhale to push myself to say more, to give him the truth medicine he desperately needs, he steps into me, grabbing my shoulder, and pushes me back several steps until my shoulder blades flatten against the refrigerator door. His chest pressed to mine, he cages me between his arms, smoothing hair from my face with his palm then drawing a line with his thumb across my mouth, pausing on the center of my bottom lip. How easily I could part and bite him, suck in his thumb and taste it with my tongue. I hate myself for having that thought. Those thoughts are why this is a bad idea, why he's right, why I should leave and not bother with this so-called failed experiment.

He leans in, his lashes long enough that I anticipate the feel of them against my face as he blinks, though he never comes close enough. I'm staring at his mouth. He's staring at mine as he looks down on me, inches separating our worlds. He licks his bottom lip slowly then bites it as he smirks, and my core pulses.

I swallow hard and search for my voice.

"Jensen . . ." His name is all I'm able to croak out before he pushes away from the fridge and leaves me standing there alone to watch him walk away and into his room, slamming the door closed and causing me to flinch.

My chest shudders with my ragged breath and my lips tingle. My body is teeming with energy, a buzz left from hope and expectation. Shameful as it is, I want him. My lungs are filling quickly. I'm so fucking angry. I'm also frustrated and hot. And confused!

Fists balled at my sides, I take two steps forward and halt, deciding to keep the distance intact. My words, however, have minds of their own.

"See? Just like I said. You quit too easily!" My own voice echoes through the empty apartment and I remain still, panting as my heart thumps in my chest. Long seconds pass, but eventually, Jensen's door opens and he steps out into the dark hallway, shirtless, in his boxer briefs, and hard as a fucking rock.

My hands fall to my sides, my body teeming with electricity. Every nerve ending is firing with heat, and my inner voice screams for me to run at him. My feet can't seem to move.

"What do I quit, Sutter? I'm not quitting baseball. I'm pissed, and I fucked up tonight. I'm mad about it. But I'm not quitting."

"Well, you're not shit, either." My voice quivers, betraying all that is going on inside of me. I'm so mad at him I could scream, but I also want to push him down on his bed and straddle his body so I can feel him inside me, finally.

I take a deep breath, my chest lifting as my breasts swell with want and desire. Jensen's tongue peeks out of the corner of his mouth, licking his upper lip. I bite at mine to test whether it's still attached to my face.

"All right. I'm not shit. But what else do I quit? You're so sure I can't finish things, but what am I not finishing?" He lifts his chin, taunting me. Fucker has me hot.

Two can play at this game. I lift my chin and haze my eyes.

"You quit me. That night? In my apartment, when I was giving myself to you. You know I wanted you. And I felt it, Jensen. You wanted me, too. But you're too scared. You act like this big tough guy, but you're really fragile, aren't you? If you let yourself have me, you might have liked it. You might give in to feelings, and oh . . . those are things you swore off forever."

His chest heaves as I get under his skin.

"But guess what, Jensen Hawke?"

I hold his stare, both of us glued to our self-made restricted spots on the floor. I tug my shirt up over my head and let it fall to the floor, then reach behind me and unclasp my bra, holding it over my breasts while he looks on, his mouth open and hungry.

"I'm over that phase." I let my bra fall to the ground. My nipples pucker in the cool apartment air and under his glare. I run my own hands over them and pinch the tips myself, the entire time imagining it's him touching me. Jensen reaches into his boxers and grabs his hard cock, slowly stroking it, and I shudder with need.

"What phase is that?" His bicep flexes as he holds himself, and I don't know where to look next. Every movement he makes is dominant and sexual and turning me on.

"The one where I think I can be friends with a guy like you."

He gulps.

"We're not friends?" His head tilts slightly, his hand

still wrapped around his shaft. I kick off my shoes, then hook my thumbs in the waistband of my leggings and slide them down my hips, stepping out of them so I'm standing bare in nothing but my pink lace thong. Jensen's eyes trail down my body with laser focus, from my chin to my navel and lower.

"We're not. Because I like you too much." I step toward him, and he continues to work himself with his hand.

"What do you like about me?" His eyes trail back up my body with every step I take in his direction until our gazes lock on one another.

"So much," I say.

He gives a nervous nod, and his lips part with a heavy breath. I reach him and slide both of my hands up his biceps, then shoulders, until my fingers find his neck and weave into his hair.

"I think it's about time you and I— We should probably fuck, yeah?" My dirty talk turns me on, and it seems to work for him as he sneers a smile then swoops his hands around my body, lifting me up against him and carrying me into his bedroom.

Jensen kicks his door shut behind him as his eyes sear into mine. His grip loosens enough to let my body slide against his until I'm standing on the tops of his feet and his hands cup my face. His thumbs sweep both of my cheeks, then his hold grows stronger. He leans in and takes my bottom lip in his, groaning at the taste of me. I run my tongue along the length of his lips, spurring him to kiss me deeper. He tilts my head back in his hands to devour me more, and the feel of his tongue probing the inside of my mouth draws a deep moan from my belly.

My calves hit the edge of the bed just as Jensen breaks

our kiss, but he still holds my head in his hands, his eyes roaming from one side of my face to the other until our gazes lock in the most honest connection I've ever felt.

"I like so much about you, too, Sutter. So very much," he says, dipping down and taking my right nipple into his mouth, suckling it hard.

I cry out as he lifts me easily, taking more of me into his mouth. My feet fumble their way up the bed as he leans me back and continues to drop wanting kisses from my breasts down my tummy until his teeth bite at the thin strap that hugs my hip.

"These have to go," he growls, running a hand up my leg and along the inside of my thigh. My legs part the higher he travels, and when his finger finds the soaking cotton strip that covers my center, I arch my back wanting to feel all of him everywhere, and hard. So hard.

Jensen moves my panties to the side then slowly strokes my swollen tender skin, coating me in my own wetness before pushing his finger inside.

"Oh, fuck!" My head flies back and I grip at his pillow and blankets, in search of anything that might keep me grounded even though I want to fly.

His skillful hands unbind me from my panties in seconds. He lowers himself between my legs and continues to stroke my pussy with long laps of his tongue.

"So fucking sweet."

His words vibrate against my center and a million tiny shockwaves buzz through me all at once. I reach down and grab his hair in my fists, wanting to keep him right where he is, his tongue on me, finger inside me, body between my legs. He works me so hard, his pressure unrelenting as he dips his fingers in two at a time then follows up with his tongue pushing into me. As he pulls away, he flicks my most sensitive area with his tongue, and I fall over the edge completely, my thighs closing in around him and holding him to me until every wave is finished.

I'm breathless, but I still need more.

"God, you're beautiful," I say as he moves above me, bracing himself on his forearms, his muscles taut and dick hard enough that it's sticking out of the top of his boxers.

Jensen chuckles and lets his head fall to rest against mine.

"I'm pretty sure I'm the one who's supposed to say that about you."

"We can both be beautiful. Fuck it," I say, rolling my head against his.

My hands at his sides, I trace every ridge of his perfect form until I find his boxers. I don't hesitate to pull them down, and Jensen helps them the rest of the way off as his cock springs out, the tip of it resting against my lower abdomen. I lift my head enough to see it, licking my lips and wanting him in my mouth, but wanting him in my pussy more.

"I think you said it best," Jensen says, taking his long shaft in one hand as he holds himself above me with his other arm. He strokes himself and I join him, layering my hands over his then taking over, working his skin up and down and running my thumb gently over the wet tip.

"What did I say?" I can't remember speaking once. All I can think about is this man and his body on mine.

"You said we should probably fuck."

I glance up to meet his cunning smile and hooded eyes. My legs spread as I rock my hips up and guide him to my entrance. His gaze is locked on mine as he rocks forward, splitting me open and slipping deep inside. He's too big for me to take him all, but I try, pushing against him, wanting to feel his cock push against my insides.

My body is already numb from one orgasm, and the build of another threatens quickly. Jensen must feel my core tighten, because he slows his rocking, sliding in and out with careful ease, at times leaving me completely only to push back inside.

I lick my lips, wanting him to kiss me. He obliges, his eyes shutting as he drops his mouth to mine. His body covers me completely when he takes my face in his hands, and I let my hands caress the contours of his back and down the curve of his ass.

His speed picks up, and that sensation of falling returns to my core. I whimper, both wanting it to come and willing it away. I bite at his lip, then lean my head back and arch so my breasts are easy for him to feast on. When his mouth finds my hard tips again, I moan. His teeth graze the pink skin as his hips work between my legs, his cock hitting me so hard that my entire body pulses. I wrap my legs around him, holding him to me tighter as his breathing grows hard at my ear.

"Fuck, Sutter. I'm going to come," he warns.

I hold him to me, not wanting him to leave me feeling empty ever again.

"I have an IUD. We're fine. Keep going," I pant.

Jensen growls, his body growing hotter, hips moving faster. I push into him, taking him deeper, already wondering when we can do this again as I chase my second orgasm of the night. Mine's building to a peak as he thrusts and growls into the crook of my neck. My body beads with sweat as my breath leaves my chest, pulses taking over my body from inside out as Jensen fills me with heat.

We revel in every sensation, his body moving against mine, slowing with each thrust until finally, we're numb and satisfied and exhausted. Yet so far from done. So fucking far from done.

CHAPTER 18

Jensen

It's morning. The only reason I know is the thin line of sunshine that starts at the edge of my dresser and slowly crawls up my wall until the sun has fully risen. It just appeared, and I should be exhausted, yet I feel as though I could be up for days as long as I have Sutter here next to me.

For once, I watched her sleep. The pink of satiated exhaustion colored her cheeks a pale rose, and yeah, I took pride knowing I put that there.

I have never been so hungry for another human in my entire life. Kissing her tore my heart open, then coming inside of her put it back together. The whole thing was so overly masculine and animalistic, like I claimed her with that act. But . . . I kind of did. And she claimed me, too.

She hums as her arm stretches above her head. The sheet slips from her body, exposing her breast, and unlike the last time this happened, I lean over her and take her nipple between my lips, sucking it into a hard peak.

"Good morning." Her voice is raspy, worn out from my name. Just how I like it.

I lick her pink skin and flick it with my tongue just to hear her moan.

"They're so raw," she whines.

"Sorry. I can stop."

Her hand weaves into my hair at my threat and she guides my mouth back where it was.

"Don't you dare."

I smile against her, deciding to be gentle so I can have more of her tonight. I kiss the tip softly, then pepper my way to the other breast and treat it the same.

Sutter twists to lay on her side and we stare at one another with our heads supported by mashed pillows and elbows.

"I feel embarrassed that Nana's quilt had to see all that." Sutter tucks her face behind her hand and pretends to hide, but I force her hand away and immediately link it with mine.

"Good thing Nana's blanket doesn't have eyes, then, or any signs of life for that matter."

She giggles and that perfect smile stretches across her face. I lean in and kiss it.

"This is what did it, you know. This is what got me." My lips tickle against hers as I speak.

"What?"

"That smile. It's unlike anything I've ever seen."

She gives it to me again and I tug her on top of me so I can kiss it into permanence. She slides down enough to lay on my chest, propping her chin on her fist. I could stare at her like this for days.

"You must be exhausted. You should sleep."

I shake my head.

"Uh uh. Can't. Way too wired from . . . things."

She buries her face in my chest, but I lift her chin and force her to look me in the eyes.

"No getting shy on me now. That's not the girl who wore me out for six hours last night and this morning." I run my finger along her lips, and she snaps at it with a playful growl.

"I'm gonna need to get to my actual job today or else I'm going to lose my shithole apartment. But maybe later we can meet at the field? Do *our* actual work?" She pushes up on my chest to lift her naked body, and as tempting as it is to grab her and coax her into spending more time in bed with me, I know she's right.

"You know, you could always move back in here if you lose your apartment. Which, let's face it, wouldn't be that much of a loss."

She glares at me playfully but then her expression relaxes into something more serious. I sit up, worried I've actually offended her over her tiny apartment, but a second later it dawns on me. She and Corbin lived here together.

"Sorry, I didn't think." My pulse ratchets up as the sting of jealousy taints my mouth.

"No, no." Sutter sits on the side of the bed, her arms halfway through one of my T-shirts. "Corbin is . . . meaningless. And let's face it, I kind of still live here anyhow."

She gives a tiny shrug and crooked smile, then we both say, "I have a key," in unison. She leans in and nuzzles her nose against mine, then stands and pulls my shirt on completely. She grabs a pair of sweats from my drawer since everything she wore here last night is still littered on the floor of the kitchen and living room. Which probably means—

"Shit, your brother is going to kill me!" This entire time, Billy hasn't entered my mind once. Why would he? I get why he's guarded about his sister and relationships with ballplayers given what happened with Corbin, but this is different. Or, I think it's different. Fuck, even if it's the same, *we're* different. Sutter was not part of my plan, and I guarantee I wasn't part of hers. We just . . . happened. And I don't think I can stop this version of us that we are now. I don't want to.

"It will be fine. I'm a big girl," Sutter says.

"No offense, but it's not your ass Billy is going to kick."

Sutter's chest bubbles with dismissive laughter as she waves that idea off, but I give it serious consideration, right down to a quick mental comparison checklist of his best skills versus mine. I think our weight is comparable, and I might be in better shape, but that's no compensation for brotherly rage. I may have to resort to running.

Sutter slips out my door quietly and I hold my breath, listening for the apartment door to open and shut. Not hearing her brother's voice gives me some relief, so I roll out of bed and slip on a pair of sweats along with my practice shirt. I'm in definite need of a shower, especially if I'm going to make it to breakfast with my sister and parents this morning. I'm still not fully convinced I'm going to go, but I gave my sister's plea a lot of thought this morning while I waited for Sutter to wake up. I need to stop being the roadblock for great things. Or as Sutter put it so bluntly, I need to quit being my own problem. If my parents and I are ever going to have some sort of relationship, it's going to take both of us coming to the table—figuratively and literally. I'm done being the party who doesn't show up.

I gather a fresh pair of jeans and my black Monsoon long-sleeve shirt, then duck into my bathroom for a quick shower. I put myself together enough to be presentable for my dad, who will probably be sporting several days' of stubble anyhow. I shoot my sister a text to let her know I'll meet them in the hotel lobby in thirty minutes, but before I make it to the door, I come face-to-face with Billy as he stands a few steps from his bedroom, his sister's discarded clothing in a neatly folded pile in his hands.

"Oh, hey." My words stop there. So does my heart. His face is heavy, his cheeks weighed down with disappointment and my shame reflected in his sloped eyes.

"Sutter will probably be looking for these." He clears his throat as he hands them to me. I take them in my palm and utter thanks.

Thanks. Like he's really handing me this as a favor. He could have given these to Sutter, but he waited for her to leave. He purposely saved things for this moment, to catch me. To talk.

"Billy, it's not—"

"Like that," he finishes, quirking a brow.

I breathe out a laugh and shake my head.

"Yeah, you're right. That's stupid to say. It's like that, but it's also . . . not. I mean, your sister. *Pfft!*" I close my eyes and shake my head as I mentally replay all of the ways Sutter has driven me batshit crazy. Her pushiness. Her invasive nature. The damn key she will never give up, on top of her complete disregard for my personal space.

"I know more than anyone in this world how great

Sutter is. She's my sister, Jensen. We've been best friends for a lifetime, and there is nothing I wouldn't do for her. And from what I can tell, you're a pretty decent guy. I think you two are actually pretty compatible. There's just this one thing."

I lift my chin in curiosity while bracing myself for what he might say.

"You're not permanent."

I hold my breath as I marinate on those words. I don't have to question them. I know what he means because it's the nature of my job, of my dream. Most things people have to work this hard for in life are like that. There's a starting place and then every step on the way up and back down. But being physically permanent is a whole lot different than emotional commitments. *Could I convince Sutter I'm committed in that way? Is that what she would want? Is that what I want?*

"I see those questions behind your eyes. They're perfectly rational," Billy says, drawing my eyes to his. His intuitiveness is startling, and frustrating. My chest feels heavy all of a sudden.

"I really, really like her, Billy. It's not just a fling for me." I more than like her, which seems irresponsible for someone I've known less than a month. But it's also the truth. I've never felt so drawn to a person before. Sutter fills all the gaps. She makes me listen. She makes me better.

"I'm glad. But you're going to have to leave one day. Not today or tomorrow, but in a month? In the fall? And you could go anywhere. And Sutter would want you to because that's how she's built. She believes in the people she cares about, and insists on letting them fly."

I nod and glance down to her clothes in my hands, the delicate lace trim of her bra peeking out from her folded-up shirt. Something so intimate of hers. I suddenly feel protective over it. Over her.

"Maybe she'd come with me." I glance up, not sure what to expect on Billy's face. His mouth is a stoic hard line, his eyes blank.

"You could try. You know she was engaged, right?"

I nod, glad she shared that with me. Finding out something like that from Billy right now would be pretty unpleasant.

"Corbin tried to convince her to go to Texas with him. But Sutter, she won't leave this place."

"Why?" Not that I want her to leave or would ever expect her to drop her life to follow mine. But what is holding her here so steadfastly?

"Has she told you about our mom?"

Her mom.

I nod slowly, understanding filling in the blanks.

"She won't leave her. Sutter thinks she has to be the one always here, always a phone call away, just in case. I've tried to convince her I can handle things here on my own. I visit Mom, too. But no one does it like she does. It's my mom's fault it's that way, and even though I love her, I'm so mad at her about it. I love both of my parents, but Mom . . . she really did a number on Sut."

My brow furrows.

"Sutter was young when my mom got the diagnosis. Dad knew about it, and I overheard enough to get that something serious was in our family now. But my mom wasn't the kind of person to burden others, so she went and made all these plans on her own. My parents are divorced because my mom insisted on it. She knew my dad loved coaching more than the air he breathed, and maybe she was afraid of the time coming when he'd have to choose, worried he wouldn't choose her. So, she chose for him. He would live out his life his way, and she would live out hers. She studied literature, taught it to hundreds of students. Even did some writing of her own. And when her mind couldn't keep up, she enacted the plans she put in place to make sure the rest of us could carry on and live our best lives. Only, Sutter was so young when those plans were made. And the adult Sutter who stepped into the fold as they were happening saw a father who was selfish, a brother who was wishy-washy—*her words, not mine*—and a woman she called Mom slowly slipping away from the picture."

I fall back on my heels a little with the weight of everything Billy just said. My breath comes out heavy and my eyes stare at the floor as if some magic answer will appear there.

"For someone who studies psychology, my sister sure is clueless when it comes to her own tendencies."

"No kidding," I breathe out.

Billy steps toward me and places his hand on my shoulder. It almost feels like a consolation, which is a bit off-putting.

"My sister has all kinds of abandonment issues. And trust fears. And the biggest heart in the fucking world. I just felt you needed to see the entire landscape, so you don't fucking break it." His hand squeezes with a slight warning and I flash my gaze to his. I don't fight back because his subtle threat comes from a place of great love.

And I need to hear it. It still doesn't stop me from wanting Sutter in my life.

I make it to breakfast about two minutes past the time I set with Amber, and my sister is already sitting at a small table on the outdoor patio when I walk up. It's a table for two, which means my parents won't be joining us this morning, and my amused expression lingers long enough for her to catch it on my face.

"Yeah, yeah. I know, you told me so," Amber says, fanning a menu in my face as I take the seat across from her.

"It's okay. Maybe I'll actually enjoy this breakfast. That's a win, right?" I smirk at her, then scan the short menu.

A waiter hovers nearby, so I wave him over then glance at my sister. "I'm assuming you're ready since I left you hanging here for a few minutes?"

She nods and we both order the protein omelet, a clear sign of siblings. The waiter leaves us with a pitcher of water and I guzzle down my glass and pour it full again as soon as he leaves.

"You run a marathon this morning?"

I spit out some of the water at her observation, which she immediately picks up on because Amber can read me like a book.

"Oh. My. God. You had sex!"

"Oh, Jesus, Amber," I chastise in a hushed tone,

glancing around the space at the few families and couples vacationing and probably not interested in hearing about my conquests over breakfast with my sister.

My sister leans in like we're at a slumber party and she's ready for gossip.

"Sutter and you are really a thing, huh? Jensen, I like her. I *really* like her."

I glance up and will away the heat crawling up my neck as I shake my head. My sister has been invested in my love life since we were teenagers, and she always wanted me to have a girlfriend she could take over as her best friend. Meghan was not that girl. Not because my sister didn't like her, but she didn't *love* her. They were too different. But Sutter, as I've said, and Amber—they are the same.

"I like her a lot, too," I admit.

My sister giggles and rubs her palms together as she prepares for a devious scheme I have to stop before she gets too far in.

"Do not start planning our wedding. I like her. And yeah, I want this to be something with her, something real and long term. But let me do it on my own, okay?"

I hold my breath as my sister's eyes study mine. I swear she's weighing whether or not I'm a big enough boy to take care of my own play dates. I can assure her I am.

"Fine," she huffs, sitting back in her seat and spreading her cloth napkin over her lap.

"But she's coming to my wedding, Jensen. She's coming, and if I have one wish, it's for her to be in it. I want my brother and a girl worthy of him walking down my aisle together. It's my bridal wish, so you must grant it."

"Bridal. Wish." My lips twist as I give Amber a sideways look.

My sister takes her water glass in both hands and brings it to her lips, pausing before taking a drink to reiterate to me above the crystal rim.

"Bridal. Wish."

CHAPTER 19

Sutter

Like all great best friends, I did Kiki the solid of calling her during my drive to work to fill her in on every sordid detail of my night and morning. Twice. It almost felt like bragging. Maybe it was.

Jensen made me feel more beautiful and seen than I have ever felt. It was like our own little world there in his room, under his blankets and in his arms. My mind never drifted away from the moment once, until this morning when I stepped out of his room and the suffocating strangle of repeated mistakes wrapped around my throat.

I've made this walk before.

That was my only thought. And it keeps popping up in my mind, even now, hours later. I kept that part from Kiki because she was so excited to see me happy. I didn't dare express my reservations. There will be plenty of time for that when things begin to fall apart.

I already assume they will. *What is wrong with me?*

Jensen is waiting for me at the field, and I promised myself to clear my mind of everything for at least the next

289

two hours. Before he and I gave in to this pull between us, we had a plan, and I have to stick to that at the very minimum. My thesis is due next month. *For real* due. I'm pretty sure I've run the course of extensions and forgiveness. Any more delays and I'll get sent back to the beginning without collecting a degree, like Monopoly jail.

I brought my laptop with me today so I could upload stats from the pitching coach and then run them through my program. Jensen will throw again in four days, and it's a road game. I'd like to go, but I just got back in town, and I promised Mom I would go to that concert in the park with her. The chances of her being in the mood to go are slim, but in case she wants to, I would hate to miss it. I don't want to let her down. That's what my dad is for.

I pull into the lot next to my dad's oversized pickup truck with dually wheels. The man has always acted like he's a rancher, I swear. He's not. We barely had dogs growing up. I gather my laptop and work bag, then step out of my car and straighten my long black skirt and the top Kiki gave me. I leave my black jacket in the back seat because the afternoon sun has warmed things well into the nineties. When I push through the gates, I'm welcomed by the usual sounds of balls slapping leather mitts and wood bats drilling line drives deep into the outfield. The day before travel day is always a light practice.

Jensen is finishing up his light bullpen session when I walk up, and the joy seems to be back in his motion. His arm moves effortlessly, and every throw zings toward the catcher like a bullet. Every action is crisp. And he's smiling.

I smile too.

"Thanks for finally getting him to not fall to his right,"

Coach Bensen says to me, doing very little to hide his loud whisper behind his clipboard.

"I was not falling to my right," Jensen grumbles.

"Of course not!" I wait until he turns to walk back to the mound before looking Coach Bensen in the eyes and mouthing *he totally was*.

We both laugh and Jensen labels us assholes, probably deservedly. He finishes his last few pitches and I follow him into the training room where Shannon starts work on his arm along with a student trainer from the college. The kid is maybe twenty-one—*maybe*—and overt about his attraction to me. After asking me my name and occupation like I'm on some interview, he goes with a classic.

"You come around here often?"

His name is Levi, according to his badge. And while I force myself not to audibly laugh, Shannon and Jensen seem perfectly fine destroying his young ego. They both spit with their laughter, and Levi steps away from wrapping Jensen's arm, his eyes darting around wondering what he did that was so funny or wrong.

"Levi, it's fine." I want to make it better, but Jensen has other plans. He wants to make it clear.

"Dude, she's my girlfriend." His voice is loud and matter of fact, and to hear him throw out that term with such ease sends my pulse racing. I think I'm scared to accept it, yet also in this strange, shocked place where I also might want to cry happy tears.

"Girlfriend, huh?" Shannon teases us both a bit, maybe to set me at ease more than Jensen. She glances down at my tapping toe more than once. She knows the Corbin history.

"I mean, I'm pretty crazy about her, and the love bite on my neck indicates it might be mutual, so—"

"Jensen!" I reach forward and cup his mouth, then note the small bite mark on the side of his neck. *Oh, my God, I really did that!*

"Ha ha, okay. You two sort that out on your own time. Congratulations, or not. Up to you." Shannon pats the wrap down on Jensen's shoulder and dismisses him to my care.

I don't know what I expected. With Corbin, it took a while for him to be willing to show off the fact he was dating the coach's daughter. I guess I thought Jensen would be the same. But when I follow him to his cubby to collect his things, he turns around and catches me off-guard, dipping me backward and kissing me in front of at least a dozen of his teammates who all whistle and hoot in response.

He bites his lip as if savoring my taste as he tilts me back up.

"In case I wasn't clear about my feelings this morning." He holds my gaze hostage for several seconds, until I nod in acceptance. It's a bold declaration, and it muddles my thoughts from earlier in the day.

This isn't Corbin.

This is Jensen.

I'm different now.

Nothing about this is the same.

My dad's office is empty, and I nod for Jensen to follow me inside so we can more easily download his stats and connect online. It takes me a few minutes to get things lined up and to import from the drive Coach Bensen left for me, but once I have Jensen's last few outings plotted, the visuals are pretty convincing.

"Looks like I took a step back yesterday. Which we knew." He points to the earned runs line, his face falling as he relives giving up a three-run homer.

I tip his chin back in my direction and shake my head.

"It's a blip. It's about the trend, not the dips and turns along the way."

That advice—something I've said before to Corbin, to Billy, to myself—it's the heart of my thesis and everything I'm studying. I wish I could take it to heart in my own life. I'm trying. I'm trying so hard. I don't want to hold my breath waiting for this amazing high I'm experiencing to turn into a low, but experience tells me that's inevitable.

Jensen opens his phone screen and shows me a few videos Coach Bensen and my dad sent to him this morning of batters he will face in Salt Lake. He walks me through his plan, half of which is in a pitcher language I don't fully follow, but I get the main points. I pull out the things that strike me in his assessment as he prepares, the way he uses the word *always* when talking about the other team's first four batters *always* getting on base. That's not true. Their percentages would be a thousand instead of three hundred if that were the case. It's the little things he needs to learn to spot himself and rework in his head. They don't *always* get on base. They're good at getting on base, but most of the time, something prevents it. Those are the areas Jensen needs to exploit.

After an hour of dissecting his stats and morphing his baseball language with my psychological perspective, I fear I've created a monster. He's completely taken over my dad's desk, creating his own plan of attack and filling one of my father's notepads. Eventually, he grows so excited to share his sudden insights, he literally commandeers my laptop and rushes out to the bullpen area to talk something through with Coach Bensen.

My father passes him as he leaves, so I take over my dad's abandoned desk and swivel in his chair.

"You seem happy. I'm guessing you found a way to keep your ace from throwing meatballs right down the middle?" My dad's mouth forms his typical pessimistic line.

"First of all, he's *your* ace. And second, you know better than anyone that he had five great innings before that. Shit happens."

My dad coughs out a laugh.

"That it does. Now, scoot." He waggles his finger at me, and while I'd like to hold my position, this isn't what I want to spend my time in here talking to him about. I get up and take the chair in the corner so he can retake his throne.

"I'm going to see Mom this weekend. I know you'll be in Salt Lake, but when you're back, maybe you and I could visit together?"

He glances up at me over the rims of his glasses, never once nodding or acknowledging my suggestion more than that. I breathe out a heavy sigh, but while I can usually tuck my ire back into that place in my head where I pretend my father's actions don't bother me, that space no longer seems willing to hide my feelings.

"You're a real ass, you know?"

He chews on nothing in his mouth as his eyes remain on the tablet he's scrolling through aimlessly.

"So you've told me before."

I glare at him, watching the reflections of names and

position numbers scroll by in his glasses. He doesn't look up, and my hand automatically forms a fist. I bring it down on his desk, knocking over a cup with a few pencils and a stack of Monsoon two-for-one coupons. The mess is annoying, but I'll clean that up later. I'm too focused on saying my piece right now.

"You want to tell me I'm an asshole again? You want me to watch you say the words?" My dad pulls his glasses from his eyes and pinches the bridge of his nose. "Fine Sutter. Tell me, what kind of asshole am I?"

I blink a few times, stunned at his absolutely clueless response.

"Um, you're the kind who was a shitty husband and who left his wife to wither away in a facility he hasn't set foot in once. That kind!"

My chest heaves with my anger, and when my dad swallows hard, I feel some vindication that I wounded him. That feeling is short-lived, however. Standing up and setting his glasses on the corner of his desk, my father rests both of his palms on the clear space on his desk mat, his jaw twitching as thoughts race behind his eyes. He brings his palm up slowly, then slams it down so hard he rustles the remaining papers on his desk. They fall to the floor with the other overboard office supplies.

"That's enough!"

It's my turn to swallow. I've heard my dad shout at his players this way, and maybe he did to me and Billy at points in our lives, like when we stole the car once and Billy let me drive at the age of fourteen. But my dad's red cheeks and watering eyes are a level above anything I've ever seen directed at me. I pushed him, and while I'm glad to see him feeling, I'm a little nervous about where this conversation is headed. The heads turning to peer into his office aren't helping much.

"You think whatever you want, Sutter. I don't care. I love you and I know you have to tell yourself stories to have peace in your life. But don't for once think any of my life with your mom, of our lives apart now, is easy for me. It is not. And one day maybe you'll be able to understand it."

My eyes widen on his, matching his challenge. Rather than stick around, though, I opt for grabbing my bag from the floor and storming out of his office. Anything more I say will only make the depth of our rift deeper, and I cling to the idea that one day my dad and I will be close again. We have to be. I need him. When Mom's gone, he's all I'll have left.

My body shaking, I take maddening steps down the corridor to the field, spotting Jensen sitting next to Coach Bensen in the front row of seats by the third baseline. I hang back, slipping into the last row of seats to calm my racing heart and let Jensen have his space and map out his game plan. He's doing so well, and I want him to leave for Salt Lake without bringing along any worries about me and my dumb fight with my dad.

Of course, the fact my father just stepped out of the corridor and is heading my way doesn't help matters. I can't even properly run away. And I'm wearing a damn pencil skirt that binds me all the way down my legs, so even if I did run, I'd probably topple over like the mustard bottle in the seventh-inning hotdog race.

I turn to face my dad as he nears, and I hold up a hand to will him away, or at least beg him to be quiet. His mouth stays in a hard line as he marches down my row and plops down in the seat right next to me. I can hear his breath tickle his thick nose hairs, and probably because I'm irritated at him, but I want to pinch his nose shut and force him to breathe through his mouth.

"Corbin called me."

"Shit. Not you too," I say, rolling my head. I don't need his opinion on Corbin. My dad knew Corbin was getting pulled up days before I did, yet he never gave me a heads up or talked to me about it in a way that would prepare me. Not that it's his job as a coach. But isn't it kind of his duty as a father?

"Sut, you need to listen. He told me about wanting to hire you, and I told him to suck it."

My head swivels in his direction, and my mouth flies open into a wide O. My dad glances my way but never fully meets my gaze. I've noticed this about him over the years. When we have tough conversations, my dad prefers not to look me in the eyes. It's a type of avoidance, according to my studies. But I think it's a coping skill and a way to overcome one anxiety with another.

"I never thought he was good enough for you. You deserve . . . better. And there's a lot better out there, believe me."

It's quiet between us for a few seconds, but eventually I utter, "Thanks."

My dad reaches over and flexes his hand over my knee, hovering for a second before patting me twice. He brings both of his hands back to his lap and picks at his nails, like I do when I'm in his position. There's more to this conversation. I just don't know what it is yet.

"Sut, he doesn't just want to hire you. *Texas* wants to

hire you. As in, the organization as a whole. As in, your big break. Thesis published or not."

It takes me several seconds to compute my dad's words. I'm not sure I actually have.

"But I'm in the middle of working with Jensen—"

I'm falling for Jensen.

"Jensen is going to be fine. He's getting his call soon; I feel it. And you know I'm never wrong."

I blink again. A lot. My chest is pounding with the beat of a college drumline. My arms are tingling. My mouth is watering. *Crap, am I going to throw up?*

"It's your dream, Sut. You have to."

"I can't." My answer is so fast it surprises even me. It's an automatic for me, but there's this ache in my belly at the sound of it. My dream is right there, on a plate. Well, on a contract being drawn up, I suppose. But I'm going to turn it down. For a boy. For my mom. For Billy, and because I would miss Kiki, and I want to finish my thesis.

"Sut, sweetheart."

I swallow down unexpected tears. My dad hasn't called me sweetheart in years. He reaches over and puts his hand on mine, and I look down to see my hands are shaking under his touch.

"I know you're afraid. But we're all going to be fine. You need to choose *you* this time. You'll regret it the rest of your life." He leans forward an inch to fully meet my eyes, and I give in to the single, fat tear that's been begging to fall down my cheek.

Just then, Jensen breaks into laughter several rows below us, and I flash my gaze to him. He's bumping fists with Coach Bensen over something he's figured out, maybe something I taught him, or maybe something he already knew and can finally see. We've only just begun. I can't possibly leave at such a beautiful start, especially for a team with my ex who Jensen quite literally despises.

"Oh."

My dad's reaction brings me back to him. I start to question what he means but then as he glances to Jensen then back to me, I see he already knows.

"It's nothing. No, it is. It's something. And that's another part of why I can't go." My stomach turns over again at my dilemma.

"I see." My dad nods and refolds his hands in his lap, returning his gaze to Jensen and his assistant coach. He looks on for nearly a minute, studying them, then moving his attention to the field where the rest of his players are putting away screens and gathering up balls from his pre-travel batting practice. He has a full team to run everything for him, yet my dad is here every day to act as guardian over it all. It's his passion.

But what is mine?

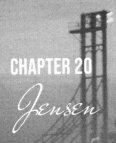

CHAPTER 20

Jensen

No more business as usual.

In fact, fuck business.

Sutter came back to the apartment after our session. I gave her the clothes her brother found, and her reaction was pretty similar to mine. A bit embarrassed, but also defiant as hell.

"Billy can't tell me what to do," she said.

And she's right. He can't. I can't. Apparently, nobody can.

But I can't help but linger on what her brother told me. Maybe it's selfish of me to wish for things to go one way —*my way*. Why does this relationship have to revolve around me and where this game takes me? Sutter shouldn't have to pack up and follow me. But also, I wish for it more than a little.

Her brother walks into the apartment and immediately freezes at the door. His tie is half undone and his brow is covered with sweat, probably from taking the stairs up today. The elevator is on the fritz.

301

"What's that smell?" His eyes narrow on me, and I glance toward the kitchen. He follows my lead and spots the steaming pot Sutter has brewing on the stove.

"It's fine. I've got it under control." She has her hair in a twist on top of her head that at some point she fastened into place with a wooden spoon. She's wearing a pair of my old shorts and an oversized T-shirt with the sleeves rolled up over her shoulders. Her skin is pink, probably from the flames she had going for some ungodly reason a moment before Billy came in.

"You let her cook." He shifts his eyes back to me, his mouth a soured slight frown, the kind you'd expect after getting off the teacup ride.

I shrug.

"I don't let her do anything. She simply does."

Billy nods, then pulls his arms from his jacket and drops it along with his briefcase on the easy chair by the sofa. Rolling his sleeves up, he moves into the galley space and slides in next to his sister, who looks a bit overwhelmed.

"Hey, Sut. What do we have brewing here?" He lifts a brow. Sutter runs her forearm over her forehead, then turns to the microwave beeping behind her.

"Shit! Well, we were going to have pasta and meat sauce, but now I'm not so sure about the sauce part." She opens the door to the microwave and reaches in without thinking.

"Oww!" She leaps back nearly two feet and sticks her burnt fingertip in her mouth.

"I'm on it," I say, dropping my phone on the coffee table and wading into the combat zone that is the kitchen. I flip on the cold water and run it until I feel the chill, then wave Sutter over to hold her finger under the running water.

"Here's what's going to happen," Billy announces. "You two are going to deal with the First Aid situation going on back there, and I'm going to salvage this dinner. Sound good?"

"Sounds amazing!" Sutter's concentration is on her throbbing finger that I'm holding in place under the cool water. It's definitely going to blister. It's a good thing she doesn't have to pitch against Salt Lake.

"Should we invite Kendra?" Sutter nudges me as she asks and waggles her eyebrows, like this is all part of her grand plan. I don't think she had a blueprint for any of this.

"Uhh." Billy stalls, and the longer it takes him to respond, the deeper the dent grows between Sutter's eyebrows.

I shut the sink off and wade through the items in the First Aid kit, pulling out some ointment that can go on her burn later, after she endures an ice compress. I get her set up with one and leave the bandage out to wrap her finger in before dinner. Sutter slides up close to her brother and links her arm through his, resting her head on his bicep and giving it a squeeze.

"I'm really sorry, Bill."

He continues stirring noodles and checking the heat on the burner for a few seconds but eventually bends his head down to kiss the top of his sister's. They leave it at that. And it's the sweetest thing I've ever seen. It makes me miss Amber more.

Despite Sutter's disastrous beginning, Billy manages to turn her bevy of ingredients into a bowl of deliciousness. His sauce is sweet and tangy, the meat tender and accented with tiny pieces of garlic, pine nuts, and whole chunk tomatoes. I slurp up a forkful of noodles that fling around between my lips and splatter sauce all over the front of my shirt.

"New rule. Billy, you are always the cook. Sutter, you are banned."

Sutter starts to protest my proclamation, but her brother cackles with laughter, and making him feel good seems to trump any insult to her. She eventually settles into her chair with crossed arms and mutters *fine*.

We devour our dishes in mostly silence, the NBA playoffs on low in the living room and occasional satisfied hums leaving all of our mouths. I help clean the kitchen while Sutter retreats to the couch and kicks her legs up over the sofa arm. I want to join her and lift her head in my lap so I can run my fingers through her hair, which is no longer carrying around a spoon. But I also don't want to make things any more awkward than they already are in front of her brother.

He must feel the weight in the room too. Between stiff grins and overdone apologies each time either of us gets in the other's way in the tight kitchen, we're on a fake politeness overload. Not that either of us is angry. But there's definitely a lot of unspoken shit happening.

"We won't bang on the couch. Sound good?" And as is Sutter's way, the tension balloon instantly pops with her crass interjection.

"That's good, because Kendra and I were all over that couch," her brother fires back.

Sutter flies up from the sofa and kicks her way to the chair as if she saw a mouse. I'm too thrilled to see her get stung back to feel embarrassed myself, and eventually I hold out a fist for Billy to pound and take a full breath as if everything is now normal. It sort of feels like it is.

We watch a few episodes of *Sing for Your Supper* before Billy retreats to his room. Eager to get her clothes off and my dick where it belongs, I flip the TV off the moment her brother's door is shut, and carry Sutter over my shoulder into my room where I strip her out of my clothes and pepper her body in head-to-toe kisses.

"Thanks for the love bite, by the way," I say as I pounce on her and cage her between my arms. She reaches up, touches the very spot she marked, and giggles. She's proud of her work, but I plan on getting revenge.

"You know what this means," I tease, dipping my head and suckling the top of her breast until a small heart-shaped bruise is left behind. I move on to her nipples as she protests me marking her, but she seems to completely forget what I've done as I bring the hard peak into my mouth and bite it gently.

Her back arches, giving me access to both of her breasts, and I swoop my arm behind her to hold her in this position until I've made her tits so raw she can no longer take it. I roll over with her in my arms so she's on top of me, and she lifts up on her knees, holding my cock until it's lined up perfectly with her wet center. She sinks down slowly, her head falling back with a sigh as she slides up and down on my cock, her hips rocking forward and back. I touch her clit with my thumb and work tiny circles into her swollen skin until she's crying for me to let her come.

I pump into her, letting myself go. As she comes down from the high, she collapses into my chest, our bodies sticky with sweat, my dick still hard inside of her, waiting to go again.

"God, I missed you," I hum.

I run my fingers through her twisted hair, a few of her

waves tangled from her cooking attempt and odd hair solution. She chuckles and reaches around to untangle her hair with me at first, but eventually it's smooth enough for me to take over and lull her into rest.

"I like you so much," she says. The same words as last night.

I smile and tuck my chin to leave a kiss on top of her head.

"I like you so much more."

"*Mmmm.*" She runs her hand up and down my chest, flicking my nipple a few times.

"Mine don't work quite like yours do." Though oddly enough, I do kind of like it. It's a jolt. But it's hard to say if it's her touch or just her that's making my cock swell inside of her.

"Can we stay here forever?" I run my hand up and down her naked back as I wait for her to answer. She doesn't for nearly a minute, and at first I figure she didn't hear me, so I ask again.

"What do you say we lay here like this forever?"

I feel her swallow against me and stop my hand in the center of her back.

"Sut?" She shifts against me and our bodies part as she moves to my side and holds herself up to look me in the eyes. The heaviness in them scares me. My throat closes, and my stomach turns. Meghan made this kind of face when she told me we were growing apart. But Sutter and I, we just started. There's nothing but growth together happening. I need more of it.

"What's wrong?" I sweep a lock of hair behind her ear, but she must feel my trembling hand because she takes it in hers and brings it to her lips.

"It's nothing."

She's a terrible liar. She knows it. I know it. I lean my head to the side and hold her gaze, unflinching.

Finally, her eyes blink lower, falling to my chin as her bottom lip quivers. When she flits her focus back to meet my eyes, it feels like a needle passes through my heart.

"That offer from Corbin—"

I feel sick, and I am certain I hide it poorly. Sutter reaches forward and cups my face with her hands, leaning in and kissing my lips then shakes her head.

"No, I said no. I wanted you to know. Corbin's offer . . . I turned it down. I won't work for one man. I'm too good for that." She pulls her cheeks high, but I can tell they aren't high enough.

"You feel regret." She has to. It was a pretty high-paying job, and I hope she didn't turn it down just for me. Though I really don't want her under his payroll. The thought of that brings out my caveman tendencies.

Sutter's eyes fall to my mouth again, and she stares at it for several seconds before leaning in and stopping with her mouth a paper's width away from mine.

"No regrets. I'm right where I belong." Her lips tickle my skin, then she suckles on my lower lip, teasing me with her tongue and grazing my skin with her teeth. I let her drive for minutes, letting her kiss me like an artist with a brush. It's mesmerizing, being adored by her like this. But there's an undercurrent that's a constant, and I can't get her brother's words out of my head.

"She won't leave."

Sleeping in a room with Dalton is a lot less enjoyable than spooning in my bed with Sutter. Spreading out in a queen bed is nice, and having someone bring me hot towels is quite a perk. But it's not the Four Seasons. It's the Salt Lake Special, and I'm ready to get back home. But we have three more to play against the Monuments. Three games in which I have nothing to do but root for the other guys in our starting rotation.

I threw the game of my life tonight. I sent Sutter the highlight videos that I could pull from the livestream when it ended. It's not the best picture, but she did get a kick out of the guy I sent back to the bench with three straight sliders. He tried to break his bat over his knee and failed. Now, he has a serious contusion on his upper thigh of his own doing. *Dumbass.*

While I would have been perfectly happy spending the night on the phone with Sutter and trying to sync our channels to watch one of the playoff games together, she insisted I practice some of her advice and try being social for once in my life. Most of the team came to this bar to celebrate our win, and even though Dalton turned in early, I decided to break my mold and be a life *at* the party for once.

"Hey, there's Jay Hawk!" Brad slaps my back as I walk into the bar. He's picked up on the nickname, and it's spreading around the clubhouse. I'm working on getting rid of the negative feelings that brew when I hear it. That name was never said in a negative way, and that's what I remind myself every time my mind threatens to replay the Kendall homerun.

"This round's on me. Toast up!" He hands me a pint

and I clank my mug to his before taking a big sip that leaves a foam mustache behind.

I don't have the heart to tell Brad that the beer is shit, so I clutch it in my hands and thank him, then carry it to the end of the bar where I slide onto the stool next to coach.

"That shit is foul." I push the mug away and Coach shakes with quiet laughter.

"I spilled mine on purpose. Here, let me get you something real." He holds up his hand and the bartender slides our way.

"Heineken for my boy here." He nods in my direction.

"Coming right up," he says.

I glance down to the other end of the bar, checking to make sure Brad doesn't see me swap out for an upgrade. While I'm looking away, though, Coach tips my mug over toward the bar and it spills into the trough.

"Ooops." His voice is flat, and I stare at my empty mug as it lays sideways.

"You are an evil genius," I say.

"Here you go, sir." The bartender pops the cap for me and I take the bottle in my hand, refusing the glass. I like it better this way. It's the way my dad drinks his beers, and I used to fantasize about the two of us sitting on the tailgate of his truck knocking a few back. That day will probably never come, but maybe . . . maybe one day after he sees me pitch in the majors. Maybe then.

"Thanks." I tip my beer to Coach, and he lifts his and gives me a nod as he grunts.

We drink in silence, both of us trying to catch the score on the game playing on the tiny TV tucked up in the corner near the expensive, top-shelf shit.

"Your daughter is pretty obsessed with this game, you know. It has to hurt, knowing she'd sell baseball out for hoops in a heartbeat." I bring my beer to my lips and take a long sip, but when I realize he has yet to respond to my joke, I set it down then clear my throat. "I mean, she loves baseball more. I'm sure. It's just, I know she likes the Suns, and . . ."

"Jensen?"

"Yeah?" My voice cracks like I'm twelve.

"Shut up."

I nod silently, doing what he says. I gnaw on my tongue with my molars, my chest fluttering with this strange need to make this man like me but to also obey his wishes. I almost open my mouth to speak a dozen times, filtering through highlights of our game and my opinion about the next draft and even the game on the TV.

"She's pretty obsessed with you. Just so you know." Coach Mason hijacks our dead conversation and pulls it offroad, taking me on a route I did not see coming.

I lick my lips and panic in search of the perfect response.

"I'm equally obsessed." I wince then drink more of my beer, wishing like hell I had take-backs for that.

"That true?" He turns in his seat, his bony knee brushing against my thigh muscle. His nearness is intimidating, and though he's smaller than me, he still scares the shit out of me.

"I mean, I hope she is. I probably should let her talk to you about us. This isn't how she'd want you to find out, I'm sure. So if you could just pretend I didn't say we were dating, that would be—"

"She turned down a job for you." It's as if he didn't hear

my words at all. I lick my suddenly dry lips again and look back at the rim of my beer bottle. I rotate it slowly in my hands as I inhale. I should have stayed in my room.

"I know." From what Sutter said, Coach wasn't real big on Corbin either. He can't be too upset at the idea of her not working for him.

"Oh, you know. You know what she gave up. For you. Who she is obsessed with." His sharp tone leads me to believe maybe she read him wrong. He seems to be a Corbin fan after all.

I hold my tongue between my teeth and consider the fewest number of words I can say and still get out of this alive.

"Sir, I really think she's going to get a much bigger job than working for one rookie pitcher. I believe in her, and I think she's going to be an incredible asset to some team someday. And I hope I'm lucky enough to be in her atmosphere and just hope to stay there."

The lump in my throat is so big I swear I could see it if I glanced down. I try to swallow it, but it does little to relieve the rising heat in my chest and my thumping heart. My temple is pulsing, and my right eye is starting to twitch.

I finally give in to the temptation to look him square in the eyes, and when I spot the light smirk on his lips, I relax —but only a little.

"What's funny?" I shouldn't ask him this *ever* because he's quick to tell me. And it's almost always something I wish I didn't know, or an insult, or both.

"Jensen. My daughter lied to you. She's so obsessed with you that she didn't tell you that the job offer she turned down? It's for a team. For Texas. For the organization. With the option to build her own team, to grow it, and to become *the* authority on that voodoo shit she's actually turned into science."

I'm not sure how long it takes for me to speak again. I know my mouth hangs open for long moments, long enough for Sutter's dad to laugh, finish his beer, and read the scores from around the league that are sliding across the bottom of the TV screen.

"I'm sorry. Texas?" I finally repeat that bit—*the* bit. My heart sank a long time ago. Now my stomach is pooled at my feet, and I don't think my legs work.

"Texas, son. Texas. For you." Coach Mason gets up from his seat and tosses a twenty on the bar, then leaves a heavy hand on my back. I turn to catch his name on his coaching jersey as he walks away.

Sutter is falling into the pattern her brother worried she would. She's throwing away her dream to stay in one place and be the touchstone for all of us. And I'm falling in love with her.

She can't do this.

CHAPTER 21

Sutter

Some girls love the fresh smell of flowers. Me? I'll take an oiled new leather mitt any day.

I spent so many months frozen and not moving forward. But knowing that an actual professional sports team sees value in what I offer, in my practice and what I do? Gah! Even not taking the job, merely the offer has been enough to renew my enthusiasm and commitment to making Jensen a future Cy Young winner.

I finally cashed the check Corbin gave me. The one that actually had the word *hush* scribbled in his horrible hand-writing in the notes section. I'm happy to never let anyone know I put that man's ring on my finger. I don't even know who that girl was anymore. Thank God she got away.

I paid off a few credit card bills, then made a special stop at Gamers on the north side of town. My brother had a custom glove from here when we were in high school. Billy was never good enough to wear it out, and I think he probably still has it in his closet somewhere. It wouldn't do me any good, though, since Jensen is a lefty.

The colors are classic, the warm honey and the red mahogany laces. It set me back six hundred bucks, but the way I look at it, that was Corbin's money anyhow. I don't want any of it lingering around, and I'd rather turn it into a meaningful gift for the man who brought my heart back from the dead.

I pull into the garage and catch Ernie walking to the main doors from his daily errands. I holler at him to wait up, then stuff Jensen's glove into my workout bag and throw it over my shoulder. Jensen texted to meet at the apartment tonight. Their bus got in around three this afternoon, and I just put the finishing touches on my thesis. I need to plot the last few charts which will require two more outings of him, but unless he completely blows it, my predictions will hold true. It will be kind of cool to see if his numbers in two weeks are where I think they'll be. I bet everything's up—spin rate, velocity, accuracy.

"Sutter Mason, how the hell are you?" Ernie holds the door open for me and I bow to him as I pass by.

"Why, thank you, sir. You know, you still owe me a game." I won't quit on him. I'm going to get him back out there one of these days.

"Yeah, I know. But that horse track is always calling. And you know I like to volunteer down at the visitor center."

I did *not* know that. My mouth agape, I shake my head. Ernie chuckles.

"Oh, cat's out of the bag. Turns out I like talking to people and telling them where to go." He winks and I laugh.

"Yeah, you like telling people where to go, all right."

The elevator dings and we both step in. I lean toward

him and unzip my bag a little for him to see my gift for Jensen.

"Ooooo-weee! She's a beaut!"

I pull it from my bag and force him to put it on his hand. Ernie was a leftie too. Well, he still is, I guess. Though, these days he's not throwing anything farther than a few dozen feet.

He turns his hand around with the glove on it, his eyes dazzling at the stitches and color. He stops at the thumb area and twists the glove enough to read the words *Jay Hawk*.

"That young man has himself a nickname, huh? Maybe I do need to see what this Jay Hawk business is all about." He hands the glove back to me and I tuck it into my bag before the doors open.

"Now we're talking. I'm going to hold you to that."

I step out on Jensen's floor as Ernie continues up to his. My legs are full of energy, and I'm glad I changed into my shorts and a T-shirt because I'm kind of pouring sweat. I'm nervous, like giving a glove equates to a proposal or something. But in our world, it kind of does.

I get to the apartment and slip my key in the lock, but before I turn it, Jensen pulls open the door and tugs me inside.

"I was watching at the peep hole." He lifts me into his arms and swings me around, the way a groom carries a bride over the threshold. He drops me on the couch, and I let my bag fall to the floor next to me so my hands can find their home on his sides and back. I weave under his shirt in seconds, his skin hot and muscles so tight.

"I missed you, too," I say through laughter before he covers my mouth with his. Jensen's kiss is instantly deep, and he moves his hands to cradle my face in an adoring way. His mouth is warm, and he tastes sweet—like mint and honey.

"I'm starving," I say between kisses. I might be hoping he will reveal a slice of cheesecake or something equally amazing in response to my hint. But instead, he sits up and lifts me with him, his shoulders sagging with a heavy exhale.

Shit.

The knees of our bent legs touch, and Jensen takes my hands in his, teasingly running his thumb over my stunted nails.

"Don't make fun."

He pulls them to his mouth and kisses my fingers one at a time, then lowers our tethered hands back to his lap. He holds my gaze for several seconds as his mouth rests in a soft smile that twitches faintly every so often. He's nervous about this.

He's leaving.

"Jensen, I'm scared."

His eyes squint as he shakes his head. Whatever he thinks, that didn't do a thing to calm me. Neither is the touch of his thumbs along the backs of my hands as he paints them in slow circles. I like it, it's just not distracting enough from the increasing ache in my chest.

"You're going to Texas."

My heart stops.

I blink a few times. My face literally melts, and all feeling is gone.

"Sut—"

"No." I shake my head as if the one small word isn't enough.

Jensen laughs, biting the tip of his tongue. He leans in closer to me and moves his hands to my face. I grab his wrists and continue to shake my head in his hands.

"Sutter, you have to. I can't let you *not*. Your dad told me."

"Well, that wasn't his right." My lifeless heart kicks once. Then again. It's beating hard but slow, like a ticking bomb. My lips quiver, and my eyes sting with the stress tears I've managed to put off for so long.

"Maybe it wasn't. But it doesn't mean you shouldn't go."

It's all I can do to stay awake. I want to pass out and wake up in his arms and have it be morning, all of this erased. A new day. Or better yet, an old day. Yesterday. I want to go back in time.

"I don't want to." It's a lie and I recognize it the moment my voice hits my ears. *I do want this.* It's all I've thought about since my dad explained it to me. And when I left the message turning it down, I nearly threw up. I had to sneak out into the building hallway to call them in the middle of the night while Jensen was asleep. I didn't want to chance someone actually answering. It wasn't Corbin I called, but the front office. Where important people make major decisions—game-changing decisions—for multi-million-dollar franchises. And someone in that office wanted to hire me.

"Maybe not now. But you will want to. And I kind of think you already do. You're just scared."

I shake my head, but he nods, cancelling me out. I start to cry.

"Sutter, this is wonderful news. Don't cry." He runs his

thumbs under my eyes, sweeping away one tear to make room for the other.

"It's not. I have my mom here. I can't leave her."

"You have Billy. And you can. And whether you believe him or not, you have your dad."

I grit my teeth and sniffle, preparing myself to argue his last point. But before I can, Billy steps out from his room and moves to take a seat in the chair across from me.

"Sut, you can count on us. I know you don't want to believe it, but Mom wanted things this way. She didn't want to be the burden." Billy's voice is soft, but his words cut.

"She is not a burden!" I lash out at him, and he holds up his open palms.

"Not on purpose. No, you're right. I misspoke," Billy backtracks. "But she wouldn't want to be the thing that held you back. I know it. And you know it."

I stare into my brother's eyes, his blue a mirror of mine. The truth is shining back at me, but it doesn't ease the clenching in my belly. The unknown is a huge part of it. But also, there's Jensen.

"But my life is here." I turn my eyes back to Jensen's beautiful face. "You're here."

"I'm here," he echoes. "But you know as well as I do that I won't be forever. And maybe I'll go to Texas soon too. Or maybe I'll be traded and sent somewhere else."

"Like the Mets?" It's a joke to pull him back into us, but it only makes me sad when he laughs at it.

"Yeah, or the Yankees."

I shake my head.

"Never the Yankees," I say through sniffles.

Jensen runs his hands up and down my arms. He must

know how little life is in them. I'm cold. And numb. And I don't think I will ever *not* be scared.

"Your plane leaves at three tomorrow."

My brother's news jolts me back to life.

"My plane?"

Billy shifts and turns his legs to gain a little more space between me and him, probably anticipating my kick. If I could move them, he wouldn't be wrong.

"I booked the flight. And I'm coming with you so you won't travel alone. You can take the meetings and review the offer on the plane, but you'll want to say yes. Sut, Jensen called in a favor." My brother leans his head toward Jensen. Everyone has been conspiring against me in the last few days and it makes me feel claustrophobic.

"It was Amber, really," Jensen explains, adding that his sister's fiancé called in some negotiating power through his agent.

"Oh, yeah. Of course. And did we bring your parents in on this? Maybe Coach Bensen and Ernie? How about Kiki or maybe my boss at the school district?" I stop my tirade when Jensen whispers my name and squeezes my hands in his again.

"Sutter, if you go to Texas and take this meeting and read the deal and still decide this isn't for you, that you don't want this, then I will personally pack up your shitty small apartment and move you in here and let you take all the room in the bed."

I look him in the eyes and see he means it. Every word. I also know, deep down in my gut, that if I open up to this idea, I'm going to stay in Texas.

"You promise?"

Jensen sits up straight and draws an X over his chest.

"Cross my heart."

I've never been in a room this nice in my entire life.

Clyde Nichelsen's assistant brought me into his office about thirty minutes ago. I'm too afraid to explore with nobody around, but the longer I sit in the same spot on this leather couch, the more my skin is bound to stick to it for good.

> JENSEN: Any news?

> ME: Still waiting.

He has messaged me every ten minutes since I left the hotel. I should have taken my brother up on his offer to accompany me. I thought it would make me seem more like a tourist and less like a professional having my big brother hovering around the lobby.

I shift my legs and curse my damn short skirt as my skin crackles with the friction of Velcro as it peels off the couch. A rush of air hits me a second later as Mr. Nichelsen, Vice President of Development, bursts through his enormous mahogany doors.

"Sutter, I am so very sorry to keep you waiting. Here, would you like a water? Or something stiffer? What can I get you?" His accent has the soothing effect of honey on a biscuit, and the way he bobs between his drink cart and me, unsure of where to go first, somehow sets me at ease. He's a people pleaser. Like Billy.

"I'm great, but thank you. And I haven't minded the

wait. I am kind of in love with your office. I don't suppose mine would be anything like this?" I stand and gesture around the space. A glass wall overlooks center field.

"Well, I can get you a corner office, but I can't guarantee this view. It took me quite a while to work up to this one." He laughs at his own joke, and I walk across the room, following after him to a corner table with four chairs. He rolls one out for me and then pushes it in gently as I sit.

"I see you have our proposal in your hands there. I hope you found it . . . appealing?" He leans back in his seat and touches his fingertips together, tapping them as he awaits my response.

This offer is more than appealing. It's ridiculous for a twenty-five-year-old untested not-yet-graduated psychologist. The offer is to have me work with some of the younger pitching staff, the guys they bring up to try for a game or two at the beginning and end of the season, unless of course there are higher stakes at play. Then, nobody moves much, and rookies have to sit tight and wait.

"I know I'm not the only person who does this, and I'm really honored that you think I am the right fit for your team." I'm going to say yes. If he says the right words, I've already committed. I was up all night on the phone with Jensen, letting him coach me for once. I spent sleepless hours building up my courage. But there's a chance he could blow it. I'll know when I know.

"I don't think it, Miss Mason. I know it. That Corbin Forsythe"—there's a pause after he mentions his name and I literally hold my breath, bracing myself for the slew of compliments I'm going to have to endure for someone I detest—"He's a real piece of work. Hard-headed as all get-out and a little bit of a prima donna, don't you think? I mean, what's with his hair? The man cannot stop touching his hair. Talking about his hair. I'm not sure if he's a pitcher or a Cover Girl."

Not where I thought he was going at all.

"He does have nice beachy waves for a dude from Arkansas, doesn't he?"

Clyde goes dead silent at my joke, his mouth agape for a full second, and I grip the arms of my chair in preparation of being admonished. But then he cuts loose with a table-slapping laugh, and I relax again.

"I forgot he's from Arkansas. That man, I tell ya. He wouldn't know how to surf if his life depended on it. I doubt he could handle a horse or tractor in Arkansas, either. I'm not sure where he truly hails from."

"Me, neither." I shake my head, wondering how I fell down this rabbit hole but loving every second of it.

Clyde finally stops the Corbin-bashing and points his finger at me.

"You, though. I know from the videos I've seen, and from Corbin's own mouth, what a difference *you* made in his arm. I won't lie to you. Half the reason you are here is because he was desperate to get you on staff. He's had a few rough innings and his spring was not so great. I know his opener was solid, but he's young. The bones, though. The bones are there. And you—so he says—are a bone artist."

Bone. Artist.

I roll that term around in my head, amused by it. I'm not sure it fits, but I love the crazy shit that comes out of Clyde's mouth.

"I like to be cutting edge. Owner does too. We never want to be following others. We like to lead. And just like the whole metrics and moneyball business was the way to go a few years back, making sure our players are in the right headspace to face or throw hundred-mile-per-hour pitches is where the future is. I see a whole division of Sutter Masons in this organization, but I sure would like the original to be the first. What do you say?"

Yes, Sutter. Say yes!

"If I could take lunch to think about it and give you a call?" *Lunch? I'm not even hungry.*

He twists in his chair while leaning back, his eyes twinkling, cheeks tanned from the sun, a line permanently drawn across his nose where his cowboy hat shades him when he's outdoors. He lifts his chin.

"You bet."

His grin wrinkles his eyes as it pushes into his cheeks. He gets up and I join him, taking the opportunity to make a slow pass along the floor-to-ceiling wall-to-wall bookcase that is loaded with memorabilia. I'm wowed by every item I see, and Clyde shares personal stories about several of them. But then one photo in particular catches my eye.

"May I?" I point to the small black frame with what looks like a young Clyde standing next to a fellow teammate, both of them in Royals uniforms.

"Oh, yeah! That's Ernie!"

It sure is!

I hold the photo still and run my thumb over the glass to get rid of the light dust that's collected. I've seen this photo before, in my dad's office. It's mounted on the wall, a copy of the original, which I'm guessing this is.

"Good ole number seven," Clyde says, taking the photo from me. He stares at the image for a few quiet seconds, the smile playing at his lips growing as what I think might be a series of memories stack up in his mind.

"You know, I'm friends with Ernie Chester," I say with pride.

"Get out!" Clyde leans his arm into mine. "What a small world. Ernie and I were rookies together. He played a lot longer, and a lot better, than I did. He stuck with the game for years. Me, I went to business school."

He glances around his grand office, and I think for a moment how different their lives are now. I wonder if Ernie would be jealous seeing this. I doubt it. I kind of think things panned out exactly the way they were meant to.

And if I was waiting for a sign, I'm pretty sure I just got it.

"Mr. Nichelsen, I'd be honored to work for your organization. When can I start?"

Clyde puts the photo back in its place and turns his smile to me, his hand outstretched. I take it, giving him the firm grip my dad taught me to give every man I meet—the kind that says I can kick your ass if I want to.

"Why, Miss Mason, I think you already have."

CHAPTER 22

Jensen

Sutter has been living out of a hotel room for about six weeks now. I'm not sure what I'm going to find when I swipe this key card, but I have a feeling it might be close to hoarder-level chaos.

She has no idea I'm coming. And if I don't get to her before she wakes up, my surprise will be ruined. She'll see the news on her phone, thanks to the dozens of notifications she set up for any mention of my name. I swear, she sometimes knows whether I lost or won a game before I do.

I press the card on the reader and cringe when the beep is loud enough to wake the entire floor. I power through, pushing the door open slowly and dragging my bag behind me. My gear is already on its way to the clubhouse. It was weird to part with things I've carried around on my own my whole life, but there's also something liberating about it.

I brace the door handle and guide it closed once I'm

inside, the click loud enough that Sutter stirs on the bed across the room. I hold perfectly still, waiting for her to fall back asleep. When she does, I kick off my shoes and jeans and toss my shirt on top of my suitcase. There's a good chance she's going to scream and punch me in the dick, so I use caution as I pull back the comforter and slowly sit on the edge of the bed. I manage to make it all the way to a laying position before she yawns and rolls to her side, blinking awake.

I smile and so does she at first. Then she starts punching.

"Mother fucking fuck fuck what the—" Her fists sail around the bed, sometimes landing on my chest, other times grazing the headboard. She's managed to turn the blanket into a churro twist and grabbed the remote in her hand, which she is now getting ready to throw at me.

I hop up and flip on the bedside lamp, holding my open palms out to my sides.

"Sutter, it's me!"

"What the hell, Jensen! You don't do that to people!"

She wads up the blanket and throws it at my chest while I laugh. I clutch it, then unfurl it and spread it back over her body.

"Uh uh. You are not getting in here." She kicks her feet to the side, but I grab them and tether them together before running my fingers up her thigh until I find her ticklish sides. She cackles then eventually goes limp, giving in to me completely. I kiss her so hard I think I might break her lips with mine. I've missed this face so much. It's one thing to hear her voice every night, and FaceTime works in a pinch. But actually getting to touch her is where the magic is.

We've only been in the same space four times since she left. I knew it would be part of the deal; I didn't think it would be quite this hard. I wasn't ready for the missing someone part. It's such a painful comfort, a strange feeling to have.

"Jensen Hawke, how did you get in this room!"

I have been waiting for this question nearly twenty-four hours. Ever since I got word about being called up for this week's series against Anaheim. Billy put in a few calls to help me get in Sutter's room. He may have told his friends in booking that I was her husband, but I'm all right with that idea. I'd like to be. One day.

I reach over to the night table and slide the card into my hand, then hold it up to Sutter's face.

"I have a key." I grin as she stares at it blankly. She swipes it from me in seconds then throws it across the room, tackling me for getting even with her. Nothing about her tackling me is a punishment, however. I would fly from Arizona to Texas a dozen times a week just to let her tackle me like this.

I hug her to me and kiss her more gently this time, enjoying it as she relaxes in my arms and rests her forehead on mine.

"Wait! What are you doing here?"

I grin at her question, and she's quick to put the clues together.

"No!" She lunges to the other side of the bed and grabs her phone, sorting through the dozens of notifications. I love watching her eyes light up as she reads each and every one.

"You did it! You're here! You are in the majors!" She leaps at me again but quickly climbs out of my grasp, scrambling across her room. She kicks a box out of the way of her closet then pushes the door wide while I scratch the side of my head and watch her mania in action.

"Sutter, it's two in the morning. You should not get this wired."

She hushes me, though, so I fold up my legs and sit back while she rummages through some bag in her closet.

She pivots when she stands, holding something behind her back as she walks over to me.

"I have a present for you. I was supposed to give it to you the day you sent me to Texas, and then I sort of forgot in the middle of everything." She shrugs.

"You were a little distracted." She was bit of a wreck, actually. It's the most frightened I have ever seen her. She was afraid of change, and maybe afraid of failure, all things she was learning to help other people conquer. I'm still not sure I did it right, but the fact she's doing so well in this job now, looking at living here permanently, makes me think I was close.

She pulls her hand from behind her back and holds out what might be the prettiest glove I've ever seen in my life. The leather scent scratches at my memories of playing catch when I was a kid and carrying my glove around on the handle of my bat while riding my bike through the alleyways in Washington.

"When did you do this?" I run my hand over the laces, then turn it over and fit my hand inside. It's still a little stiff, but I can break it in.

"Right before I left. I know a guy in Tucson who runs a glove shop. He did me a solid." She twists my wrist until I see my nickname stitched in gold.

"Wow! Sutter, I—" I swallow down my emotion. I've never been given something so thoughtful in my entire life. I'm glad I'm not proposing tonight because I might not be able to live up to this. I'm also going to need to up the size of that diamond.

"I wanted you to have something to remember me by, you know." She shrugs, not wanting to finish that thought. But I know her fears. I know what haunts her. She wanted me to remember her in case we didn't make it. In case I left her behind. I bet she never considered once she would be the one leaving me in the dust. I'm just glad I caught up.

"Well, good thing I have the actual Sutter Mason in my arms instead. I mean, I love the glove, don't get me wrong. But the girl? I love her more."

I've said those words a few times over the phone, at the end of conversations and usually when she's dozed off to sleep. My mouth is instantly dry now that I say it to her face. And the way she seems suddenly catatonic has me a bit worried I jumped the gun.

"Say it again." She tosses the mitt on the floor to rid anything from the space between us as she settles in and sits so her legs wrap around my waist.

I suck in my bottom lip as my body reacts to her slowly inching forward.

"I said I love the girl, Sutter. I love *you*. I love Sutter Mason. TLF. True Love Forever." She closes the remaining space and wraps her arms and legs around me, kissing me until she's breathless. I don't think I've breathed since I got into this room.

"I love you too, you silly boy. I love you more. So much more, Jensen Hawke. *Jay Hawk*." She giggles, half with nerves and half amused at the way she pokes fun of my nickname.

She can make fun of it all she wants. As long as she takes it for her own someday.

Epilogue

Six Months Later
🔴 Sutter

Our magic number to make the playoffs came and went. While that meant life for Jensen got a lot less stressful, it meant my side of the business was about to get red hot. When we were mathematically eliminated from making the post season, Clyde put me to work with six of his prospects from the farm system. Two of them are lefties, which I have decided are nothing but a pain in my ass.

Maybe I'm biased. Lefties have a certain quality that just needles at me. One lefty in particular. Yet I wouldn't trade him for anything in the world. I think half the reason I fell so hard for Jensen Hawke was because of the way he simply refused to roll over and give in no matter how damn persuasive I was.

I was able to hire two students from a nearby university to work with me for the last three weeks of the season. I kind of like the teaching aspect of this job now that I'm in it. They're interns, and though they aren't much younger than me, the learning journey between us is mountainous. In a good way. They are going to have so many great wins when our guys excel. The losses will come, too, though. And that's the part I'm trying to get better at handling personally.

For me. For Jensen. Neither of us like the way mistakes feel. But mistakes come with opportunity. Or as Jensen likes to joke with me, *one should always BEE on the lookout for opportunity.* He found my HR poster mockups during a late-night snooping session on my computer. I may never live them down.

Jensen headed back to Arizona a week ago. He promised to unpack the dozens of boxes he stored from my old apartment when I left for Texas months ago. There was one box I told him to go ahead and burn, and that's the one that had Corbin's things in it. I have no need for any of those letters or photos. They're all laughable now. There isn't a drop of nostalgia among them. Now if I can just get that rumor of him being traded to New York to pan out.

As my plane touches down at Sky Harbor, I take in the familiar orange horizon and purple mountains that cut jagged lines around the Valley. I feel the heat seep in through the jetway as I roll my bag into the airport. I breathe in the hot air. *Home.*

Kiki is literally bouncing on her toes beyond the security checkpoint, so I jog toward her out of fear that she'll break the rules and run at me, getting herself arrested for crossing the line. We collide in an epic besties' reunion complete with squeals and hugs and promises of mojitos.

We make our way to baggage claim and she helps me

haul my stuffed suitcases out to her car. They barely fit in the trunk, but with a few good shoves—and Kiki sitting on the trunk—we get it closed.

"I forgot how hot it is here in October." I fan myself by pulling my T-shirt away from my chest until my friend gets her AC cranked up high enough.

"Arizona reminds you real fast that it can bring the hell." We both laugh. She's quoting one of our favorite sayings from the local radio station in Tucson. That's part of an Arizonan's survival kit: making fun of their own habitat and its ridiculous climate.

It's about a ninety-minute drive home from Phoenix. I should have switched the flight my brother booked for me for one that went directly to Tucson. It got me in later, but as it is, I'm going right to bed the minute my feet reach my door.

Our door.

Me and Jensen's door.

For most of the drive, Kiki fills me in on the latest drama between her and the "outfielder" as she likes to refer to Chris Marte, the man she's been on and off dating for months now. I think she thinks it makes their fling something hot and secret, but literally everyone in our circle knows who the outfielder is. Lots of people do since he's super famous.

And thanks to a turn at some big Chicago fundraiser that he flew her out for as his date, half of Chicagoland knows about them, too. They were *the* photo on the paper's society page. My friend likes to pretend she's embarrassed by it, but I guarantee you that newspaper clip is tacked on a wall somewhere at McGill's.

Now that I think of McGill's . . .

"Keeks, I know we were going to stop to grab drinks and a bite on our way in, but I don't think I can handle McGill's tonight. I'm exhausted. And Jensen is probably anxious for me to get home."

"Aww. Come on, just one. I already asked him, and he said it was fine." She glances at me a few times and puffs out her lip, a trick that worked on me when we were in college but has little effect on me now.

"I don't think so." I yawn and push the butt of my palms into my eyes. Kiki's car slows and I pull my hands away, glad to see our exit. But when we get to the light where she's supposed to turn left, she hooks a right and starts to speed.

"You know you can't literally run away from me not wanting to go out drinking. You can drive as fast as you want but I still want to go home."

"No, you don't," she says back, her voice curt and robotic.

"Uh, no. I do."

She makes a hard stop at the light and flips her left blinker on.

"Sutter, you're my girl. But if you don't go out for a drink with me at McGill's tonight, I swear I'm going to knock your teeth straight out onto that sidewalk." Her jaw flexes with her threat and my brow draws in, a little worried that my friend might have fully cracked. But then it hits me.

"Kiki." I say her name with urgency, and she glances at me but looks away fast.

"Kiki, look at me right now. Look me in the eyes."

She shakes her head and mouths *nuh uh*.

The light still red, I reach over and grab her chin. Her

jaw and neck are surprisingly strong as she fights against me, but eventually she gives in and stares me right in the eyes. It takes about two seconds for her to break out into a scream.

"Oh my God he's going to propose and you better act like you had no idea, but *oh my God!*" The light turns green in the middle of her blubbering secret-spill and the guy in the car behind us lays on the horn.

"Fuck off, buddy!" I say, holding up my middle finger. He probably can't even see it through the tinted windows. I don't care.

"Kiki. I look like shit. I can't do this. I'm in sweats. And this shirt." I pull my oversized sweatshirt up to my face and sniff. "Oh, God. I can't let this moment happen while I'm in this. Please, Keeks. I swear I will pretend it's a surprise and sell it like a Meryl Streep performance when it happens, but you have got to circle this neighborhood one more time while I fish out something decent from my carry-on in your back seat.

The light has already gone yellow and since we haven't budged, the angry driver behind us zooms around us and lays on the horn one last time.

"You better be fast. That boy is nervous as hell, and I swore I wouldn't get you there late." She twirls her finger in the air to urge me to get moving. I unbuckle from the front and climb over the console so I'm in the back. I dig through my carry-on duffle and fish out the strappy cotton dress that I rolled up and tucked in there last minute. I was afraid I'd be hot when we landed. Now, I'm sweating bullets, but it has nothing to do with the damn sun and concrete vortex or whatever the hell it's called.

I worm around Kiki's back seat while she meanders

through the neighborhood streets, careful not to pull right next to anyone so they can't see me as I strip out of one outfit and into another. I slip my arm through the final strap right as she pulls into McGill's. A full parking lot isn't completely strange since the college crowd comes here, but for a Tuesday, it's still a little weird. I wonder if I would have noticed.

We both get out and I flip my head over and run my fingers through my hair a few times while my friend sprays citrus body spray around me to get rid of the airplane stench. We toss it in the passenger seat and she locks up, then squares my shoulders with hers to give me one final inspection.

"Tell me this one will stick." I hold her gaze and mentally beg her to take my silly request seriously. I know Jensen loves me. But there is still this lingering worry that nags at me sometimes that the good things are going to fall apart.

"This one will stick. And he was what you were waiting for."

I nod at her sage advice, words she has said to me more than once.

I take my friend's hand and let her lead me into McGill's. She drops our hold the second we get inside, and almost instantly I recognize faces.

Amber smiles bashfully from the back corner, where Ryan is standing behind her with his arms wrapped around her from behind. I still can't believe she insisted I was part of their wedding. My dad is by the bar. I wish my mom was sitting next to him, but evenings are hard for her now. That's when the dementia is at its worst. My dad has been going to visit her several times a week since I've been gone, and Billy told me he started wearing his old wedding ring again because he likes that sometimes she still believes they're married.

Jensen's parents are next to my dad. They've made it out to two of Jensen's games in Texas. Granted, Amber had to basically drag them there and plan every step of the trip, but they saw their son pitch his major league debut. And whether his dad shows it publicly or not, I know there's a kernel of pride in there somewhere.

Behind them, Ernie has his favorite stool. He's actually been out to several games to watch Jensen. The two of them have formed a special bond. My dad says Ernie's been showing up in his office from time to time just to chat, too. I scan the bar for my brother, and when I spot his plaid shirt, I call out his name and begin my performance.

"Billy Mason, you came to a bar just for me!" My brother spins around with wide eyes. Clearly I've caught him off-guard and ruined his plan.

"Oh, yeah. Uh . . . Kiki invited me. And so . . ."

"Relax. She knows," Kiki says close to his ear.

"Oh, thank God." My brother holds his hand over his chest, then glances to his right. I follow his gaze, and that's when the world slows down.

There is nothing simple or subdued about the way Jensen Hawke is standing in the middle of a suddenly parted crowd of people. Light blue jeans hug his godlike muscular legs. Black leather dress shoes point from his feet. His black button down fits his chest like it's painted on, the silver buttons dotting up to his throat. His hair is slicked back with a hard part, and his devilish half smile is the icing on one fine slice of cake.

"Sutter Mason." He says my name and a hush falls over the entire bar.

I don't have to act this out because even knowing this was coming I could not have been prepared for this scene. I cup my mouth and shiver as my friend steps to the side to leave me alone, the center of attention—*his* center of attention.

Without pause, Jensen drops to one knee and holds out a Tiffany blue box. *Oh, good gracious, this is it.*

He flips the box open.

That's a ring. That's the most beautiful ring I've ever seen. That is my ring. For me. From him to me. Mrs. Sutter Hawke.

"In front of all these people, in the very place where I first saw you move like a vixen on that dance floor, where we drank—well *you* drank—way too many beers and broke through my stubborn-ass armored heart . . . will you do me the honor of saying yes to watching years of bad reality shows and hiking up thousands of mountains with or without pants for the rest of our lives?"

My cheeks are hot behind my hands, and I peek around my fingers to read the faces of our friends in the room. I think the pants thing really puzzled them. But for me? That pretty much sealed the deal.

I start nodding and Jensen gets to his feet, sweeping me up and kissing me while we spin in dizzying circles. He sets me on my feet, then tosses the box out into the crowd before holding my hand in his trembling ones to slide the ring onto my finger. It glistens under the flashing TV lights and catches the blues and oranges from the old juke box in the corner. I hug it to my chest then step up on my toes to kiss him again.

To kiss my future husband.

And pose for a candid photo that will get pinned on the McGill's wall of fame, where it will yellow and curl around the edges over the years to come until one day, someone plucks it from the wall and remarks about what an incredible couple those Hawkes are and what an amazing family they've built together.

THE END

If you enjoyed this series, you might also like:

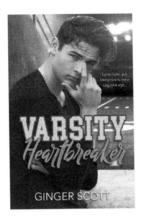

The Varsity Series

A New Adult Sports Romance Trilogy

Begin Your Binge with Varsity Heartbreaker

Lucas Fuller is a lot of things.

He's the boy next door.

He's the first crush I ever had.

He was my first kiss.

He's also the only person who has ever broken my heart.

For two years, I've wondered what happened to the us I used to know.

We were best friends, and then suddenly...we weren't.

I tried to run away from it. I even changed schools just to make the hurt disappear.

But no matter how hard I tried to not think about Lucas, I just couldn't stay away from the high school quarterback with perfect blue eyes and so many secrets.

I'm back. We're seniors now. We've grown—all of us. And Lucas Fuller might be different, but I'm different too.

This is my time to take risks, to experience life and to fall in love for real.

I want Lucas Fuller to be a part of my story, but I know for that to happen, I need to know the truth about our past.

Acknowledgments

Man oh man. I hope you enjoyed the journey. This book was bliss for me. If you've been a reader for more than a few years, you've probably come to know that I have quite a love affair with baseball. I love sports, period. But this one . . . it gets me right in the heart. There's romance in baseball, and I will defend that to my dying breath.

There are so many people I need to thank. This book came to fruition thanks to my husband and son, who tolerated me writing at odd hours and requesting ample amounts of Diet Coke. To my editor, Brenda Letendre, for guiding, teaching and helping me to make sure Sutter and Jensen's story was exactly as it needed to be. To Autumn, Wordsmith Publicity, my life source, who is always willing to read my haphazard chapters and crazy-hour texts of self-doubt. Thank you for being my champion, and for shouting about me and this book from all the rooftops—real and virtual. To my girls Dylan Allen, Kennedy Ryan, Rebecca Shea and Jennie Marts for meeting me online (and in Panera) to get the words out no matter what time of the day. To my mom for being my eagle eye and my bestie Jen for the undying faith that I can write a book because every single time I wonder if I truly can.

And most importantly, thank YOU! You have so many ways to spend your time. I mean, you could watch a baseball game for Pete's sake! The fact that you give your precious time to me and my words means the world to me.

If you enjoyed Southpaw, please consider taking the time to leave a review in your place of choice. It is the greatest gift you can give an author. Well, that and a pair of World Series tickets. ;-)

About the Author

Ginger Scott is a *USA Today, Wall Street Journal* and Amazon-bestselling author from Peoria, Arizona. She has also been nominated for the Goodreads Choice and RWA Rita Awards. She is the author of several young and new adult romances, including bestsellers Cry Baby, The Hard Count, A Boy Like You, This Is Falling and Wild Reckless.

A sucker for a good romance, Ginger's other passion is sports, and she often blends the two in her stories. When she's not writing, the odds are high that she's somewhere near a baseball diamond, either watching her son swing for the fences or cheering on her favorite baseball team, the Arizona Diamondbacks. Ginger lives in Arizona and is married to her college sweetheart whom she met at ASU (fork 'em, Devils).

FIND GINGER ONLINE: www.littlemisswrite.com

facebook.com/GingerScottAuthor
twitter.com/TheGingerScott
instagram.com/authorgingerscott

Also By Ginger Scott

The Boys of Welles

Loner

Rebel

Habit

The Fuel Series

Shift

Wreck

Burn

The Varsity Series

Varsity Heartbreaker

Varsity Tiebreaker

Varsity Rule breaker

Varsity Captain

The Waiting Series

Waiting on the Sidelines

Going Long

The Hail Mary

Like Us Duet

A Boy Like You

A Girl Like Me

The Falling Series

This Is Falling

You And Everything After

The Girl I Was Before

In Your Dreams

The Harper Boys

Wild Reckless

Wicked Restless

Standalone Reads

Southpaw

Candy Colored Sky

Cowboy Villain Damsel Duel

Drummer Girl

BRED

Cry Baby

The Hard Count

Memphis

Hold My Breath

Blindness

How We Deal With Gravity